The
BOURNVILLE
~ BARGE ~
MYSTERY

For Brigitte,
for ever and a day

The
BOURNVILLE
~ BARGE ~
MYSTERY

A.S. Baker

BREWIN BOOKS

BREWIN BOOKS
19 Enfield Ind. Estate,
Redditch,
Worcestershire,
B97 6BY
www.brewinbooks.com

Published by Brewin Books 2019

A CIP catalogue record for this book is available
from the British Library.

ISBN: 978-1-85858-707-3

Cover art by Zora Payne.

Printed and bound in Great Britain
by Severn, Gloucester.

FOREWORD

The fictional events of *The Bournville Barge Mystery* are based upon the factual diary of my grandfather, Stanley Johnson, written as a fifteen year old employee of Cadbury Brothers in the summer of 1921. Stanley had joined Cadbury's a year earlier to work in the General Office, replenishing stationery items, running errands and delivering messages between departments. He was happy to be there and he was lucky, for a job at Cadbury's brought with it the benefits of the founding family's commitment to the social and physical welfare of its employees which, in Stanley's case, extended to one day's free education every week.

George Cadbury had established the Bournville Day Continuation School in 1913, making attendance from every young worker compulsory for half a day each week, with a further half day offered to those who wished to volunteer for Saturday lessons. Cadbury employed R W Ferguson to bring his philanthropic dream to fruition, appointing him as the company's Head of Education and building two impressive school buildings, one for girls and the other for boys, at the heart of Bournville Village. Ferguson committed his teaching philosophy to a number of books, including *A Day Continuation School At Work*, co-authored with W J Wray (Longmans Green, 1920), elements of which are woven into my narrative.

As part of the curriculum, students participated in the annual Camp School, a week of outdoor lessons and visits to sites of interest, with nights spent under canvas. For working class youngsters from Birmingham, many of whom had never before ventured beyond the confines of their city, these weeks in the shires were unforgettable. And lest they ever did forget, each student was required to write a diary of the week and to illustrate it with sketches and postcards. Stanley's diary of his 1921 canal adventure provides the framework and chronology for my story: all other aspects flow from the long-imagined spirit of a man I never knew.

A.S. Baker, August 2019
abaker17@me.com

1

77 MELTON ROAD, KINGS HEATH,

BIRMINGHAM: AUGUST 13TH, 1921

The young man sat on the edge of his bed and watched the second hand click around the tin clock's face. Beyond the window, the rain beat down: huge droplets drumming on the slate roof, gushing along the wrought iron guttering and gurgling into the mouth of a drainpipe fixed against the red brick wall. The young man cared nothing for the rain. His heart beat along with the clock, pumped by the anticipation of the glorious week ahead.

Tickety-Click. Tickety-Click. Tickety-Click.

At last, the minute hand hopped its decisive beat onto the six and the bell sprang into clanging action, instantly to be silenced by a deft flick of an index finger. For a moment there seemed to be no sound at all in the tiny bedroom, not even a heartbeat, before the teeming rain and ticking clock crowded in once more.

Stanley Johnson stood up in his summer pyjamas and wire-rimmed spectacles and stretched his thin arms above his head in a luxuriant yawn. He was fifteen and a quarter years old and this was the most exciting morning of his life.

Hitching up his pyjama bottoms, he tiptoed to the bedroom door and gingerly turned the brass handle to the left. The latch clicked softly. He pulled the door inwards and stepped out onto the landing: all clear. He took a breath, then descended the stairs, avoiding the creaks and groans that so often betrayed his father's forays upstairs to stamp out candle-lit adventures within the pages of *Boy's Own*.

In the kitchen, Stanley's father had already set the enamel wash bowl on the table and half filled it from the kettle, now back on the range beside the teapot. A towel and a bar of soap lay alongside a florally patterned jug of cold water. To the right, at the other end of the table, sat the remains of yesterday's loaf on a board. His father was nowhere to be seen.

Stanley padded across the red brick tiles to the table, tugging his pyjama top over his head. He tested the temperature of the water in the bowl with his index finger, added a generous splash of cold water from the jug and carefully laid down his spectacles on the table next to the folded towel. His morning ablutions consisted of a series of shallow face dives into the bowl, during which he would blow a stream of bubbles whilst humming a sound that he liked to think represented submarine engines. He would then gather up a quantity of water in the cup of his two hands and vigorously rub his forehead and hairline with his wet fingers. The soap remained untouched.

Just as Stanley was making his final ascent from the bowl, his father strode in through the yard door.

"Stanley! How many times has your mother told you to use the lav *before* you have a wash?"

"But you were in there, Dad," spluttered Stan, reaching for towel and glasses and upsetting the soap instead. "I was going afterwards."

"Well mind you do, my lad. And you'd better take some more paper with you, an' all. I've just finished the last lot."

William Johnson still talked with the gruff Lincolnshire accent of his farming boyhood, from which he had escaped, at fourteen, to seek love and employment in the grimy metropolis of Birmingham. Employment came first, with the Birmingham Corporation Tramways in Aston and, later, as a driver at the Kings Heath garage. Love had followed in the plain but homely form of Mary Yeomans, born to an Aston family of glass cutters whose wedding dowry had included a beautifully cut crystal beer tankard bearing the date of their union: October 9th, 1898. Stanley's teetotal mother used the glass as a celery jug.

The rain pelted down on the cobbled yard behind the grey kitchen window. Inside, William shuffled around the range, busy with the teapot and caddy. He was trying valiantly to keep to a daily routine that did not usually include his youngest son.

"Come on, lad. Look lively. Time and tide. Time and tide."

Stanley gathered up his spectacles and made for the back door.

"And don't forget the paper neither," called William as his son hurtled across the back yard towards the toilet. "I swear you'd forget your blessed head if it warn't screwed on."

Stanley raced back into the kitchen, grabbed an old copy of *The Sports Argus* and shot out once more into the yard. His father stirred the tea in the pot and smiled behind his white moustache. William's greying hair and weather-lined face gave him the look of a man much older than his forty-eight years. The lean, upright frame and steel grey eyes suggested a strict demeanour, but Mary was the disciplinarian of the family, as his three children knew only too well. This morning, as on most mornings, he was dressed in the worn trousers of his Corporation uniform, held up by thin braces over a collarless white shirt, open at the neck. In winter, he would place a folded newspaper between vest and shirt as extra protection against the cold that seared through the open front of his tram, but there would be no need for such measures today. Just an oilskin cape by the look of things. He pulled a starched white collar from the washing basket beneath the table.

Stanley erupted back into the kitchen at high speed, spraying rain drops and leaving wet prints on the tiled floor beneath his bare feet.

"For heaven's sake, Stanley! Can't you slow down a bit in the morning? You're like a whirling blinking dervish around the place."

William clung on to his teapot as though his very upright stability depended upon it. His son sped through the kitchen, along the hall and into the front parlour where his mother had laid out his clothes and kit bag the night before. Such excitement! The kitbag's khaki canvas had been fiercely scrubbed into respectable cleanliness for whatever inspections the week might bring. Stanley's first day clothes hung from the back of a chair, his stout walking boots beneath. The Camp School booklet lay upon the dining table, open at the page marked "<u>Hints to Campers</u>."

The first hint concerned "<u>Luggage</u>" which, the booklet suggested, *should be brought in a kitbag or hold-all and should be securely packed and labelled. It must be conveyed to the Barge at the place of Departure by each member of the school.* Stanley noted the neatly written label, securely tied around the drawstring of the kitbag: *S. Johnson, General Office.* A good start. There then followed three hints emphasised by heavy underlining:

1. <u>Space on the Barge is very limited. Avoid bringing anything unnecessary</u>.
2. <u>It is undesirable to have best Sunday hats about the Barge, they are a nuisance. Please bring nothing more than a cap</u>.
3. <u>Put your knife, fork and spoon at the top of your bag or keep them available for immediate use</u>.

He was encouraged to read that food was going to play such a key role in the adventure. And he hadn't got a Sunday hat anyway, so there were no problems on that front. Excellent! The next hint was the authoritative "What To Bring:"

In addition to your ordinary clothes a change of under-clothing is necessary in case of wet weather. (A pencil tick indicated Mrs Johnson's approval of this counsel). *The following should also be brought:-*

Footer Shorts or Flannel Trousers
Jersey, Sweater or Flannel Shirt
Bathing Costume
Boot Brushes and Polish
Mackintosh or Raincoat
Sleeping attire
Towel and Soap
Tooth Brush and Paste
Knife, Fork and Spoon

Eating references underlined again! This was going to be so good!

Each item had been gathered together by his mother, scrupulously cleaned, folded and packed into the kitbag, then ticked off in pencil on the page. The words *oilskin cape* and *umbrella* had been added, followed by a question mark. Stanley's mother had clearly foreseen the morning downpour.

Ground Sheets will be provided but each member is required to bring three blankets or rugs.

Three grey blankets lay neatly folded on the table, tied together with coarse string: the best summer blankets, virtually free of darning. Would they fit into the kitbag or should he carry them separately? He prodded the bulging kitbag with his big toe. Separately, then.

Stanley dressed quickly, discarding his pyjama trousers on the floor as he grabbed the summer underclothes from the chair. Socks, cotton shirt and shorts followed in rapid succession, before he threaded his trusty leather belt through most of the loopholes and fastened it tight around his skinny waist. He picked up the boots in one hand, his pyjamas in the other and headed back to the kitchen.

"Your mother was up until goodness knows what time last night sorting out that lot. I swear our Jack had less clobber to carry when he got called up. Lord only knows how you're going to lug it all the way to Bournville."

"But it's all in the book, Dad, and the Firm says that we have to go by the book. Mister Ferguson made a big thing of it at yesterday's meeting and he's practically a Director. Anyway, Mister Biddle said that he would take me as far as Cotteridge in his motor lorry, provided I can get to his shop by ten past five."

"Well you'd better look lively, then. Time's marching on and Mister Biddle won't wait if you turn up late. Let's get some breakfast into you."

Stanley slid his skinny backside along the wooden bench behind the kitchen table and came to rest directly behind his mug of tea. William carved a chunk of bread and pushed it towards his son.

"Do you want some of your mother's jam with that? Or would you prefer something edible?"

Father and son giggled together. Despite this being a long-established running joke between them, it still provided a joyous moment of close complicity. William glanced over his left shoulder, just in case his wife should make an unannounced appearance at the door.

"What is it this time then?" giggled Stan

"Raspberry, I think," replied his father, "Although it could be mushroom." They dissolved into laughter once more.

"Shhhh," struggled William. "It wouldn't do to wake her at this hour."

"I'll just have the bread, thanks."

Stanley wolfed down the thick slice of bread and butter, slurped up most of his tea and wiped the back of his hand across his mouth. The mantel clock above the range showed five minutes to the hour. It was time to go.

"Your mother has dug out an old oilskin cape of mine for you to wear," said William, as his son pulled on his boots. "It should be big enough to cover both you and that stack of best blankets she's given you. Be sure you wear it, or I'll be for the high jump."

"I will, Dad," puffed his son, tugging at his left boot, "and I'll be sure to take good care of it."

Laces tied, Stanley raced back into the parlour to pick up his baggage, pushing the Camp School booklet into the top of his kitbag where he was pleased to feel his knife, fork and spoon tied together with garden twine. He folded down the waterproof flap and pulled the drawstring tight. His father's old cape hung by its hood from a peg on the back of the parlour door and Stanley donned it in a trice. It felt as big as a marquee and smelled strongly of damp. The arms were at least six inches longer than his own, and the hood flopped over his face. "I look like a Zeppelin," he thought. But there was no time to ponder on matters sartorial. He hitched up his oilskin, grabbed the pile of blankets by their string and stowed them against his hollow chest, clamping them in place with his left forearm. He let the cape fall back into place before hoisting up his kitbag and swinging it over his right shoulder where it hung, lopsidedly, from a single canvas strap. Ready! He swung round towards the door and knocked over the dining chair with his kitbag.

"Stanley!!" His father's strangled whisper hissed from the kitchen, "What on earth are you up to now? You'll wake the whole blessed house!"

"Sorry, Dad" whispered Stanley, exiting the parlour, "I'm a bit overloaded."

"You look like Scott of the bloomin' Antarctic. Come here and I'll do something about the hood."

William rolled back the edges of the material with his thick fingers until Stanley's steamed-up spectacles reappeared.

"There, lad. At least you'll not be walking into any lamp posts. Now, let's be off with you. And be sure you have yourself a good time."

Father and son exchanged a brief smile and Stanley headed for the front door.

"Oh - and your mom said to tell you to do everything the teachers ask of you and not to get into trouble" recited William.

"Tell her I promise, Dad. See you next week."

And with that, Stanley headed out into the rainy morning and shut the door behind him. The moment had finally come.

The walk to Sid Biddle's shop took seven minutes: left at the front gate, down to the end of Melton Road, right onto Addison Road and straight on to the T junction with the main road into town. Here, Stanley turned right towards Birmingham and walked past a run of small shops whose names and window displays he had come to know by heart: *Wrensons*, the grocers, where Jack used to work as a Saturday delivery boy, and *Sadler Brothers*, the corn and seeds merchants, whose window advertisements for blood-fish-and-bone at a shilling a peck could still make him feel squeamish. On down the row, past the ironmonger and the butcher and the baker, until Stanley arrived at the boarded up shop front of F & S Biddle Limited, Greengrocers of Distinction. There was no sign of Mister Biddle.

The rain splashed up from the paving stones and down from Stanley's oilskin. The clock on the church spire showed twelve minutes past five. His heart jumped. What if he was too late? What if Mister Biddle had already headed off without him? Should he stay and wait, or should he try to walk it? How long would it take him to walk it, anyway, what with all of this kit and caboodle? The sense of panic was rising. Stanley scanned the road in both directions. The tram lines were full of water, which would make for some terrific splashes when the next tram passed, but that wouldn't be for ages. Anyway, the trams went nowhere near where he was going. Maybe he could thumb a lift? But from whom? There was nobody about.

Just as Stanley was preparing for a brisk march along Vicarage Lane, Mister Biddle's lorry lurched out from a side road, made a sweeping left turn across the width of the main road and groaned to a halt in front of the shop, where it shook itself like a wet dog and conked out.

"What a beauty," breathed Stanley, his eyes wide behind misty glasses. "AEC Y-Type and just like new."

"Don't stand gawking, lad. Get over here quick. We're late enough already."

Stanley bounded across to the open cab of the lorry, within which Sid Biddle was wedged behind the huge steering wheel.

"I'm sorry, Mister Biddle," he apologised, though the lorry's late arrival was hardly his fault. "Where would you like me to put my kit?"

"Sling it in the back behind the cab. That'll be about the driest place on the whole bloomin' wagon. It'll certainly be a whole lot drier than up front with us!"

Sid Biddle was one of life's great moaners. Even throughout the glorious summer days of the past few weeks, when his takings from strawberry sales had broken all previous records, Sid could be heard grumbling about the weather.

"They're swelling up something rotten in this heat, Missus. I'm telling you. Me poor legs. I'm in bloomin' agony just stood standing here serving you."

Stanley heaved his kitbag over the wooden side boards and scrambled up into the cab. It was a long way up, especially with only one free hand with which to pull himself onto the soaking passenger seat, but he made it into position and was instantly ready for the off.

"Not so fast, young lad," carped Mister Biddle, "How are we supposed to go anywhere, stalled like we are? Jump down and give the 'andle a turn for us, will you. But mind: it's got a kick on it like a bloomin' cart 'orse."

Stanley jumped down to the wet pavement and positioned himself by the radiator grill in front of the imposingly long bonnet.

"On my command, lad," bellowed Mister Biddle. "*Swing!!*"

Stanley hesitated. This was not the command that he had been anticipating. Something like "Go!" perhaps, or "Now!" might have been more obvious, but the invitation to "swing" puzzled him.

"What the bloomin' 'eck are you doing, lad?" exploded Mister Biddle. "Fallen asleep on the job, 'ave you? When I say swing, you *swing*. Comprendo?"

"Er, yes Mister Biddle, Sir. Perfectly. Sorry. Er, what is it, exactly, that you want me to swing?"

"The *'andle*, you bird brain. Swing the bloomin' 'andle. Lord save us." The exasperation was palpable. "Now... On my command: *Swing!*"

Stanley bent his back and swung his whole weight into the task. The motor caught immediately, yanking the handle violently out of his grasp and pulling him sharply over to land on his side on the wet pavement. Winded, he nevertheless clung valiantly to the three blankets beneath his cape. The engine roared its appreciation of Stanley's sacrifice and he struggled back to his feet.

"Told you it had a bit of a kick," lamented Mister Biddle, humourlessly. "Now get yourself back up here sharpish so we can be on our way."

Mister Biddle's lorry really was a marvellous machine. He had bought it - for cash, as he liked to tell anyone who appeared even vaguely interested - in the Spring of 1919 from an Army surplus dealer in Manchester and had driven it all the way to Birmingham in a day! With his new possession safely stabled in the warehouse behind the shop, Mister Biddle had begun a long and loving "improvement" of the vehicle. Over the course of several months he had replaced one of the wooden wheels, fitted a new set of solid rubber tyres to all four of them, installed hinged wooden boards around the flat bed platform at the rear and, most obviously of all, painted the whole in a splendidly deep shade of greengrocer green with illuminated gold signage. It was his pride and joy.

This morning, as the vehicle roared and bounced along Vicarage Road at a heady 18 miles per hour, Mister Biddle's smug pride warmed the milk of his human kindness: "So, young Stanley. What's this great adventure you're about to enjoy, then? Or should I say, endure?" He even had a twinkle in his eye.

The lorry veered right as the road crossed the railway bridge, then left as it swung into Fordhouse Lane. Stanley gripped the dashboard with both hands as Mister Biddle double-de-clutched into a lower gear.

"I'm going on the Bournville Day Continuation Camp School barge trip, Mister Biddle" proclaimed Stanley. "The firm has organised everything, including the food, and we're going all the way to Warwick and Stratford upon Avon." His face beamed with pride.

"Well now. Isn't that grand! Warwick *and* Stratford. That certainly is an adventure and no mistake."

Conversation lulled as Mister Biddle stamped and heaved his way through the gear box and it was a while before he spoke again.

"I reckon that the best I can do for you, lad," he stated, once they were back on a straighter course, "is to drop you over there, beyond the canal bridge. You can scoot down onto the towpath, turn left and you'll be at Cadbury's within ten minutes. How does that sound?"

"Marvellous, Mister Biddle. Thank you very much for the lift. It has made all the difference."

"Well, you be sure to have a good time, young Stanley," advised the greengrocer, bringing his lorry to a halt at the kerb. "And stay out of mischief an' all."

"I will, Mister Biddle," he sang as he bounced down onto the pavement and dragged his kitbag from the back of the lorry. "And a very good day to you, Sir."

The gears of the AEC crunched once more and Stanley slithered down the steep banking besides the road bridge. He adjusted the oilskin, hitched the kitbag onto his right shoulder and headed off, squelching and whistling, towards the forest of factory chimneys in the distance.

2

THE OFF

Stanley could hear the boys' low chatter well before he arrived at the Cadbury Wharf. They had gathered on the rough ground alongside the canal, arriving in dribs and drabs from the packed suburbs of South Birmingham: twenty-five in number and ranging in age from fourteen to eighteen, clumped together beneath a scattering of black umbrellas and waterproof capes. The sweet smell of chocolate hung limp in the grey clouds. It was a quarter to six.

Despite the rain, the pitter-patter chatter of the boys betrayed the high level of excitement amongst the group of rough and newly broken voices, the scarcity of umbrellas keeping everyone vaguely in the right place for the imminent arrival of Mister Ferguson, whose motor car had just been spotted trundling into the adjacent car park. Stanley muttered a low greeting to a chap called Barnwell, who worked in the cash office, before heading off to join the broad figure under a floral umbrella who had taken up position a few dozen yards away, close to the canal's edge. The figure was Fred Parker. He was Stanley's best friend.

"Or'right, Stan?"

"Alright, Fred. You?"

"Or'right, ta."

Stan pulled the oilskin hood from his head and shuffled in beneath the ancient whalebone umbrella that Fred's grandmother had insisted he use. They stood immobile, gazing intently into the distance, hoping to catch their first glimpse of the work's barge rounding the bend on the far side of the aqueduct.

"D'you think it'll be a diesel or a steamer?" whispered Fred, pink-faced and plump, "I do hope it's a diesel. God forbid it's the donkeys." His voice was barely audible, as if the very act of speaking out loud might break the magic spell of a day so long anticipated. "They wouldn't give us the donkeys, would they?"

"It'll be a diesel," affirmed Stan solemnly. "Jack Bolas says it's a diesel, and a new one at that. Anyhow, I heard they've put all the old steamers on the milk run to Knighton, so that pretty much settles it."

Stan's earnest rhetoric was as much to convince himself as to reassure his best friend, but it seemed to have worked. Fred sighed his relief. Stan blinked his pale blue eyes behind the magnifying lenses of his spectacles and the worrying moment of doubt passed. They resumed their intense peering into the distance, planted at the wharf's edge like two leaning stalks of the same flower.

Stan and Fred had been firm friends ever since bumping into each other on Stan's first day at the vast Cadbury Brothers factory, a year previously. Stan's mind had been spinning from the grandeur and scale of the Bournville site, his eyes looking everywhere except where he was supposed to be going. Hypnotised by the sheer number of electric light bulbs hanging from the ceiling, he had meandered straight into Fred's hurtling path towards a seat in the men's dining room. The ensuing crash had sent Stan's spectacles somersaulting onto the dinner plate of a clerk from Cocoa Buying and had left Fred in a heap of tangled overalls beneath an adjacent table. As Fred's disheveled form uncoiled itself from the parquet floor, a firm friendship had appeared the least likely outcome of the coming together. But to Stan's amazement, Fred's big, honest face broke into a huge grin as he staggered to his feet and he held out a pudgy hand.

"What a bloomin' lark that was!" he chortled. "Bloke over there thought I was gonna land in his liver an' onions." He took a deep breath. "My name's Parker, by the way: Fred Parker. Pleased to meet you, mate."

That is how it had begun: an unlikely meeting of minds following an unfortunate meeting of brawn. Stan, a pale and stringy messenger boy from the General Office; Fred, a tin box solderer from Biscuit Packaging whose appetite for food and enjoyment knew few bounds. And here they were together once more, standing in the rain alongside a prickly canal at the foot of a wilting umbrella, staring keenly into the distance like eager children on Christmas Eve.

"Are you chaps expecting someone?"

The surprise of Mister Ferguson's intervention, from a position immediately behind Fred's right shoulder, caused the two chums to jump three inches off the ground. Hearts thumping, neither dared to turn into eye contact with Cadbury's esteemed Manager of Education.

"Sir?" they stammered into the rain.

"Are you two privy to some special source of information as to what we might be expecting to arrive from that particular direction?"

"Sir, we're, that is, we are waiting for the barge, Sir," stumbled Stan.

"And which barge would that be, Johnson?"

"Our barge, Sir. The one we're going to camp on.... in," he affirmed feebly. "The Camp School barge, Sir. It's a diesel."

"How very interesting, Johnson. Does this mean, therefore, that you and Parker have booked your own transport to Camp School? Or will you be joining the rest of us on the barge that lies behind me?"

"Sir?"

"Regardez!"

Mister Ferguson presented the vessel in question with a theatrical sweep of his left arm as Stan and Fred wheeled round to face twenty-three gleeful young faces beaming out from the barge's misted windows. A plume of smoke rose from a narrow chimney at the stern, whilst in the foreground, two donkeys chewed at the grass between a pile of railway sleepers.

"Come on, young men. Let's get you aboard."

Red-eared and shame-faced, Stan and Fred discarded their wet weather clothing and baggage at the entrance to the barge and made their way as quickly as possible through the grins of fellow campers to a vacant wooden bench near the front. They sat close together, side by side, eyes downcast.

The air inside was warm, humid and bursting with juvenile excitement. Anticipation was heightened by the dimness of the interior. The window flaps had been closed and fastened against the rain that drummed down on the canvas roof. The hum of voices grew louder. When he lifted his eyes from his boot caps, Stan's first thought was just how spacious the barge was. The deep draft of the hull allowed plenty of headroom, whilst the seventy feet of the boat's length had been skilfully fitted out with wooden benches and tables to create a floating classroom. Narrow, it certainly was, but not claustrophobic and on sunny days the side flaps would be tied up to give the impression of more space. Unfortunately, this morning's view was anything but sunny. Still, no matter. How lucky they were!

At the front of the barge, amidst a controlled eruption of galoshes and umbrella, Mister Ferguson made his formal entry aboard. A dapper man in his early fifties, he was of medium build and greying hair, with a neatly trimmed moustache beneath a large aquiline nose. His suit dated back to the old queen's reign, sombre and slightly worn, but immaculately clean. The fragrance of Macassar hair oil preceded his arrival at the wooden crate that would serve as his temporary throne. He lowered himself into a sitting position, adjusted the spectacles on his fine nose and levelled his gaze upon the congregation. Voices hushed away, boots shuffled to order, eyes swivelled front. Attention rapt, the great man began his speech:

"Good morning, boys."

"Good morning, Mister Ferguson," they chimed.

"Welcome to the Bournville Works Camp School barge for this year's voyage to Warwick and Stratford upon Avon."

He paused for effect.

"I am pleased to say that such adventures have now become an annual event in the life of the Day Continuation School. We are much indebted to the firm in this regard and I am sure that you will want to join me in thanking Cadbury Brothers for its generous support of our educational endeavour thus far."

A spattering of weak applause broke out, largely emanating from the members of staff at the rear.

"Eight years ago, Mister Merrett and I had the pleasure of leading a group of boys on our very first Camp School. It was held in the village of Rubery and was a splendid success. We repeated our experiment the following year, but, alas, the War then intervened. Our efforts at practical instruction outside the classroom environment had, by force, to be placed on hold. The world was obliged to attend to business of a very much graver nature."

"What's 'e on about?" whispered Fred to Stan. "I can't 'ardly understand a word 'e says."

"It is not, however, my intention to dwell upon the horrors of the Great War," proceeded Mister Ferguson. "That particular subject is all too familiar. Instead, let us look to the future; to youth, as represented here upon this vessel of learning. You boys can now look forward - *must* look forward - to a future of peace, harmony and economic prosperity, the like of which humankind has never before known. The modern learning techniques of our annual Camp School have been specifically devised to help equip you for the marvellous opportunities that lie ahead."

The headteacher's ponderous efforts at product marketing were met with profound silence. Fred mimed a look of puzzlement and somebody at the back stifled a yawn. Stan's brow was furrowed in concentration. The air inside the barge was getting hotter. Mister Ferguson ploughed on.

"As Mister Merrett has recently written: 'Camp School is essentially a school, but it is conducted under camp conditions; the warp is camp, the weft is school, and the fabric is a most delightful recreation for body and mind.'"

"Blimey, it's a bloomin' dressmaking course we're on," whispered a tall lad called Coley, loudly enough for the boy behind him to have to snort back laughter by disguising it as a violent sneeze.

"Bless you Ironmonger," smiled Mister Ferguson. "I do hope that you haven't caught cold in this morning's rain?"

"No, Sir. S'oright, Sir," replied Ironmonger, red in the face. "Just got something up me nose."

Mister Ferguson hummed a brief reproach and forged on:

"The primary aim of the Camp School is, therefore, educational. But instruction will be largely practical. As we travel, we must endeavour to learn more - by lesson, visit and observation - of the villages and parishes through which we pass. Many places and features of interest will command your attention: architecture, history, scenery, geology, literary associations and industry. If your work during the week is done well, it will furnish material for many a pleasant reflection. Above all, Camp School will give you a more complete appreciation of the wonder and complexity of life."

The preacher surveyed his flock from the pulpit prow of his barge of learning. A mixture of wide-eyed reverence and bleary-eyed incomprehension washed back. He continued.

"The success or failure of a venture such as the Camp School rests with everyone on this barge. We are all in it together, so to speak." He afforded himself a brief smile.

"You coming with us then, Sir?" piped up the tiny Alfie Bedlow from his position behind the front desk.

"No, Bedlow, I am not. I was employing a figure of speech, do you see? For demonstration purposes." Mister Ferguson sighed faintly and moved on.

"Each of you will have been provided with a printed booklet containing notes on certain aspects of the topography, architecture and dwellings that we will encounter along the way."

He lifted a copy of the booklet above his head, inadvertently squashing it against the canvas roof.

"Do you all have these with you?"

"Yes, Mister Ferguson," replied the chorus.

"Very good. Some of the text within the booklet has been reproduced from Doctor B.J. O'Brien's seminal work on the county, *Words On Warwickshire*, published last year. These extracts have been selected to accompany and inform you at every stage of our journey. They will illuminate the wonders of our voyage and I can certainly vouch for the scholarship that lies behind them, for the author is a close personal acquaintance of mine."

Mister Ferguson lifted his eyes in expectation of a gasp of admiration which did not materialise. Instead, a boy near the back mined a bogey from his left nostril whilst the others remained uniformly unmoved. Mister Ferguson cleared his throat.

"A number of maps and guide books have been placed at various points on the barge to allow you to follow our route. By way of an enrichment of the general subject matter, the firm has provided a new edition of the complete works of Shakespeare and I have added my own copy of *The Deserter, and other stories* by Harold Frederic. We can't have you studying local history all of the time, now can we? Please treat all of these books with the utmost care."

The boys earnestly nodded their solemn promise so to do.

"As you can see, space aboard is very limited. Please do not, therefore, clutter it up for everyone else by leaving books, boots, items of clothing or half-eaten sandwiches strewn around the barge. Anyone who has brought along an umbrella or his Sunday hat will be obliged to leave it behind with me on the wharf. I can't think why I am looking at you in particular, Bushell."

The boys giggled at Bushell's embarrassment.

"Your kit bags are to stay aft, where you have stowed them, until we reach the evening camp site. For the benefit of land lubbers amongst you, aft is at the back."

Another wave of laughter rippled through the barge.

"Mister Barker and Mister Pickup, who you all know from the School, will be leading this week's excursion. The Master of the vessel is Mister Reid who, with the help of Mister Phipps, will also be acting as ship's quartermaster and cook. Young Doran will be leading the donkeys. Needless to say, I expect you to give these gentlemen your full attention and obedience at all times. Discipline on board is of paramount importance."

Somebody near the back dropped his pencil and made a dive to retrieve it under the desk. The ensuing mini fracas gave momentary pause to Mister Ferguson's flow, but he was soon back into the swing of his discourse.

"Finally, but most importantly, is the question of your diaries. You are all expected to keep a diary of the week ahead and the firm will offer prizes for the best examples. Your diary will be your own permanent record of the school afloat, so be sure to write it carefully. And feel free to make its contents as interesting as possible. Drawings, snap shots and post cards may all be inserted, along with anything else that you think will add colour. Mister Pickup has a new notebook for each of you and will distribute them presently."

Three or four of the boys turned around to catch sight of Mister Pickup and were rewarded by a smile from their teacher and a glimpse of a pile of brand new notebooks on the desk beside him.

"So, without further ado, it is time for me to bid you *Bon Voyage* and to disembark. Have fun, boys, out there in the wild beyond, and above all, behave yourselves."

With that, and without applause, Mister Ferguson disembarked to the starboard side and scuttled off into the pouring rain. Behind him, an expectant buzz of excitement swelled within the barge. Mister Reid busied himself at the tiller; Mister Phipps untied the ropes and at precisely 6.11 a.m., under leaden skies and torrential rain, the work's barge slipped away from the wharf and headed south. To the boys' right, a shunting locomotive, wreathed in steam and raindrops, tooted farewell as it fussed around Waterside Sidings, its flock of empty coal trucks clanking to a halt at the buffers. Ahead lay the Bournville Lane aqueduct, broad enough to carry not only the Birmingham and Worcester canal, but also the twin tracks of the mainline railway. Beyond that, almost everything for the boys would be new.

From his seat beside a side flap, Stan could not see Bournville Lane below. Neither could he see the sweet shop on the corner of Victoria Road that he had been looking forward to viewing from above. Even those next to the windows were struggling to see much of anything outside, so dense were the droplets of condensation rolling down the glass. If it had not been for the gentle swishing of water beneath the hull, nobody on board would have known that they were really moving. But moving they most certainly were, at a steady 2 miles per hour and in the direction of adventure. How exciting!

The weather quickly improved and by the time the barge reached Kings Norton Stop Lock the order had been given to lift and peg up the side panels to let in the morning air. But just as the warmth of the day began to dispel condensation, the barge came to a graceful halt before the forbidding obscurity of Brandwood tunnel.

Young Doran led the donkeys up the steep path that sliced into the bank to the left of the barge as the boys watched on. Tall, wrinkled and slightly stooped, Doran appeared to Stan to be the living antithesis of everything young. Beneath his greasy flat cap, the weathered skin of his brow was ploughed into furrows of servitude and resolve. His grizzled chops sprouted white stubble whilst the toothless mouth clamped a short briar at its corner. He wore brown moleskin trousers beneath a coarse canvas smock, pulled tight at the waist by a length of string. His boots were caked with dried mud. It was impossible to pinpoint Young Doran's age. He could have been fifty or a hundred, but probably nobody had ever thought to ask.

Stan thought it a good time to scan the first extract from Doctor O'Brien's *Words on Warwickshire*:

Brandwood Tunnel is the first major landmark along the Stratford Canal that sprouts left from the Birmingham and Worcester just beyond Kings Norton Junction. It is the only tunnel along the whole 25 mile length of the canal and represents a portal between the growing urban landscape of Birmingham at its northern end, and the sleepy green Warwickshire countryside to the south. The tunnel was designed and engineered by the great canal architect, Josiah

Clowes. It measures 352 yards in length and was officially opened to traffic in 1796, some three years after the first plans had been drawn up and two years after the death of its architect. Work on the rest of the Stratford Canal was to be frequently hampered by funding difficulties and disagreements amongst the backers. The section to Kingswood Junction was formally opened in May 1802, but the final stretch into Stratford was not completed until 1815.

Even when fully open, the canal never represented the huge step forward in local transport that its backers had originally promised. Coal was its principal cargo and, for the first thirty years or so, the tolls that were levied brought in enough profits for the owners to pay themselves a modest annual dividend. But ongoing issues of flooding in the upper Avon, along with falling revenues and increased competition from the railways, led the owners to seek a buyer. In 1845, in a move full of irony, the canal was sold to the Oxford, Worcester and Wolverhampton Railway Company. With the railway age dawning bright throughout the country, dusk came quickly to the Stratford canal. One hundred years after its ceremonial opening, it is now derelict, unloved and virtually redundant.

With the long hauling ropes now coiled on the prow, the barge was once again under way - but only just. In the absence of the donkeys, locomotion through the tunnel was powered by the strong arms of Messers Reid and Phipps, pulling on a rickety handrail that ran along the right-hand wall. The air was damp and cool. Ancient brickwork, blotched with green and occasionally streaked with white, arced up out of the black water. For the boys, it was like a ride on the ghost train at the fun-fair. Their voices whooped and yelled in the semi-darkness, claiming doubtful echoes and daring virgin swear words. The temptation to touch the wall was irresistible. Arms flailed in the dampness; finger nails scraped the moss from the mortar; hands dipped into the chilly water. Boys seated towards the middle of the boat scrambled to where the action was. Smiles lit up the dimness. The barge swayed to the movement of happy campers.

It took them a quarter of an hour to navigate the tunnel and when the barge finally re-emerged into the light of day it straight away made its first scheduled halt at Mill Pool Hill Wharf, where Young Doran was waiting with the donkeys. The clouds were thinning and the sun made a fleeting appearance. It was time for breakfast.

Excitedly, the boys spilled out into the long wet grass and set about arranging half a dozen wooden benches, in a higgledy-piggledy arc alongside the barge. Mister Reid erected a trestle table and, with the assistance of the dumpy Mister Phipps, brought forth a steaming tea urn from the barge's galley. Given the difference of at least twelve inches in their respective heights, the grey-haired porters arrived at the table with a decidedly lop-sided demeanour, but the urn was sited without mishap, its brass tap overhanging the table edge. The two then returned to the barge in search of a tray of enamel mugs and teaspoons, three loaves of bread, a bread knife and a quart of damson jam.

In an impressively ordered fashion, the boys filed forwards for Mister Reid to give each of them a steaming mug of sweet, milky tea.

"Hurry along, now," he implored, "Take your slice and sit down quietly."

Mister Phipps, perspiring and flustered, quickly fell behind in his task of cutting the unwieldy loaves and the line of boys concertinaed to halt in front of him. Tea was spilled, but the delay in service was short. Before long, heaped spoonfuls of jam were being dolloped onto thick slices of crusty bread as the procession wound towards its conclusion. Within five minutes, each boy was seated on one of the forms, head bowed over breakfast. Discussion between mouthfuls was minimal: the jam was simply too delicious! As conversation gradually resumed, it was of cricket and the unstoppable might of Warwick Armstrong's Australians. The summer's final Test match was to begin at The Oval that very morning.

"I can't see England winning this one neither," grumbled Barnwell. "The Ozzies are unstoppable."

"We just don't have the bowlers," asserted Bushell. "We need someone to do to them what MacDonald and Gregory have been doing to us. And then we need someone to bat. There's only Woolley and Tennyson who can stand up to them, what with Hobbs being crocked, and I can't see old Mead being the answer."

"Sounds like you want to change the whole bloomin' team!" laughed Duggan, one of the older boys from Chocolate Moulding.

"How'd you know all this stuff anyway, Bushell?" asked Coley.

"Follow it in the newspapers," grunted Bushell. "You know. Big white things full of black words. Must have seen them, even if you've never managed to read one."

"Now, now, Bushell," crooned Mister Pickup, looming into the conversation. "Less of the teasing, if you don't mind. It's high time we were making tracks. And that means it's first turn on fatigues for the boys I am about to name." His thick white hair glinted in the sunlight as he reached for a paper in the rear pocket of his shorts.

Mister Pickup had come late to education, availing himself of a wartime recruitment drive to cast off twenty-five years of commercial travelling in garden trowels and achieve a long held ambition to impart knowledge to young people. Tall and angular, he exuded earnest intent in every deed, but educational authority was periodically compromised by a propensity to mix up his words and speak in malapropisms. The teacher cleared his throat. The boys furthest from him continued to chatter and giggle.

"Er hem. Pay attention, boys. Come on, lads: settle down now. Quiet please. Settle down at the back."

The throng settled down.

"Today being Saturday, the following campers are required to carry out fatigues. That is, washing, drying and storing the foodstuff and serving accoutrements. Those lads are: Pickles, Clarke, Bedlow, Ironmonger, Armstrong, Cooke and Shaw. Your turn at fatigues continues until lights-out. Thereafter, you will be liberated of your burdensome burden for the rest of the week."

Mister Pickup paused for reaction, received none, and continued.

"All boys are subjugated to fatigue duty, so do please consult the list that I will affix prominently to the notice board onboard."

"Is that two boards, then?" asked Coley.

Mister Pickup looked down his nose disdainfully before pursuing his instruction.

"Would you now please return your cups and plates to the table, clean your irons in the bowl provided and assemble before the barge prior to embarkation. And would the Fatigue Squad now repair to post!"

Mister Pickup's directive was followed by a moment of confusion as boys dispersed in several directions at once. A bench toppled over and a mug was knocked to the ground.

"Excuse us, Sir," asked Clarke. "Where *is* our post?"

"At the trestle table, of course. You and the other boys are to pack away the dirty items and stow them on board for ulterior cleaning when we arrive at camp. Now, hurry along boys, will you. Hurry along. We must be getting on."

3

LESSONS ABOARD

A t 8.30, with the breakfast items finally loaded and all of the boys aboard, it was time to cast off. Fifty yards along the towpath, Young Doran whispered into the ear of the lead donkey and the straining tow rope rose dripping from the black water. Mister Reid guided the barge towards the middle of the canal, passed under the Yardley Wood Road bridge and set course for Happy Valley. Stan turned once more to the words of Doctor O'Brien.

In 1793, Josiah Clowes chose to follow the winding course of the Chinn brook when planning this stretch of canal between Yardley Wood and Shirley. The meadows around the brook had long been favoured as a Sunday picnic spot by the inhabitants of Birmingham, offering a truly happy escape from the soot and grime of their cramped town, but the arrival of the canal increased the popularity of Happy Valley still further. By the end of the last century there were regular Sunday concerts on the wide lawns and in the adjacent pavilion, with several tea shops offering sustenance before the long walk home. Pleasure boats could be hired from the old coal wharves and there was even a small fairground.

Happy Valley's heyday came in the last decade of the nineteenth century, by which time it had become the favoured holiday destination of the working people of Birmingham. But the Great War brought such idle pleasures to a halt. The Valley lost its popularity just as summer weekends lost their fun.

On this damp morning in August 1921, no crowds congregated at Happy Valley. The city had devoured much of the meadowland and choking weeds narrowed the waterway. Mister Reid steered his barge past the rundown facade of the *Happy Valley Refreshment and Tea Rooms* and on towards a road bridge spanning the canal. Stan knew this stretch of the waterway well. He had been here often with Jack, his brother, fishing for sticklebacks with a jam jar and a bent pin tied to a length of twine. Here, the canal was but a short walk from the tram terminus to which on Saturday afternoons the brothers would proudly travel aboard their father's tram; sandwiches in a brown paper parcel and dreams a-plenty of the one they would not let get away.

Those days of innocence suddenly seemed a long way off to Stan. Back then, he was a child; today, a proud employee of Cadbury Brothers, travelling in the work's barge past the very spot were he and Jack had unhooked their tiny catch in pre-war summers. Stan watched the shadows of his childhood slip by with a sense of happiness and pride.

Ahead of the barge and to the right, Young Doran and the donkeys plodded along the towpath, past the site of an old stop lock and on towards the Yardley Wood Aqueduct. Viewed from the barge, the meadows seemed to fall away on both sides as the barge glided forwards, whilst the canal maintained its level course across a mounting bank of piled up earth. Soon, the banking, too, disappeared and the barge floated out across the aqueduct, held aloft in its cradling channel by eight red brick arches over thirty feet high. Below raced the river Cole, a shallow but unruly tributary of the River Blythe that criss-crossed many of the local lanes and byways around Birmingham. The broad ford that bisected the lane directly beneath the aqueduct was its last such crossing before the river joined forces with the Chinn brook, near Yardley. A girl in a blue smock was racing twigs through the bobbling current.

At the far end of the aqueduct, the fields and trees to the right gave way to mountainous piles of black ash, tipped from a thousand Victorian refuse barges. A city's waste matter brought out to bury the fertile countryside: an immense and ugly stain on a once Happy Valley. Fred looked down the black slopes of compacted ash to the lane below. Two young boys in filthy clothes were struggling up the lower reaches pushing a wheeled contraption that appeared to have been cobbled together from a soap box, two perambulator axels and four assorted wheels, no two of the same size.

"Blimey," declared Fred in awe, "I reckon they're gunna race that perishin' thing down the heap!"

Stan pushed past his friend to get a better view. The barge drifted on. The racing contraption had disappeared from sight, but Stan could see a hundred wheel tracks scored into the black ash, criss-crossing the humps and hollows of the vertiginous descent to the road below.

"They must be mad."

"Mad? Bloomin' lucky, more like. I'd kill for a go at that, wouldn't you? Blimey! The speed of it!"

"Pretty sure you'd be killed if you had a go, you big Nelly."

"Oh come on, Stan," insisted Fred, beaming at the thought. "It'd be brilliant!"

The barge was approaching the Drawbridge Inn, a small whitewashed public house standing next to the bridge after which it was named. Fred made a mental note of the place. He would definitely be back with a soap box on wheels one day.

"Now then, lads," admonished Mister Pickup in response to an increasing level of chatter. "Let's all pay attention, shall we."

The boys turned noisily around on their benches to face the teacher who was standing at the back of the barge next to the pile of notebooks.

"Settle down, now. Settle down," he requested. The boys settled down.

"I am about to issue each of you with a lined exercise book in which you will be expected to write up your camp diary. Please take good care of the book and be sure to write legibly within it."

Mister Pickup handed a pile of ten books to each of the three boys sitting closest to him. "Take one book from the top of the pile and then pass the remainder to the boy immediately behind you. I will collect any spare books in due course, once I have made my way to the front of the barge."

Stan took a book from the dwindling pile that arrived over his left shoulder and quickly passed on the others to Duggan, sitting in front of him. A box of sharpened pencils arrived next and Stan took one for himself before handing the box to Duggan and awaiting further instruction from Mister Pickup, now installed in the bow. This turned out to be somewhat vague.

"Right-ho, Boys. Settle down now. The whole barge is waiting on you, Armstrong. Thank you. Right then. That's better. Now, as Mister Ferguson remarked to you this very morning, the keeping of a diary is a paramour of importance. Not only will it become a constant reminder to you of your week at camp, but it also represents the chance for you to receive a handsome reward."

"Oooo," chorused a number of the younger boys at the front.

Suitably heartened, Mister Pickup continued his recital.

"The writers of those diaries that reach a sufficiently high standard of excellence - not just excellent, mark you, but highly excellent - will receive suitable books in recognition of their good work."

To Mister Pickup's surprise, the murmuring that ensued amongst the boys following his pronouncement proved less positive.

"Books?" whispered Fred to Stan, "Why couldn't they give us a bag of chocolate waste?"

Stan was actually quite excited by the prize on offer and determined that his would be the very best diary of the week's camp. He did not, however, share this new objective with Fred.

"Yes, well, I'm glad that you approve," said Mister Pickup unconvincingly. "So, without further ado, may I suggest that you all make a start. We have a long stretch ahead of us and it will be after midday before we stop for dinner."

Stan lowered his eyes to the book and searched for inspiration. There seemed to be an awful lot of pages between the mottled covers and he wondered how on earth was he going to fill them. Fred was looking out of the barge, watching a moorhen scamper into the undergrowth. Duggan was already bent over his labours, sketching out an elaborate frontispiece design of serifs and copperplate. The barge was strangely quiet; the water audible as it swished against the hull. Where to start?

It came to Stan in a flash: a chart. He would create a chart in which each activity and place of interest would be recorded against the time and date of its occurrence, thereby creating a densely packed fact list that would be both easy to understand and brilliant in its originality. And he would include page references, too, allowing the reader to turn to relevant sections in a flash. What a marvellous idea! He looked quickly around the barge to see if anyone else had thought of the same thing. Duggan certainly hadn't, if his ornate calligraphy was anything to go by, and Armstrong was too busy picking his nose to have come up with anything at all. Stan appeared to be in a happy minority of one. He allowed himself a smile and, without quite knowing why, looked out towards the towpath on his right. To his surprise, Young Doran was there, framed in the open window of the barge, leaning on a wooden staff and peering directly at Stan from beneath his greasy cap. Was that a wink? Stan quickly averted his gaze. Surely not. He must have imagined it. He turned back to the window but Young Doran was no longer to be seen.

"I have a number of rulers and erasers with me here at the front - er, bow - should anyone have need of them," offered Mister Pickup.

Stan shook his head, as if to clear it, and his thoughts returned to the exciting prospect of his chart. "Me, Sir. Please," he replied, thrusting his hand in the air. "May I borrow a ruler, Sir?"

"Come forward to collect it, Johnson, but be sure to put it back in the same place once you have sufficed of it."

As Stan drew the final straight line of his master chart fifteen minutes later, the barge passed the principal feeder channel of the Stratford Canal, through which the waterway draws replenishment from the Earlswood Reservoirs. He set down the ruler and turned once more to *Words on Warwickshire*:

Clowes's carefully planned canal runs flat for the first ten miles of its course, from Brandwood Tunnel all the way to Hockley Heath, but the subsequent decent into Stratford upon Avon comprises a total of 55 locks and demands a consistent supply water to remain operational. Work on digging the necessary reservoirs began in 1820, at Earlswood, where the River Blythe could be diverted to fill them. It was a huge undertaking. Construction of the three artificial lakes took five years to complete and employed hundreds of workers, including many prisoners from the Napoleonic wars. Today, the benefits of their labours still endure, extending well beyond the sporadic demands for water from the decaying canal system. The reservoirs have become popular boating lakes and summer swimming pools, attracting hundreds of weekend visitors from Birmingham who arrive by train at Lakes Halt, a request stop on the Birmingham to Stratford railway line.

By 10.35, the barge was at Warings Green and Stan, bang up to date with diary entries on his master chart, was able to write: "Weather quite fine, sun shining brilliantly."

The Warwickshire countryside slid lazily by. Stan stretched his arms above his head and yawned, his eyelids suddenly heavy in the sunlight. He was saved from slumber by an announcement from the bow:

"Alright now, boys. Settle down please. Settle down now. That includes you, Armstrong. Thank you. Well, the time has come for our first lesson of the day. I must, therefore, ask you to give your full attention to Mister Barker as he imbues you all, as I know he will, with today's lesson on church architecture."

Chair legs grated and boots shuffled as the boys brought their anticipation and attention into line. Mister Barker was not to be missed. His quiet authority had a way of capturing potential mischief and holding it, caged, until the lesson had been thoroughly learned. Mister Barker had what politicians call *presence*. He had talent, too. He could enthuse a group of excitable, working class boys for forty-five minutes on the subject of medieval church masonry without recourse to hypnotism. This extraordinary hold on his class owed little to Mister Barker's stock of ripping yarns, for in this regard his cupboard was bare. Neither could you say that Mister Barker was a particularly strict and disciplinarian soul who bullied his charges into docility. He certainly was not. What really held the attention of the boys was their master's most singular appearance.

Above average height and as slim as a bean stick, Mister Barker stood to attention in his tailored tweed suit and leaned his weight upon an artificial right leg, the silver top of his walking stick gripped tight in leather-gloved hand. His left profile still bore the handsome traits of his youth, but when he turned to face the benches of the camp school barge, the physical scars of Mr Barker's war were clear to all. Much of the skin on the right side of his face had been burned and stretched to a mottled-raw appearance, like that of an old man, yet curiously unwrinkled. A dark leather patch covered what used to be Mister Barker's shooting eye. His right ear, disfigured by blast and burns, was recognisable only from its position on the side of the head. The burns extended up into the hairline, creating a rather lopsided crown of wavy blond hair, held in place with fragrant oil. His mouth bore an odd, permanent smile, lips stretched at the corner by tightened skin, which forced Mister Barker to lisp on difficult words, like "cerebral" or "spiritual", but which never allowed him to express his sadness. Sadness was the deepest of Mister Barker's scars. A bleak, dark sadness that periodically eclipsed his bright outlook like a fall of soot in a sunlit room. Once upon a time, everything in his life had been bright; every challenge achievable, every opportunity within reach. But that was before.

Arthur Charles Barker was born in Edgbaston and educated at King Edward VI High School, where he excelled as a scholar and shone as a sportsman. In 1909, he played a summer's cricket for Warwickshire before going up to Oxford to read Classics at Brasenose. He enjoyed his studies and loved his sport, gaining Blues for association football and athletics, as well as for cricket, at which he was university captain for two of his three years. He breezed to his First Class honours degree and went down from Oxford in the summer of 1912 to train as a barrister. He was called to the bar in 1914 and celebrated his general contentment with life by taking his mother for tea at The Ritz. Two months later, in a crowded Birmingham recruitment hall, Arthur signed up as a volunteer for the 15th Battalion, The Royal Warwickshire Regiment. He was commissioned as a Second Lieutenant and posted to the Western Front where he would spend the rest of his war. He proved himself a brave and popular young officer, being mentioned in despatches once and promoted twice, and by a combination of good luck and quick thinking had managed to escape any kind of serious injury for the better part of two years. Then, on the morning of September 25th, 1916, on the road between Ginchy and Morval in the valley of the Somme, his run of good fortune ran out.

Arthur had first learned of Cadbury Brothers' pioneering attempts to provide complementary education to their young factory workers at one of his mother's social gatherings. Mister Ferguson, whose upward mobility through the Edgbaston social clique had finally brought him within reach of the Barker family, had trapped the injured son in the corner of the drawing room and regaled him with a forty minute introduction to the cause. Arthur had neither the heart nor the mobility to escape. Yet strangely, as the minutes rolled by, Mister Ferguson's animated exposition of his educational thesis began to strike a chord. Arthur began to envisage a road away from the shattered promise of his youth. A chance to reconnect with the lost concepts of innocence and trust; with hope and with education. Arthur liked the idea a lot.

And so it began, in the tea-scented drawing room of his family home. Within days, Arthur had been accorded the honour of accompanying Mister Ferguson to tea with Mister George Cadbury and the matter of his future career had been settled. The old man had simply bowled him over with his shining eyes and enthusiasm for the continuation of learning. It had been quite impossible to say no.

"No, Armstrong," insisted Mister Barker softly, "I do not think that Sweeney Todd was the culprit, regardless of what you may have read in your Penny Dreadfuls. Indeed, the facts may actually predate your source by some 400 years, although I could be wrong. In either case, you should all make this a subject for close investigation if ever you have the opportunity to visit the church."

The subject in question was the tower of Saint Michael's, the tiny church at Baddesley Clinton, a village still several hours distant. In typical fashion, Mister Barker had begun his narrative on the architecture of the church, not with a detailed résumé of the merits of its nave or chancel, but with a murder. The murder of the local priest, no less. And it appeared that Nicholas Brome, the Lord of the Manor, had been the murderer. According to Mister Barker, old Nicholas had been wandering through his grounds one day when he happened upon his beautiful wife, locked in a passionate embrace with the priest. The sight of his wife thus engaged had rather upset Nicholas and he attacked the priest, killing him stone dead. Such acts of anti-clerical violence were generally frowned upon in the late fifteenth century and Nicholas was in fear for his life. Happily for him, however, the gods were on his side. Or rather, the Pope and the King were on his side, which amounted to pretty much the same thing. Nicholas was pardoned for his crime and straight away set about making reparations, investing all of his money and what remained of his time in the renovation of Saint Michael's church, including the construction of a new tower, in which he installed a peal of three bells. It was a labour of love to follow a crime of passion, but definitely not the act of Sweeney Todd. At least, that's what Mister Barker said.

The barge slipped deep into the sunny morning, winding around the contours of Warwickshire at the clip-clop pace of the donkeys. Mister Pickup had joined Mister Reid for a spot of conversation at the stern, but now dozed in the wicker chair by the tiller. Mister Phipps bent over his knife in the tiny galley, chopping up bread for dinner. The unheated stew slopped gently in its pot. Further along the barge, the unfurling of Mister Barker's lesson hummed along like a well oiled motor, whilst thirty yards ahead of him, trudging down the towpath, Young Doran, unhurried and unheard, hummed a strange tune to the trees.

At 11.40, Mister Barker's lesson came to an orderly conclusion and the boys indulged in a spot of leg and arm stretching. Stan reached for his diary. Glancing right, he caught his first glimpse of the red brick spire of the Church of Saint Thomas and gleefully filled in the next line of his chart "11.40: Hockley Heath Church sighted." This was all going jolly well!

Mister Pickup made his way through the desks towards the front of the barge, stifling a yawn.

"Now, boys. Pay attention will you, please. Settle down now. Settle down. That includes you people at the back. Right. We are presently proceeding through the village of Hockley Heath and those of you sitting on the starboard side will soon be afforded a splendid visa of Umberslade Park and its fine house."

Most of the boys guessed correctly and looked right. The few who found themselves gazing at woodland, to the port side, quickly rectified their mistake before Mister Pickup had noticed.

"Umberslade Park is the property of the famous Mister Muntz and his family. Now, can any of you boys tell me something about Mister Muntz?"

The boys murmured amongst themselves, cluelessly.

"Anyone?" implored Mister Pickup.

An arm was raised at the back.

"Yes, Duggan? What can you tell us about Mister Muntz then?"

"Me Uncle Tommy lives in his road, Sir."

There was a burst of laughter. Even Mister Barker smiled. At least, he seemed to be smiling. It was always so difficult to tell.

"Would you mind explaining yourself, Duggan?" requested Mister Pickup, composing himself.

"Muntz Road, Sir. Me Uncle Tommy lives in an house in Muntz Road: number 89. It's in Small Heath, Sir. Me Aunty Hilda lives there an' all."

Duggan was smiling broadly, evidently rather pleased with himself. The other boys were rather pleased with him, too.

"Oh, I see," responded Mister Pickup, who didn't, "Very good, Duggan, I am sure. Yes. Well."

In floundering for something else to say, his eyes met the Cyclops gaze of Mister Barker, standing near the galley. To Mister Pickup's great relief, his fellow teacher came to his aid.

"Well, clearly Mister Muntz must have attained great success in his field if the City of Birmingham has chosen to name a street after him, Duggan," encouraged Mister Barker. "But can anybody guess just what that field might have been?"

The shuffling of feet under desks was the best that anyone could muster by way of a response.

"I will give you a clue," proposed Mister Barker. "It is something for which the city now enjoys world renown. And I am not talking about chocolate, Bushell."

"The Austin, Sir?" ventured Bushell, unconvincingly.

His father worked at the Longbridge plant, a mile or two from Bournville, but even as he said it, Bushell realised that he was wide of the mark.

"I think that you will find that Mister Herbert Austin is responsible for that particular enterprise, Bushell. The clue being in the name."

Bushell's face reddened as the other boys giggled.

"But well done for trying," soothed Mister Barker. "Anyone else going to hazard a guess?"

"Guns?" attempted Bert Morris.

"Almost guns, yes. Good. We are getting warmer. Indeed, without Mister Muntz and his business, we would have no guns at all."

"It's iron, Sir," trumpeted Clarke from Display Materials. "Yeah: Muntz's Ironworks."

"Exactly, Clarke. Iron it is. Well done. In fact, Mister George Frederick Muntz founded his iron manufacturing company almost one hundred years ago and its success made him a very rich man. He swiftly became one of the city's leading benefactors and went on to represent the city as a Member of Parliament. After his death, the business passed to his sons, as did his magnificent home."

Right on queue, as if the teacher had been deliberately timing his speech for dramatic effect, the lawns and grand buildings of Umberslade Park floated by on the starboard side. Stan smoothed the page of his diary and carefully recorded the event:

"Umberslade Park is on the right hand side of us. It is the property of Mr Muntz, the great Iron Manufacturer."

He liked the look of "Iron Manufacturer". It made him think of some fantastical creature from a story by H G Wells; a huge manufacturer made of iron, rampaging through a future Britain and casting fantastic iron structures at will. Mister Pickup shook him out of his reverie with a further pronouncement from the bow.

"Right-ho, lads. Very good. Well done. I think that we have now safely asserted exactly who Mister Muntz was and how he came to own such a splendid property. Bedlow, please stop chewing the end of your pencil, will you? They don't grow on trees, you know."

Bedlow dutifully stopped chewing his pencil, leaving a flake of bright red paint stuck to his front tooth and a number of tiny wooden splinters hanging from his lower lip.

"There's a good lad. Now, in the few minutes that remain before dinner, I thought that I might run through the key itinerant features of the rest of our day."

Mister Pickup retrieved another stencilled sheet from his back pocket, cleared his throat and unfolded the paper to its full extent.

"Er hem. We are due to arrive at Lapworth top lock in approximately twenty minutes, whereupon the barge will commence its descent of one of the longest fleets of locks anywhere in the country. In point of fact, there are over twenty locks for our barge to negotiate, and all of them are in a downwards direction."

A number of boys, including Stan and his near neighbour Duggan giggled at this point, which caused Mister Pickup to jerk his gaze away from the stencilled sheet.

"Is something amusing you, Duggan? Is it Johnson, perhaps?"

"No, Sir."

"Then do please attend to what I am telling you a little more closely from now on, will you? I am not going to repeat myself twice."

The boys pulled themselves together and settled down to endure the rest of Mister Pickup's travelogue.

"We will have dinner at Lapworth, whereafter you lads will take part in an outdoor class whilst Mister Reid ensures the safe passage of our vessel down the locks and on to Shrewley. There, we will re-communicate for tea before undertaking the last part of our day's journey, to Hatton. It will be a very full, er, thing. Schedule, that is. May I remind all of those lads on fatigue duty that they will be required to help set up the forms and tables and that they should report to Mister Reid after dinner in order to help with the washing up?"

A low hum of voices indicated that Mister Pickup may, indeed, remind those boys.

"And so, in the few minutes that remain before we touch shore once more at Lapworth, it would probably be a good idea if you all got on with your diaries."

A clatter of desks and chairs ensued, as the boys made themselves comfortable for the next bout of recording the day. There was a good deal of jostling for elbow room in the confined space and, in the ensuing scramble, the ear of one boy was poked with a pencil.

"Oi! Watch it, mate," squealed Armstrong, whose ear had just been pierced, "or I'll knock your bloomin' block off!"

"Oh yeah? You and whose army?" sneered Edgington, a sickly looking boy from packaging who nobody liked.

"Hey! Hey, boys. Settle down. Settle down. Come on, let's have a bit of decorum, shall we? A bit of peace and quiet. Armstrong, I shall see you afterwards."

"But, Sir," spluttered Armstrong indignantly. "'E started it. He stuck his blinking pencil in my ear. And it's bleeding, Sir," he added as an afterthought, although it was not.

"That's enough!" insisted Mister Pickup. And it was.

Stan opened his diary at the page before his embryonic master chart, and set about designing a frontispiece. To his left, Fred gazed out at the Warwickshire countryside. All noise in the barge died away and, once again, the gentle swishing of the water on the hull was the only sound to interrupt the bird song and the distant clip-clopping of the donkeys. They drifted deeper into the green Warwickshire sunshine, past a timber yard and round a sweeping right hand bend. To Stan's left, a noisy threshing machine slapped away at a wheat field's harvest, fed by a posse of labourers. It was a thing that Stan had never seen before: a wonderful thing, alien and new. He smiled in deep happiness and leaned back in his chair to reflect upon the marvellous good fortune that had come his way.

4

THE BRIEFING

*A*fter more than ten miles without a single lock, the Stratford-upon-Avon canal hits something of a jackpot as it approaches its junction with the Warwick and Birmingham at Kingswood. No fewer than twenty-six of them tumble down from the Birmingham plateau, between Lapworth and the Dicks Lane bridge at Rowington, over a distance of less than two miles. The impressive flight includes a run of nine locks, from six to fourteen, which lie immediately next to one another, like long steps cut into the green hillside.

Because the locks are so narrow and short, with room for only one barge at a time, Josiah Clowes designed a series of pounds, or pools, between them where barges might wait their turn or pass others coming in the opposite direction. These pounds also act as mini reservoirs, able to supply water to the flight during busy periods of transit without draining the upper reaches of the canal.

Today the flight was anything but busy. The Camp School's donkey-drawn barge was the first of any description to arrive at

Lapworth all summer and the open top lock gate was draped thick with weed. Young Doran walked the donkeys beyond the gate to a patch of lush grass and watched the barge slip into the narrow channel. Holding the tow rope short and fast, he proceeded to bring the vessel to a smooth halt in front of the bottom gate.

"Right-ho, lads," cried Mister Pickup. "Time to jump off and lend a hand. Orderly, mark you. Let us all disembowel in an orderly fashion. We don't want the ship to sink beneath us, now do we?"

The boys largely ignored their teacher's plea for order and charged for the port side exits, causing the barge to knock heavily against the lock wall.

"Steady on! Hey! Steady on! You'll have us all in the drink at this rate."

Mister Pickup felt queasy. He held on tight to the front desk, the colour draining fast from his face, knuckles shining white beneath his jacket cuffs.

"Come on, lads. Play the game, will you. Play the game."

The lads were definitely playing the game, but not noticeably the one that Mister Pickup had in mind. They cascaded from the barge onto the stone quay, collectively letting off steam, stretching limbs and raising their voices for the first time in hours. Young Doran eased his grip on the rope and smiled into his chin stubble. Mister Phipps and Mister Reid pushed the top gate shut as the barge boy positioned himself next to the sluice winch. Amidst the general hubbub, Mister Pickup gingerly disembarked with conspicuous relief.

"This way, lads. Follow the path to the right."

The teacher herded his boys along the towpath to observe the work of the crew from beyond the second lock. The men and donkeys proceeded to work in silent harmony, lowering the barge through two locks before steering it towards the appreciative boys, now grouped together on the grassy bank a few yards beyond the gate.

"Well done, everybody. Very good, Mister Reid. Excellent. Excellent." Mister Pickup was clapping like a seal. "Now, lads. The plan is for us land-luggers to walk alongside the barge until we attain the next lock. We can then partake of our midday repast together at the appointed place. Dinner, Parker, is what I am talking about. It will soon be time for dinner!"

"Why does he always look at me when he mentions food?" Fred grumbled.

Young Doran and the donkeys passed through the clump of boys, forcing several of them to duck under the towing rope for fear of being swept into the canal. Disarray, however, was temporary and the boys were soon sorted into their familiar twos and threes, straggled out along the towpath, ambling towards the prospect of food. Here, the canal path ran parallel to the main Warwick Road and the excited chatter was briefly interrupted by the grinding gears of a small delivery van, making an assault on the shallow rise back to Hockley Heath. Several of the boys swerved off the path in order to observe the vehicle's travails, peering through the thick hedgerow. Stan and Fred found themselves at the head of the group, walking just behind the donkeys.

"They don't really look strong enough to pull it, do they?" marvelled Stan. "I mean, how much do you think it weighs anyway? Got to be a ton, wouldn't you say? Maybe more."

"Easy a ton," answered Fred sagely. "I mean, the bottom's made of iron isn't it. Bloomin' miracle it floats at all, when you think about it."

Stan did think about it and was about to offer up his own hypothesis on the flotation properties of iron when he was interrupted.

"Seventeen tons six hundredweight, old Sal."

It was a strangely deep and sonorous voice which, to Stan and Fred's great astonishment, emanated from somewhere beneath Young Doran's flat cap, suddenly beside them.

"Er, s-seven... Seventeen tons? Well! Who'd have thought it?" Stan laughed nervously. "Well, well."

"Forty year old last winter and sound as a bell. Don't make 'em like Sal no more."

"Who's Sal?" asked Fred stupidly.

"Shhhhh! You dope. It's the boat, he's talking about. Barge, I mean. Isn't that right, Mr Young... er...Mr Doran?"

But Young Doran had moved along the path to whisper to his donkeys and the question remained rhetorical. Within a few seconds he had unfastened the animals' harness and was waiting for Mister Reid to nudge the nose of the barge into the grassy bank so that he could tie it up to the iron stake that lay upon the prow. Dinner time had arrived!

Upon Mister Pickup's command, the fatigue squad unloaded the wooden forms and serving table, whilst Mister Phipps fussed about in the galley. The operation to set up facilities on the grassy bank proceeded in an agreeably swift and orderly manner, much to Mister Pickup's surprise. Once everything had been arranged, Mister Barker made his lop-sided exit from the barge and limped heavily towards the serving table. The boys quickly formed a raggedy queue behind him, cutlery clutched, sniffing the air for a foretaste of Mister Reid's neck of lamb stew. Rarely had they been so hungry.

The camp school's open-air dining room had been pitched on a broad expanse of grass that stretched away from the pound to the right. On the left hand side, squatting close to the main road, a string of ancient cottages, from one of which there presently emerged a stout woman, her grey hair tied up in a bun. She was wearing an apron over her dark dress and carried a large earthenware jug, a pewter tankard, a brown paper parcel and a newspaper. With her cargo clamped tight to her bosom, the woman made her purposeful way towards the lock gates. Here sat Young Doran, pipe in hand, watching the woman's progress across the grass with no apparent interest. As she drew near, he tipped the peak of his cap with his right thumb. The woman made a brief curtsy in reply, before placing the items of her burden on the gate beside him and taking two steps backwards.

"How extraordinary," said Stan who had been watching the proceedings from his bench on the other side of the pound. "Would you believe it?"

"Believe what?" asked Fred, his mouth stuffed full of bread and stew.

"I think that Young Doran may have an admirer," said Stan. "Or at least, a lady friend from these parts. Look over there."

Fred looked over there and saw Young Doran pouring ale from the jug, the woman watching from a distance. Young Doran filled, then drained the tankard in three draughts and set it down upon the beam. He untied the paper packet, took out a thick sandwich and chomped into it with toothless gums.

"Well, I'll be blowed," said Fred between chews. "The old bugger! He's only gone and got himself a private buffet service!"

"Do you think that's his wife?" asked Stan, transfixed.

"His bit on the side, more like," suggested Fred. "Look at the way she's looking at him."

The woman certainly did appear to be gazing at Young Doran in admiration, standing deferentially in front, slightly to the left, watching every mouthful. The old barge boy paid her no attention, finishing his sandwich with a mighty bite and pouring himself a second tankard of ale. He unfolded the newspaper and dipped his cap into its subject matter.

"You've got stew on your chin, Fred," said Stan. "And your mouth's open like you are trying to catch a fly."

"Sorry, Stan," replied Fred wiping his mouth and chin with the palm of his left hand, then wiping the hand on the grass between his feet. "Would you believe it? Young Doran is being waited on like a bloomin' Pasha!"

"Oi, you two. Got any bread left?"

It was Edgington, buoyed by his recent pencil attack on Armstrong's ear, who now fancied his chances of supplementary rations at the expense of Fred and Stan. He got short shrift.

"Push off, Edgington."

Edgington pushed off.

The excellent lamb stew was universally enjoyed, as was the pudding that followed: a generous slice of "dead flies' graveyard", home baked shortbread with currants. Mmmm! The whole thing was rounded off with a mug of sweet tea. What a feast! Amidst the hum of contented conversation emanating from the satisfied diners, Mister Barker struggled to his feet and limped towards the centre of the gathering to stand on a flat piece of turf, feet together. He rapped his silver topped cane against his artificial leg. The hubbub died away.

"It is time for me to talk about this afternoon's activities," began Mister Barker with a twinkle in his eye.

Alfie Bedlow leaned forward, elbows planted on his skinny knees and chin cupped in both hands. He had the look of a tiny gargoyle, neck-less and frowning as he squinted into the sunlight. Everybody was paying attention to Mister Barker.

"Now, are any of you fellows up for a spot of physical activity?"

A cheer of happy affirmatives roared back.

"Very good. Then the first practical lesson of our excursion will be a hiking trip across the Warwickshire countryside."

"Oooo," chorused a few of the younger boys.

"There is good reason for us to undertake such an exercise this afternoon. For the remainder of the day, the progress of our barge will be somewhat laboured. Mister Reid and his crew have no less than sixteen locks to navigate on the descent to Kingswood Junction and then a further eight locks to cope with beyond there. It will be heavy work."

The boys nodded in silent respect.

"At Kingswood, the barge will switch canals, from the Stratford to the Warwick, before heading off in a south-westerly direction towards Shrewley. You fellows will go along on foot. However, as you may have already suspected, it is definitely not our plan to simply allow you to follow the canal path. That would be much too easy for chaps like you, now wouldn't it! Especially for the bright and brawny lads sitting over there."

Mister Barker pointed his cane towards some of the older boys, loafing around together at the back of the group.

"Coley's definitely brawny, Sir, but I'm none too sure how bright he is!"

It was Duggan who called out, swiftly to receive a thump on the top his arm from the aggrieved Coley. The other boys cheered in appreciation, but were quickly cowed into silence as the fearsome Coley wheeled round to stare them down.

"'E's only joking, Coley," offered up Barnwell, unconvincingly.

Coley grinned and sat back down on the bench next to Duggan. No offence taken: no harm done. The good natured Coley was well used to such jibes, especially from his old chum Duggan.

"As I was saying," continued Mister Barker, "this will be a test of stamina as well as intelligence, for the course stretches over several miles and your path will be largely unmarked."

"How we gonna know where we're bloomin' well going then?" whispered Fred to Stan, but Mister Barker got in first with the answer.

"Maps will be provided to guide you, along with a list of directions and clues."

"Is it like a treasure hunt then, Sir?" squeaked Bedlow.

"Indeed it is, Bedlow, although the treasure that you seek will be purely informational: a collection of facts for you to bring back to camp this evening."

A hum of conversation followed. Mister Barker allowed the assembly to come to terms with the task ahead.

"This will be an exercise in team work and collaboration," he continued, "so I would like you all to pick a dependable partner to be your team mate. Once you have settled upon your choice, you should form a line of pairs in front of Mister Pickup."

Mister Pickup waved a helpful arm above his head, just in case any of the boys were unaware of his precise location, though none of them were.

"Who you gonna choose then, Stan?" asked Fred.

"Why, you of course, you big Nelly. Who did you think I was going to choose?"

"Just asking."

"Well, you're the chosen one. So let's get on over to Pickup, shall we?"

"On your command, Skip."

"Shut up, Fred."

Stan and Fred joined the double line of boys, snaking out in front of Mister Pickup.

"I haven't got no one to be with," complained Edgington from the back.

"*Anyone*, Edgington," corrected Mr Pickup. "I haven't got *anyone* to be with."

"That's what I said, Sir."

"Well, never mind, Edgington. Why don't you just join Hendry and Bushell? Make up a threesome."

"Sir!" protested Hendry. "Not Edgington, Sir. Please? Why's he got to come with us, Sir? Wouldn't he be better with somebody his own age?"

"He *is* your age, Hendry."

"But it's not fair, Sir," contributed Bushell. "I mean, he's such a pri... I mean, he'll slow us down, Sir."

"Nonsense, Bushell. On the contrary. The three of you should have a distinct advantage over everybody else. I confidently predict that you will be amongst the first to arrive. Now, let us hear no more about the matter. Do I make myself clear?"

"Yes, Sir," moaned Hendry, casting a look of loathing at the horrible Edgington. "Very clear, Sir."

"Jolly good! Now, settle down everyone. I am about to disseminate the rules of this afternoon's exercise."

The boys hushed themselves to listen.

"To avoid the possibility of you all simply following one another around the countryside like so many lost sheep, Mister Barker has hit upon an idea of pure ingeniosity. He has devised four distinct routes, each with its own list of facts to be collected and its own itinerary to follow. This means that no more than three pairs of you will be working to the same agenda at any one time. And those three will set off at intervals of five minutes, so there will be little chance of cheating. Do you all follow?"

"No, Sir," said Coley.

Mister Pickup cleared his throat and set off again:

"I shall recapitulate. You will see that you are now sub-divided into twelve pairs of two. As I have already explained, we have devised four different routes for you to follow. So, by a simple process of reduction, twelve by four equals three. In other words, each of our distinct itineraries will be followed by just three pairs of hikers. Which, Coley, is what I just said. Do you now see what I was driving at?"

"No, Sir."

Mister Pickup sighed. Barnwell attempted clarification:

"Does that mean we should all be in threes, Sir? Like Bushell and Hendry?"

"No, Barnwell, it does not." Mister Pickup was becoming flustered. He took a deep breath, composed himself by looking hard at his toe caps, then confidently set off up another blind alley:

"The rules state that we should all be in pairs of two and that's just what we are: in twelve pairs. Hendry, Bushell and Edgington are also in a pair, like the rest of you, but it just so happens that there are three of them in their pair. But the fact that they are three is not actually important in the greater scene of things."

"It's important to us, Sir," whined Bushell. "We've got Edgington."

"If I may, Mister Pickup?" Mister Barker's calm intervention washed like a soothing balm over his colleague's fraying nerves.

"By all means, Mister Barker. By all means." Mister Pickup's relief was palpable.

"Let us proceed with the distribution of the booklets," comforted Mister Barker. "I am sure that everything will become clear once the boys have them to hand."

"Indeed. Indeed," gabbled Mister Pickup and he scuttled off to retrieve the booklets from the barge.

"Teamwork," proclaimed Mister Barker, looking proudly along the line of boys, "is about working together for the common good. It is about pooling resources and sharing ideas. It is an existence wherein the needs of the team must always take precedent over the interests of its members: where the output of a team's endeavours must, of necessity, be greater than the sum of its constituent parts."

A pin dropping onto the grass would have made more sound than the twenty-five boys listening. Their attention to Mister Barker's discourse was total, even if their comprehension of what he had just said was not. Mister Pickup panted back into the gathering, clutching the precious booklets to his chest.

"I'm back," he announced pointlessly. "And I have your booklets."

Mister Barker ignored him, continuing his theme at even pace. "You are now, each and every one of you, members of a very special team: *your* team. Henceforth, your loyalty must be to your team and to your team mates. You have no other focus. Your prime objective is to ensure that your team fulfils its mission and that it does so, if possible, ahead of your rivals. It is a mission of the utmost importance, not just to you and your team, but to the very well-being of the entire camp."

He paused, four long seconds, counting them out under his breath. "Now, men: are you ready for the challenge ahead?"

The roar of affirmation that swept across the open grassland caused Mister Pickup to take a step backwards. Away on the lock gate, Young Doran raised a curious eye from his newspaper.

Mister Barker issued the final instructions to his troops: "As I announce each team, would its members please come forward to receive their allotted brochure from Mister Pickup. Thereafter, if each team could repair to a vacant corner of the field to study its contents, we should be in a position to give the off at 2 o'clock precisely."

Mister Pickup whispered something into Mister Barker's ear.

"Indeed. Yes. Once you all have your booklets, would the fatigue squad please report to Mister Reid? There are a few items that will need to be reloaded into the barge before we leave."

The distribution of the booklets passed off smoothly and Stan was soon sitting cross-legged on the grass with his team's booklet. He polished the lenses of his spectacles on his shirt tails and glanced at Fred, lying full length on his back, gazing at the sky.

"Now, Fred. Let's see what they expect of us, shall we?" Stan refitted the wire arms of his spectacles behind his ears and adjusted the frames to sit comfortably on the narrow bridge of his nose. He raised the cover of the booklet into focus.

"Hiking Itinerary C, is what it says here, Fred. We must be one of the three teams working to booklet C." He seemed to have taken on a little of Mister Barker's military conviction as he spoke.

"If you say so, Stan," replied Fred. "It sounded like a load of cobblers to me, especially when old Pickup was having a go."

"Yes, well it all seems pretty clear from the way it's been written down here. Look, there's even a proper map for us to follow."

And so there was; a web of thin white lines stencilled onto a deep blue ground, along with a handful of place names and arrows. On the next page was a short list of basic directions: *proceed five hundred yards along the path to your right*, or *immediately after the stile, turn left and follow the hedgerow*. It all appeared to be very professional. On the final page was a list of *factual requirements*, such as *which species of tree predominates in the garden of Packwood House Farm? What is written on the municipal horse trough at Kingswood market?* Stan scrutinised every detail of the booklet, underlining key sentences with his pencil. Fred chewed on a blade of grass and watched the clouds. It was almost two o'clock.

5

LOST AND FOUND

At precisely fourteen hundred hours, the hikers gathered at the lock gates where Young Doran had earlier enjoyed his fine lunch. Mister Barker ordered that the four youngest pairings should set off first, followed by two further releases of four pairs at five minute intervals. Fred and Stan, as the youngest members of "C Brigade", were detailed to the first wave. It was all very exciting! Mister Pickup kept his final instructions short:

"Now, lads. Gather round and pay attention. I shall repeat myself only once."

The hikers crowded into a small semi-circle around their teacher.

"Here are your final mantras for the journey. They are simple and they are important. Stick to public roads and public footpaths; do not trespass; do not play with the farm animals and do not indulge in scrumping. Is that clear? I'm looking at you, Parker."

Fred's face reddened with indignation. Why was it always him?

A thousand years ago, much of the land into which the boys now ventured was covered by the Forest of Arden. *Words on Warwickshire* set the scene for the intrepid explorers:

The forest was a dense primeval woodland that stretched for hundreds of square miles between the rivers Avon and Tame. It blanketed more than half of Warwickshire, from Stratford upon Avon in the south to Tamworth in the north, including land now occupied by the huge industrial cities of Birmingham and Coventry. So forbidding was the forest to the Romans that they never attempted to cut a road through it. Instead, Icknield Street, Watling Street and Fosse Way all skirted it, leaving the crossing of the forest a famously hazardous occupation. Settlements of any size within the forest were rare. Henley-in-Arden, established as an Iron Age hill fort, was the largest of them, growing in linear fashion along its original track to become an important market village that served many of the outlying forest hamlets.

During the Middle Ages, great swathes of the woodland were cleared and enclosed for farmland. By Shakespeare's time, the Forest of Arden had all but disappeared, even if a large number of remnants remained, along with Shakespeare's own romanticised and largely imaginary memory of the forest in which he set "As You Like It".

One of the larger remnants of the old forest was Hay Wood, lying close to the village of Rowington. It featured on the boys' blue stencilled map as a white blob to the north-east of the canal. Such an area of woodland really should have been easy to spot along the route to Shrewley, but it was proving decidedly tricky for Stan and Fred to locate. Hot and sweating, they had come to a halt alongside a milk churn standing on a wooden platform beside a country lane.

"Where the blinking heck are we, Stan?"

"Just getting our bearings. Give me a minute, will you?"

Stan was turning Booklet C through his hands like Mister Biddle's steering wheel, desperate to get a fix on anything that might resemble a landmark.

"Shouldn't we be going towards the sun, by now?" suggested Fred helpfully. "You know, south?"

"Yes, yes. Don't rush me, Fred. I just need to get my bearings."

Half an hour earlier, it had all seemed so easy. They had made a near perfect start, racing to the first major landmark on their itinerary and collecting the relevant factual information without a hitch. From the lock, they had crossed the Warwick Road, climbed a stile and followed a rough path through a meadow on the other side. Picking their way through the deep clover, swerving around clumps of thistles and jumping over mole hills, Fred and Stan had emerged, seven minutes later, on Packwood Lane, just below the duck pool on the edge of Pratt's Pit Wood (another forest remnant). From there, it was an easy five minute stroll to Packwood House Farm and its ancient walled garden of yew trees.

Viewed through wrought iron gates, the garden made an immediate impression on Stan, who thought it quite the most interesting he had ever seen. Fred was less enthused.

"Looks like a load of fat people waiting for a tram," was his interpretation, "A right bloomin' muddle."

In fact, the garden had been laid out with clinical precision, over two hundred and fifty years earlier, by a certain John Fetherston: lawyer by profession, christian by calling and gardener of rare symbolism. With pious conviction, and not a little eccentricity, Fetherston had succeeded in creating a stunning arboreal depiction of The Sermon on the Mount. Twelve huge yews, known as the Apostles, evenly spaced around the garden, enclosed a further four large yews, christened the Evangelists. At their centre rose up a bulbous grassy mound, sporting a path of double box hedges that spiralled up to a narrow summit upon which stood a single, massive yew called "The Master". At the outer reaches of the garden, beyond the Evangelists and the Apostles, congregated "The Multitude": dozens of smaller yew trees, standing upon their Master's every word. It really was an amazing sight to behold.

"There must be a hundred of them," marvelled Stan with no idea of Fetherston's grand design. "What d'you reckon they're supposed to represent? A chess game, perhaps? A battlefield?"

"Still looks like a Saturday afternoon tram queue to me" repeated Fred. "What are they, anyway? I mean, what sort of trees? That's what we've got to find out, isn't it?"

"I'm pretty sure they're yew trees, Fred. We've got a couple of yews in the graveyard of our church. My dad helps to trim them now and then."

"So that's the answer to the first question, is it? You trees?"

"Yes, Fred. Yew trees. And I'd say that we're off to a bit of a flyer!"

Fred smiled broadly and clapped his chum on the shoulder, causing him to drop the pencil with which he had been filling in the booklet's first *factual requirement.*

"That's the ticket, Stan. Where next?"

And that was when the boys' navigational accuracy had gone awry. In a recklessly intrepid manoeuvre, they had struck out across farmland in front of the yew garden in an attempt to cut off a large corner of the designated route. But it appeared that something must be wrong with the map, for they had walked through fields of sheep for at least fifteen minutes and when they finally did find a road it was not the one they were looking for. Or perhaps it was the *right* road, but pointing the wrong way.

"Does this look like Rising Lane to you?" Stan was turning the map through a series of new angles.

"How would I know? Never been here before, have I?"

Fred wandered a few yards down the lane towards a whitewashed milestone that poked up from the middle of a clump of grass. Crouching on his haunches, he parted the strands of grass with his pudgy hands and peered at the writing on the stone.

"Over 'ere, Stan. I think I've found something."

"What's it say?" Stan hurried over, glad for whatever help he could get with his bearings.

"Actually? Nothing. Blinking useless. Just two numbers and two arrows. Doesn't say where we are and doesn't say where we're going."

"Shove up, then," said Stan. "Let the dog see the rabbit."

Stan could make no more sense of the stone than Fred. The arrow to the left was surmounted by 1½, whilst the arrow pointing right promised arrival within ¾. But where to? And where from?

"It's useless," Stan concluded.

"Told you."

The milestone was about two feet high. For want of something better to do, Fred scrambled up and stood on top, gazing out across the hedgerow. The stone wobbled slightly beneath Fred's weight, an unexpected occurrence which briefly perturbed him, but the warmth of the sun on his face quickly dispelled the unease from his mind. Stan turned his eyes once more to the map, sitting down on the grass verge next to the milestone in an attempt to improve his concentration. Behind the hedge and out of the boys' sight, a young bull chewed a mouthful of grass.

It may have been a bee that spooked the bull, or a horse-fly venturing up one of the giant nostrils. Whatever it was, the effect was dramatic. First came a rasping snort, like the sound of a heavy hose being cut from a steam compressor. Then, almost instantaneously, a bellow of such incredible volume that Stan immediately rolled into a foetal position on the ground, hands clapped to his head, fearing that the very sky might fall in on him. Fred, who had been lost in an innocent fantasy about Ada

Farrington from Cocoa Packing, jumped upwards and backwards from his perch with such a start that he managed to uproot the milestone, toppling it forwards into a ditch full of cow parsley as he fell. He landed with a thud on his back, an inch from the soles of Stan's boots.

There was an instant of calm before, as one, the boys let out a scream of eyes-shut terror, causing the bull to scamper away from the hedge in surprise. They stopped their bawling together and breathed hard. Stan uncoiled his thin body and adjusted his spectacles. Fred groaned in pain.

"You alright, Fred?" Stan's face was white, his hands shaking.

"No," groaned the prostrate hiker. "I think I've broken my arse." He whimpered a little for effect. "Bloomin' cow frightened the shit out of me."

"Me, too! But I wouldn't worry about broken bones. I mean, there aren't any down there to break, are there? You'll be alright. You're probably just winded."

"It's me bloomin' arse that's winded. I must have fell six feet and landed right on it. Blimey, it hurts somethin' rotten."

Stan looked down on his stricken friend with concern and tenderness. It certainly had been quite a fall. "Take your time, Fred. We've still got plenty of time."

Fred eased himself up to rest on his elbows and blew hard.

"That's it. A couple of deep breaths and you'll be as right as rain," soothed Stan, turning his gaze towards the wreckage of the milestone. "Crikey! But you've made a right mess of that though!"

He inspected the gaping hole in the turf and glimpsed the earth stained base of the stone, upside down in the ditch amongst the crushed stems of cow parsley. "Crikey!" he repeated, scratching his head.

"The thing was loose when I got on it, you know? Rocky, like. It wasn't my fault, Stan: honest. Could have happened to anyone."

Fred watched Stan's inspection of the damage, propped on his elbows, the pain in his rear end beginning to fade.

"We're never going to be able to lift that thing out of the ditch and put it back, Fred. Not in a million years." Stan was staring down into the ditch, passing back and forth in front of the fallen milestone like a hen on spindly white legs.

"What if we just fill in the missing turf, Stan?" Fred suggested. "You know, smooth it over a bit; maybe plant a flower in it, or something. Nobody'll be any the wiser if we fill it all in and make it look natural."

"Yes. Yes, that's good. Can you get up yet to help me? Let's fill it in and be on our way as quick as we can."

Stan was beginning to imagine the repercussions back at camp if their accident should ever be reported. Old Pickup would have a fit. He might even write a letter home to the boys' parents. Stan's heart beat faster at the thought of having to explain such an act of vandalism to his mother. He would be in the dog house for weeks. Fred struggled to his feet, holding his lower back in both hands and attempted a few stretching exercises. They did not help.

"Blimey, Stan! Me back's killing me. God only knows if I'll be able to make it all the way to Shrewley with you. That's assuming we ever find it, of course."

Stan took to his hands and knees, scrabbling about amongst the torn turf and upturned earth. Fred arrived clumsily next to him and proceeded to adopt a position of tortured prayer at Stan's side. The hole gouged in the verge was surprisingly deep, perhaps as much as two feet, its soil walls dry and crumbly. Fred leaned forward to peer inside.

"Hang on. There's something down there."

He plunged his right arm in and scratched about in the soil. The act of bending down was sending shooting pains through his backside. Stan craned over his friend's shoulder, hoping to get a view of whatever was down there.

"What have you got?" he asked. "Can you reach it?"

"Hang on. There! Got it." Fred withdrew his arm from the hole and tossed a small object onto the grass.

It was a slim rectangular box, no more than four inches long and covered with dust and dry mud. It looked like one of the pencil tins that Stan sometimes distributed around the Bournville offices, except that it was shorter and filthy. Neither of the boys felt inclined to pick it up.

"What d'you reckon it is, then?" asked Fred. "I mean, apart from a dirty box."

"Dunno." Stan moved his face close to the object and scrutinised its every particle of dried mud. "Where d'you think it came from. I mean, do you reckon it was down there all the time or did it fall in when the stone fell?"

"Must have fallen in, I'd have thought. It wasn't really compacted when I pulled it out. Perhaps somebody dropped it behind the stone when they sat down for a rest."

"Or somebody hid it there. You know, for safe keeping," surmised Stan.

"Aren't you gonna open it and find out?"

"Find out what?"

"Well, what's in it, for a start off. Give it here, Stan. I'll have a look."

Stan picked up the box as he would a melting chocolate bar and placed it in the palm of Fred's right hand. Fred was less delicate. He rubbed the box vigorously with his plump fingers in order to remove as much of the dirt as he could, half expecting to see some well known brand name appear and reveal a clue as to the box's contents, but no words or images came to light. He could feel a finely engraved pattern beneath his thumb, cut into what turned out to be a dull brown metal box, hinged along one edge, with a simple clasp fastener on the opposite side. He spat on what he took to be the lid and rubbed it hard on the seat of his trousers, like a bowler shining a cricket ball. This lightened its colour by a couple of shades and brought out some more finely engraved lines and patterns, but its message was still unclear.

"Looks like a G and a B to me," announced Fred, angling the box towards the sun, "and a whole load of squiggly lines and crosses. Pretty old, too, I'd have thought. Here, take a look." Fred lobbed the box towards Stan who almost dropped it.

"Careful, Fred!"

"Don't panic. It's not a grenade!"

Stan positioned himself with the sun at his back and tilted the box into the light, holding it close to his spectacles. He examined the clasp and deduced from its position relative to the hinges that the monogrammed G and B were probably on the base of the box, whilst on the lid Stan could just make out the form of a mounted horse, but the markings were very faint and the dullness of the metal made it impossible to see much more. It was obviously very old, probably belonging to someone of rank or importance, but there was not much else to learn without opening it.

"Shall I open it then, Fred?"

"Blimey, Stan. Yes! Get on with it, will you. The suspense is killing me."

The clasp was no more than a simple, flat hook, fixed to the lid by a tiny rivet and designed to swing through an arc along the side of the box to couple with a tiny metal eye, screwed into the base. Stan pushed the tip of the hook to the right. It was stuck fast.

"It's stuck fast, Fred," he said rather obviously. "Have you got a penknife on you?"

Fred searched the deep pockets of his long shorts for several seconds, his friend watching in fascination.

"Nope. But I've got an old nail."

"Perfect. Give it over, will you?"

With the nail, Stan was able to free the tiny hook and push it out of its coupling. He then adjusted the box's position in his hands and, holding his breath against every eventuality, pushed open the lid. The contents proved rather disappointing: just a single piece of aged paper, neatly folded several times to fit into the box. The inside of the box itself, however, was much more interesting, sparkling gold in the sunlight and covered with intricate engravings. Stan's heart pounded. On the underside of the lid, there appeared to be a medieval knight in armour, bizarrely wearing an animal skin hat and holding a church in his right hand. At his feet lay, in two distinct pieces, the dead body and severed head of a second knight. Stan gulped. He removed the folded paper and studied the shield engraved on the inside of the base. It was incredibly detailed: quartered, with the two left hand segments containing a bewildering array of lines, chevrons and graphic devices that seemed to represent nothing at all. The top right hand quarter contained something that looked like a necktie displayed next to a rampant lion, whilst the bottom right quarter was its mirror image: lion first, then the necktie. It was all very curious.

"Fred, I think it's made of gold," whispered Stan, his eyes wide behind his spectacles. "At least, the insides are gold, I'm pretty sure. Look at the detail in those engravings, too." He handed the box to Fred.

"Beautiful. A real craftsman's job. Just imagine the hours of work in the hinges alone." He was holding the box like a baby mouse. "What'll we do with it, d'you think?"

Stan had been asking himself the same question. "It doesn't belong to us, does it, so I suppose we need to give it up to the authorities."

"Authorities?" Fred was aghast. "Who do you mean by the authorities? Not the police, I hope."

"Well, yes, actually. The local police. Who else would you suggest?"

"Anyone. I'd suggest anyone but the police. Can't you think of an authority that isn't the police?"

"Er. No." Stan pondered, nevertheless. "I suppose that we could hold onto it and show it to Mister Ferguson when we get back," he offered. "He might know what to do."

"I like that idea a whole lot better," said Fred, relieved. "But would you keep it for us 'til then? I'm worried I might accidentally squash it, or something."

Stan slipped the box into his pocket. "We'd better get on and repair this hole," he suggested, keen to change the subject. "And then let's be on our way."

It was as he knelt down on the grass that Stan became aware of the tightly folded paper, still clutched in the palm of his left hand. He looked at it stupidly for a second, unable to remember even why it was there, then, mechanically, he unfolded it and turned the small creased sheet the right way around.

"It's a poem," he said at length. "Or a song. It was in the box. Look." He held the paper under Fred's nose.

"Well, sing it to me, then," he chuckled. "What's it say?"

Stan squinted through his glasses at the tiny copperplate handwriting, his lips moving silently as he read the first two lines to himself.

"Come on then, Stan. Let's be having you. What does it say?"

The words were proving difficult for Stan to understand. "Just a sec, will you. It's like a poem, written in old English. At least, a sort of English. I'm not sure I can make any sense of it at all, to be honest."

"Well, give it a go," encouraged Fred.

The ink had faded to a light grey but the words were perfectly legible. Stan took a deep breath and began his recital in monotone:

Arden's forest now in splinters
Cleared as fuel for many winters
Where once the oaks stood thick and tall
Now grows the wheat for Clinton's hall
Nearby a splinter named for hay
There lies the grave of Joseph Bray
Within the churchyard do not cower
From the gate to Lord Brome's tower
Count out your paces carefully,
No more or less than twenty-three,
Turn south towards the third of stones
The secret lies on Joseph's bones
My rhyme sleeps heavy on his heart
Unlock the sense and gain a start.

There was a brief silence before Fred ventured an opinion: "Load of bollocks, if you ask me. What kind of bloke would write stuff like that?"

Stan took no notice. He was too busy reading the poem again, thin lips chewing each word, brow frowned in concentration. What on earth could it all mean?

6

A VISION OF DELIGHT

They decided against planting a flower. Instead, they pushed the loose earth back into the hole, covered it with handfuls of long grass and rearranged the cow parsley in the ditch to hide the upturned milestone. They worked quickly, spoke little and wiped the palms of their hands on their khaki shorts when they were finished. Stan had been lost in contemplation throughout their efforts and Fred thought better of interrupting him until they were gathering up their belongings from the side of the road.

"So? What d'you reckon, then? Any ideas about what it all means?"

"Not really. Well, yes - sort of - but I'm not sure."

"Blimey, Stan! Is that a yes or a no?"

"I dunno."

"Then give me the bloomin' paper here and let me have a look."

Stan meekly handed over the folded paper. He felt ashamed at his inability to understand some of the words, yet alone their collective meaning, and he hoped that his chum might have a bright idea. Fred planted his feet wide apart and stood with his head bowed over the paper, mumbling to himself as he read. His head moved slowly from side to side. Stan watched for signs of light. Time passed. Eventually, after a near eternity of tension, the longed-for dawning glowed forth:

"Wasn't Brome the name of that bloke old Barker was telling us about? You know, the one who killed the vicar for shagging his wife? Built a tower to make it up to God."

Stan beamed in the light of revelation.

"Why, of course! Yes! Lord Brome, of Baddesley Clinton. Why didn't I see it myself?"

"Because you lack my superior powers of deduction, of course," smiled Fred.

"Read the bit about Lord Brome again, will you?" Stan had positioned himself just behind Fred and was peering at the paper over his left shoulder.

"Right. Here it is. *Within the churchyard do not cower, from the gate to Lord Brome's tower*. Doesn't make much sense, does it?"

"Read the next couple of lines as well," encouraged Stan.

"*Count out your paces carefully, no more or less than twenty-three.*"

"Yes. That's it. From the gate. Do you see?"

"Er..."

"No, it's simple. Look." Stan thrust his finger at the paper, indicating the gap between the second and third verses. "*From the gate to the tower count twenty-three paces.* You've got to read the two sentences and ignore the space. Do you get it?"

"Think so. But then what?"

"Well, I suppose we need to try and make sense of the rest of it, don't we? Give it here a bit, will you."

The sun beat down and the boys headed for the shade of a chestnut tree, towering in the hedgerow behind them. Stan held the paper close to his spectacles and studied the first verse. Fred gazed up into the tree; up through the cathedral lattice of branches and summer leaves to the outer reaches of climbing range. Boy, what a climb that would be! What a place to hide! No one would find him for days. He would be safe there, ruling the roost. King of his own majestic castle. But how would he even begin to get up there? He mapped out a course in his mind: start in the hedge, swing up to the first branch, move along to the trunk and shuffle round to the other side. Pause for breath. After that, push up to the next branch use that deep crack as a foothold… He began to get a crick in his neck.

"I think I've worked it out, Fred. Some of it, at least." Stan lifted his eyes from the paper, in search of a response from his friend. "Oi! You alright? What are you looking at up there?"

Fred shook himself from his dream climb and rubbed his neck. His face was red. He focused his eyes on Stan.

"Sorry, mate. What were you saying?"

"I was saying that I've worked out some of the poem. Actually, all of it, I think: mainly. Except the last bit."

"So what's it mean then?"

Stan came close to Fred and the two boys re-examined the paper together.

"The opening bit didn't make sense at first, but then I got it. Look, the Forest of Arden is now in splinters. Not literally, you see. Not smashed to smithereens. The splinters are the bits of the forest left behind after the main lot was cut down for fuel. You know, for logs and stuff? Splinters must be woods and coppices."

Fred followed closely, his eyes narrowed to wrinkled slits of concentration. He rubbed his neck again. "Go on."

"Well, one of the bits of forest left behind is called Hay - see, *a splinter named for hay*? Get it? And Hay Wood is on our map. It's what we've been looking for for the past fifteen minutes."

"Ahh. Right. Got it." Fred was beginning to warm to the subject. He offered up a textual critique: "If Hay Wood is really what he's on about, then why couldn't he have just said so? I mean, instead of blathering on with this rhyming cobblers?"

Stan was glad to see that his chum was engaged. He pursued his interpretation.

"So, Baddesley Clinton church, where Brome built his tower, must be near Hay Wood and Joseph Bray's grave must be in the churchyard." Stan sounded triumphant.

"So what?" asked Fred, bringing his friend down to earth with a bump. "I mean, what's all that got to do with us and the price of fish?"

"Well, nothing, you big lump. Except that there might be a whole lot of treasure waiting for us." Stan was peeved. "Don't you see? This is a clue: a clue to where something is hidden: where a *secret* is hidden. See? Look at that line, there. Don't you want to go and find out what it is, for goodness sake?"

"Well of course I do, Stanley, you stick insect. It's just that we've been looking for Hay Wood for hours already and we haven't found a trace of it. I don't see how this piece of paper is going to help us find where the bloomin' heck we actually are." Fred's voice was rising in volume. "Don't you remember? We're lost, Stan. Miles from the barge, cut off from living civilisation. We might never even make it home. And we've got nothing to eat either," he added for emphasis.

The tring-a-ling ring of a bicycle bell came as a surprising interruption.

"Hullo, you two," chirped a sing-song female voice from beneath a floppy straw hat. "What are you up to?"

Stan and Fred froze, looking to the ground between their feet, ears reddening. Stan stuffed the poem into his pocket along with the metal box and kept his hand on it.

"Er, nothing much, Miss," he mumbled into his bootlaces. "Just trying to find our way to somewhere, that's all." It seemed an inadequate reply. "Thank you very much," he added dumbly.

"My name's Fred Parker," blurted out Fred, wringing his hands in front of him. "And this is John Stanson. Er, Stan Johnson."

"Pleased to meet you, Fred Parker. My name is Kathryn Moore. Kathryn with a 'y' that is, but you may call me Kate if you so wish."

Fred definitely so wished. He had no idea how you might spell Kathryn with a 'Y', anyway. Surely that would be Yathryn?

"Hello Kate," he whispered, avoiding her eyes. "I love your bike." Stan groaned. This was not going well.

"Why thank you, Fred Parker. Do you know a lot about bicycles?"

Fred blushed a deeper shade of crimson. "Er… Bikes? Me? Ha!" He laughed nervously. "I've never had a bike me-self, Miss. No. But I know all about 'em and I can ride one alright."

Kathryn Moore lifted her pretty left leg through the low-slung frame of her bicycle and walked towards Fred, pushing her machine. Strands of golden blonde hair floated beneath the brim of the straw hat that shaded her pale complexion from the sun. She looked to be about nineteen or twenty; a slight, wisp-like figure beside the solid ironwork of her bicycle. She was wearing a calf-length summer dress of cornflower blue, with long sleeves fastened at the cuffs and summer weight boots, laced down the front. To Fred, she looked like Mary Pickford, magically removed from the flickering screen and made flesh before his very eyes. A dream girl, walking towards him with a bicycle. It actually made his knees knock.

"Here," she said. "Would you like a go?"

Kate's eyes sparkled green beneath her hat. Her thin lips parted in a delicious smile, her teeth flashed polished white. Fred swallowed hard.

"Fred!!"

"Eh?"

Stan was addressing him from somewhere in another life. "Shouldn't we be getting on?"

Fred's eyes were glued to Kate's bicycle. He answered without moving them. "Er. Just a minute, Stan. Thought I might just try out the bike for a bit. You know: if that's alright."

"Wasn't it you who was worried that we were lost and might never get home just a couple of minutes ago? You know, scared we might die of starvation? And now you want to go for a bike ride?"

"Come on, Stan. Just for a couple of minutes. It's a Raleigh Ranger!"

"Oh, do please let him have a go, Stanley," purred Kate on Fred's behalf. "And don't worry about being lost. I know exactly where we are."

Fred's wide eyes met those of Kate. He nodded a request for permission, to which Kate bowed demurely in return and released to him her steed. Fred took the handlebars reverentially in his pudgy hands and wheeled the bicycle towards the middle of the lane. With no crossbar, mounting was a simple affair, especially as the polished leather saddle was set low for Kate. Fred could touch the ground with feet flat once seated. He glanced over his right shoulder towards Stan, wrapped his fingers around the India rubber handle grips and pushed off towards exhilaration. Kate and Stan watched him go, wobbling and snaking between the cart wheel tracks, leaning low over the handlebars, teetering on the limit of balance.

"I should probably have told him about the gears," mused Kate, watching Fred's blurred legs propelling the machine away from them at little more than walking pace.

She turned her summer smile on Stan. "So, Stanley. Where is it that you two boys are trying to get to, then?"

Stan thought quickly. He was pretty sure that Kate would not have noticed the missing milestone and he certainly had no intention of telling her about the poem in the box. He tightened his grip on the paper in his pocket and came to the point.

"Baddesley Clinton, Miss. We're on a camp school walk to Shrewley and we've been told to pass by the church on the way. But we got a bit lost in the fields. You wouldn't happen to know how to get there, would you?"

Kate's smile broadened. "Why of course, Stanley. The manor house is less than a mile from here and Saint Michael's is just a few hundred yards beyond that. I'll set you on your way if you like. You are really very close."

Stan was delighted. His heart quickened in anticipation. What an adventure! There should still be just enough time to pick up whatever treasure awaited them at the church, before getting back on track and heading off to Kingswood. Kathryn suddenly seemed far less intimidating. The day was going to turn out fine after all.

From down the lane came a metallic crash, followed by a soft moan and a low expletive. Stan dared not look, but Kate turned swiftly in a half jump to face the worst, hands over her ears as if in denial of the sound. Stan turned slowly to join her gaze. Three hundred yards down the lane, Fred righted the fallen bicycle and brushed the dust from his shorts. He inspected the machine minutely, walking slowly around it whilst holding onto the saddle at arm's length. Kate and Stan looked on anxiously.

"It's alright," bellowed Fred from the horizon, waving his left arm above his head. "No damage. I'm fine."

A light breeze ruffled the broad green leaves of the chestnut tree.

"I'm really sorry about him," Stan said to Kate quickly. "I mean, about your bicycle."

Kate did not reply. She stood perfectly still, arms stiffly by her side. Beneath the floppy hat her green eyes shone cold. Fred ambled back towards them, head bowed, pushing the bicycle. It felt like a very long walk. Stan decided to meet him half way.

"What on earth are you playing at, you dimwit?" he scolded in a harsh whisper. "You've really gone and done it now. She looks awfully cross."

Fred gave a plaintive look towards his left knee, skinned and bleeding through the dust that covered much of his left side.

"Got stuck in a bloomin' rut trying to turn round. Didn't do it on purpose, Stan. Honest. And don't worry about the bike: I broke its fall. It hasn't got a mark on it."

In the end, Kate took it pretty well. As soon as she had assured herself that the bicycle was still in good order, her concerns melted away. "Come on then. We'd better be getting you both on your way to Saint Michael's. Have you got all of your belongings?"

"Yes, Miss," responded Fred. "Thank you."

As they set off, Kate told them that they were nearing the end of Chessetts Wood Road, an ancient thoroughfare running perpendicular to Rising Lane which, it transpired, was a mere two hundred yards distant. At the junction of the two lanes stood The Punch Bowl, a small public house set back from the road, snoozing in the afternoon sun. Hens pecked around the parking area and an ancient four-wheeler, its shafts vacant and upright, leaned against an outbuilding. Behind the main house, a young serving girl hummed a slow tune as she pegged out a row of towels. From inside the bar came the sound of three soft chimes of a grandfather clock.

"Are you two thirsty?" Kate was all smiles once more.

"Oh, thank you, Miss, but no: we really must be getting on." Stan was earnest in his reply. "And anyway, I'm afraid that we haven't got any money."

Stan and Fred had both left their pocket money in their kit bags on board, saving it until Warwick and the chance to buy postcards.

"I could murder a lemonade," mumbled Fred, disappointed at his friend's intervention.

"Don't be silly," insisted Kate. "It's such a warm afternoon and I'm sure that a drink would do you good."

"Oh go on, Stan," encouraged Fred. "I'm parched."

"But we've got no money, Fred," hissed Stan. "Don't you remember?"

Kate tripped off lightly towards the entrance to the pub. "Wait there. I'll only be a minute."

"I don't like this, Fred," said Stan. "My mother always told me that I should never talk to strangers. And definitely not accept gifts from them! Why has she brought us to this pub anyway?"

"Don't be daft, Stan. Blimey, she didn't bring us to the pub by herself, did she? We were coming past anyway. And she's hardly a stranger. I can't see how accepting a drink from a lady on a hot day is the same as taking sweets from a dirty old man in Birmingham."

They watched Kate lean her bicycle against the wall of the house and skip through the front door. Fred's eyes were widely glazed in admiration.

"And did you see that bike?" he crooned. "A blinking Raleigh Ranger, for goodness sake. Out here, in the middle of nowhere! And her teeth? Oh Stan, she has such lovely teeth, don't you think?"

Fred's eulogy left Stan momentarily lost for words and he had still not found any by the time Kate re-emerged into the bright sunlight. She was carrying a round tray upon which were balanced three empty glasses and a stone jug of chilled ginger beer.

"Crikey!" gasped Stan.

He had never had ginger beer before, especially not "bought" ginger beer. His mother always said they could never afford it, nor any of the other delicious beverages offered by the much maligned pop man, whose weekly round brought him to Melton Road every

Thursday morning. Though his mother may not have approved, the pop man's standing amongst the children of the road placed him on roughly the same level as Father Christmas, his cart laden with delights like Dandelion and Burdock, Pink Lemonade and Shandy by the crate full. Most of the boys wanted to be the pop man when they grew up and Stan could never understand his mother's aversion to his goods. After all, the Jenkins from down the road appeared to drink gallons of the stuff and they were no better off than anyone else.

"I hope that you both like ginger beer," sang Kate as she approached. "It's my absolute favourite."

"Mine too, Miss," replied Stan.

They drank their delicious refreshment sitting on the grass by the side of the lane. Kate put Stan's mind at rest about the cost of the ginger beer by explaining that the pub belonged to her uncle and that she was staying there during her summer break from university, earning a few shillings helping out behind the bar.

"He has a pretty foul reputation around here, I understand, but he is always kind to me and he lets me help myself to whatever I like from the bar."

"Blimey," declared the awestruck Fred.

"We close for the afternoon around half past two," she went on, "and I usually take a bicycle ride to clear my head of all the bar talk and smoke. I had only just set off when I saw you two, so engrossed in whatever it was you were discussing that you didn't even hear me coming!"

Relishing his first taste of ginger beer, Stan had already drained his glass to the last drop, whilst Fred had not even taken a sip, his lower jaw sagging in admiration of every lilting word that tripped from Kate's exquisite mouth.

"Well, you *do* like ginger beer, don't you Stanley!" giggled Kate. "Would you like a drop more?"

A few minutes later, the flagon of ginger beer drained dry, it was time to be getting on. Stan burped softly behind his hand and got to his feet. The boys thanked Kate for her kindness and she, in turn, gave them directions to the church:

"Stay on Rising Lane, cross the railway line and the canal bridge and keep going straight. When you see Hay Wood - you really won't miss it, Stanley - look for a crossroads. Here, you should turn right. This will be the long drive that leads up to the manor house. Skirt to the left of the outbuildings, take the path that runs along the edge of the cow field and follow it all the way to the church. It should take you no more than twenty minutes from here."

The boys set off along Rising Lane at a brisk pace, refreshed and purposeful. Behind them, Kate gathered the empty glasses onto her tray and called out a cheery farewell: "Take care, boys. Do be sure to come back and see me if you get lost."

Fred turned to give her what he hoped might be a winning wave, but stumbled in so doing and felt foolish. Stan waved, too, then burped again, a rush of ginger beer molecules fizzing in his nostrils. He set his eyes on the road ahead and focused his mind on thoughts of treasure. What a splendid way to spend the afternoon!

7

LOVE AND CLUES

The village and manor house of Baddesley Clinton owe their distinctive name to a young knight named Sir Thomas de Clinton of Coleshill who, in 1225, married one Mareza de Bisege, fifteen year old daughter and sole heir of James de Bisege of Baddesley. It was a good marriage for the Bisege family, bringing new blood and welcome funds to the lands that they had owned for four generations. For the Clintons, to whom the North Warwickshire manor of Coleshill had been granted by Henry II some sixty years earlier, it was also an excellent union, extending their land holding by several hundred acres of forest and newly cleared pasture.

The Clintons' decision to embellish the title of their new manor by the addition of the family name was apparently made in order to differentiate it from the Warwickshire village of Baddesley Ensor, lying some twenty miles away to the north, near Atherstone. Given the distance between the two Baddesleys, this may be disingenuous, with personal vanity holding sway rather than any desire to save travellers from the inconvenience of mistaken identity.

Sir Thomas de Clinton and his descendants lived at Baddesley Clinton until 1349 when, through want of male heirs, the manor passed by marriage to John de Coningsby. Several further changes of ownership succeeded until, in 1438, John Brome appeared on the records as "lord of this vill". John was Under Treasurer of England at the time and an important man. He lorded over the manor of Baddesley Clinton for thirty years until, in 1468, he was killed in London by a certain John Herthill. The house, lands and church thereby passed to his son, Nicholas Brome, who promptly avenged his father's death by killing Herthill. A penchant for murderous vengeance had developed early in Lord Nicholas.

Between them, John and Nicholas Brome extensively rebuilt the semi-fortified manor house, installing an inner courtyard, gun-ports, a moat and a drawbridge. At Nicholas's death, in 1517, the house passed to his daughter Constance and her husband, Sir Edward Ferrers. It was the beginning of a very long tenure by Sir Edward's family. As devout Catholics living through turbulent times, the Ferrers oversaw the construction of a number of "priest holes" within the fabric of the building, including one concealed in a toilet. They built tunnels and hiding places under the house and under the courtyard, an exercise in forward planning that turned out to be extremely fortunate for a convention of Jesuit priests who, in 1591, were saved from a raid by the local authorities by hiding beneath the South Wing.

In August 1921, the Ferrers were still holding court, robustly embarking upon their fifth century as lords of the manor of Baddesley Clinton. Stan and Fred strode purposefully up the main drive, admiring the ancient oaks that thrust up through the parkland. A pair of sheep scurried to safety at the sound of the boy's gravel-crunching footsteps. To the left, Hay Wood towered above the hedgerows, sucking in sunlight along its ragged edge, dark and forbidding. Ahead and to the right, the magnificent old manor house rose into view from behind the crest of a small hill. Fred gasped.

"Blimey! It's so old!"

The boys' pace slowed as they took in the wonders of the ancient structure; its fairytale battlements, bridge and moat. It was like no building they had ever seen before, not even amongst the illustrations and photographs of the Day Continuation School text books. A mixture of castle and palace; house and fort. Elegant red brick chimneys rose into the blue sky, contrasting with the weathered grey stone walls and clay roofing tiles. The leaded windows were small and numerous, their thick panes twinkling sunlight to the boys through the branches of the clinging wisteria. The formal gardens, extensive outbuildings and spacious coach house all added to the sense of grandeur. That such a house could exist at all was so far beyond Stan and Fred's own sense of reality that they struggled even to describe it to each other.

"Crikey!"

"Yeah. Blimey!"

The boys struck off to the left, cutting across the grass towards a coppice where they picked up a path, bordered by the woodland to the left and by a rusting fence to the right, on the other side of which chomped a herd of cattle. Reassuringly, a pointed sign marked "Church" had been nailed to a tree stump nearby.

Within three minutes, they had arrived at the church gate; a tiny iron-barred affair, hanging off its top hinges and wedged open with a brick. Beyond the gate, an unkempt footpath curved between a sprinkling of gravestones to the main church door. The whole thing looked so much smaller than Stan had expected. The gate, the graveyard and even Lord Brome's fabled tower all seemed to have been built to half scale. But it was undoubtably a most beautiful spot. With not another soul in sight - at least, not a living soul - the secluded churchyard slumbered in neglect. The grass grew long between the graves, spared from the scythe and a trampling Sunday congregation for many a long decade. Truly a place in which to rest in peace.

"Well. Here we are then," announced Stan in a suitably reverential tone. "There's Brome's tower and this must be the gate, so all we've got to do is pace out the distance to the grave."

"And collect the booty," confirmed Fred. "Let's get on with it."

The boys counted out their twenty-three paces and arrived beside three narrow gravestones, stretched out in front go the church like bread soldiers before a boiled egg.

"Third one, Fred. Does it say Joseph Bray?"

"Yep. Looks like it."

They approached as if to defuse a bomb. The gravestone was weathered by scores of Warwickshire winters, mottled grey and yellow by lichen. It lay on a slight incline, tilted from the horizontal by tree roots. A brownstone flower vase, no bigger than a pudding bowl, sat at the centre of the tomb, its last floral tribute long since perished and removed. There was no headstone, but the identity of the grave's inhabitant remained chiseled upon the tomb in bold serifs:

Here lies Joseph Bray, Bachelor and Churchwarden of Baddesley Clinton, born Dec. 6th, 1771, departed this life Nov. 7th, 1838. At peace in heaven.

Beneath these lines, the text was hard to make out; the carving lighter and worn. Hardly anything that was legible had survived the seasons. Stan ran his fingers across the dusty lettering like a blind man.

"Something from the scriptures, I think. Part of a psalm, or something."

Fred grunted a brief acknowledgement. Stan swished his hands about in the long grasses that fringed the gravestone. He was searching without a clue for something that might be a clue, muttering to himself as he circled the stone on all-fours like a bloodhound with a blocked nose. Abruptly, Fred began to recite a low monologue:

"*The Lord is my shepherd I shall not want. He maketh me to lie down in green pastures. He leadeth me beside the still waters. He restoreth my soul. He leadeth me in the paths of righteousness for his name's sake.*"

"Fred?" stammered Stan, incredulous. "I didn't know that you knew anything from the bible."

"S'not the bible, Stan. It's a sarm. And I've no idea what it's on about. My mother used to say it to me - sing it to me, really - over and over when I was little. When I was in bed, laid up with the coughing."

Stan's eyes were like saucers. "But I thought you said that your mother died when you were five. I mean, before you could remember things."

Fred was staring straight ahead. "She did, Stan. Passed away the day after my fifth birthday. Along with the baby that she was trying to have. First time that I've thought about that bloomin' sarm ever since. Funny that I should think of it again now. I mean, here in a graveyard of all places."

"It's lovely," reassured his friend. "And it's Psalm 23: from the bible. We learned it at church. Sang it just like your mother must have done. Do you remember the next bit? Spooky, I always think: *Yea, though I walk through the valley of the shadow of death, I will fear no evil. For thou art with me…*"

"*Thy rod and stuff they comfort me,*" completed Fred. "*My cup runneth over the moon.* Yeah. It's all coming back to me, Stan. Perfectly."

"Well, I am amazed, my old chum. Simply amazed!"

"Yeah, well. It's been and gone from me head again already," mumbled Fred. "So we best be getting on with looking for the bloomin' treasure before I drift off again."

The two friends resumed their contemplation of the gravestone, side by side in front of the tiny church. A breeze ruffled the trees as the sun dipped into a cloud. High up and away to the left, a noisy argument flared up in a rookery, dying swiftly down. A butterfly flapped to rest on a nearby stalk of grass. Stan was trying hard not to feel crestfallen, but doubt was welling up. He could not bear to think that he might have misunderstood the clue. Or was it a clue at all? Maybe it was just a prank. But who would play such a prank? And why? He pulled the crumpled paper from his pocket and read it again, out loud:

> *Turn south towards the third of stones*
> *The secret lies on Joseph's bones*
>
> *My rhyme sleeps heavy on his heart*
> *Unlock the sense and gain a start.*

"We *have* to be in the right place, Fred. Surely. I mean, how many other Josephs have we seen around here? And this one's exactly where he's supposed to be. So why's there nothing to find? I mean, what's so different about old Joe's grave from any of the others in here?"

"Nothing, I s'pose."

"Exactly. So where is it?"

"What?"

"The thing we're looking for, you dunderhead. The treasure, or whatever it is."

"But that's just it, isn't it. We don't actually have any idea of what we're looking for. We can't even understand half the words yet alone what they're s'posed to mean. It could be the gravestone itself for all you know."

"Now why would somebody go to the bother of making up a clue and then hiding it behind a mile post just so that we could find a gravestone? What's the point?"

Fred reflected upon Stan's question and came up with no response. Instead, he asked a few of his own: "What's a churchwarden supposed to be then? I mean, what's he do? It says here that old Joe was a bachelor and a churchwarden. Does that mean you can't be married and still be a churchwarden?"

"Of course not," replied Stan, irritated. He paused. Then his eyes lit up. "By goodness, Fred, that's it! You've found it. Of course! Why on earth didn't I see it before?"

"Er, what?" enquired Fred, bemused.

"It's the vase, don't you see? It's got *My Beloved Husband* written on it. Yet it says here that Joseph was a bachelor. It has to be the vase, doesn't it?"

"Not necessarily," countered Fred. "I mean, what if somebody just bought the wrong one? You, know; his brother or someone."

Stan gawped. Fred ploughed on.

"Imagine if he goes to the shop to buy a vase, only to find - blow me down - they're clean out of 'Beloved Brother', so he gets a 'Beloved Husband' instead and trots off back to the graveyard with the next best thing."

There was a long pause.

"It could be, eh? Couldn't it?"

"Fred, for goodness sake! Whatever we are looking for is definitely in that vase; I promise you. Look where it is: *my rhyme sleeps heavy on his heart*. The vase is right over old Joe's heart, see?"

"Only if they buried him that way round."

"Oh for goodness sake! Just give me a second and I'll prove it to you."

Stan bounded onto the gravestone and hunched down over the vase. His heart was beating fast as he lifted the sacred object and peered into its mouth. There was definitely something in there. He inserted two fingers and, scissor-like, caught hold of a roll of cloth which he carefully removed. In a trice he was kneeling alongside his friend, carefully unfurling the treasure on top of the gravestone. It turned out to be a piece of grey linen, about eight inches long by four inches wide, upon which was written, in black indelible ink, five short sentences. Or it could have been a collection of letters, arranged in groups and lines of varying lengths. The handwriting was exquisite, but the words were impossible to understand and definitely not English. If, indeed, they were words at all:

Vi trovis la tombon ekster la kapelon.
Kia nun trovi la kapelo kiu portas mian nomon,
Kvankam mi mem ne dormi tie.
La skatolo vin teni enhavas indikon,
La sekva estas če la piedoj de la dektria de miaj parencoj.

"What on earth do you make of that?" asked Stan, more to himself than his accomplice. "Any idea what it might be?"

"None. Give it here and I'll have a go."

The cloth was passed to Fred who held it in his hands like a tiny sacrament. Puzzlement creased his features. He could not understand a word of it.

"Beats me, chum," he said in a resigned tone. "Doesn't look to be very valuable either. Feels like a bit of a dead end."

"No, it can't be a dead end. Give it back here, will you. Let me see if there's a maker's mark or something."

Stan laid out the cloth again and scrutinised both sides of the material. There were no other marks. He tried to make sense of the groups of letters.

"It's not a code, Fred. It's a language. It has to be. Look at the word 'la'. There's four of them and I bet it means 'the', like in French. Except that this isn't French. At least, it doesn't look like French."

Fred glanced back at the cloth over Stan's shoulder. "What's it look like then?"

"I don't know. Like Greek or something."

"What, like an ancient Greek scripture or something?"

Stan shook his head, staring at the cloth. "No idea."

"Looks a lot more like gobbledygook than treasure."

Stan ignored him and pursued his linguistic tack. "All I can recognise is the 'la', like I said, and then this word here: *vin.*" Stan pointed his grubby fingernail at the word. "It's the French word for wine. You know, as in *vin blonk*. But I'm not sure that the rest of it is French."

"If you say so, chum. But it's definitely not a treasure, is it? I mean, it's not going to make us rich."

"No. I doubt it."

"So what are we going to do with it?" asked Fred, once more voicing the question that Stan had been pondering. "Have we reached a dead end?"

"Will you shut up about your dead ends, for goodness sake."

Stan was flustered. Fred decided against pursuing his dead end theme and, instead, made a surprisingly bright suggestion: "Why don't we take it to old Barker and ask him what he thinks? He knows loads of stuff about languages and all that. Even Greek. He might be able to tell us if it's sacred, or whatever."

Stan liked this idea, but his response betrayed anxiety. "We mustn't tell him about the milestone, though. What are we going to say about where we got it?"

"Just tell him that we found it on the road. You know; like it had fallen out of someone's pocket or something. He'll never be any the wiser."

This sounded plausible enough, but doubt flooded back. Stan was suddenly not sure that they should be taking the cloth at all. "Shouldn't we just put it back, Fred? You know, walk away and forget we were ever here? It doesn't seem right to take things from a graveyard."

"Blimey, Stan. We're not Burke and Hare, you know! It's only a rag, not a bloomin' corpse."

"I didn't say we were Burke and Hare did I, you numbskull. They've got nothing to do with it. I'm just saying that we're on the point of almost stealing something from a graveyard! A blessed graveyard, for goodness sake!"

"Look, Stan. We're not talking about robbing a bank here. It's a piece of handkerchief from an old pot surrounded by dead people who couldn't tell on us even if they wanted to. They're hardly going to alert Scotland Yard are they?"

Stan sulked and said nothing.

"Alright. How about this? We'll take it to show Barker and if he goes doolally on us, then we'll just bring it back and forget about it. How does that sound?"

Stan maintained his silence.

"Stan?"

"Alright. We'll do it your way. But let's get out of here and back on track as quick as we can."

"That's the ticket."

Stan rolled up the cloth and pushed it into his pocket, alongside the box and the paper, checking at the same time that they had not left anything behind. Fred tried the heavy church door behind them, but found it locked.

"Church is locked," he reported, puzzled. "Where do the dossers go for shelter then, if the church is shut?"

Stan took an exaggerated look around him. "What dossers?"

"Good point, Stan. Let's be off."

The boys marched away from the churchyard at a brisk clip, anxious to get back on the right road as quickly as possible. It seemed from the map that the right road would be Hay Wood Lane which ran parallel to the driveway along the western edge of the woods. By sticking to public roads, Fred estimated the distance to Shrewley to be no more than four miles, making the arrival deadline of 5.15 achievable. However, the new route would pass well to the south of Kingswood, thereby ruling out the opportunity to collect their second piece of required factual information.

"Better to be on time without the information than late with it," reasoned Fred. "Anyway, we can always ask one of the others the answer before we have to give it in. And if no one wants to help, we'll just duff up Edgington until he tells us."

Stan thought this a very reasonable approach.

The boys spoke of many things as they walked together along the dusty road that afternoon. The profusion of new sights, sounds and smells astonished them: the kestrel hovering over a corn field, its whole body in motion except the head, wonderfully still. Blackberries growing thick in the hedgerow ("it's not scrumping, Fred. Go ahead and eat as many as you like"). Enormous cowpats and tiny song birds. Scuttling rabbits and lumbering shire horses. Wild honeysuckle, humming thick with bees. Women binding sheaves of wheat; men pitchforking them onto a wagon. Such strength: such toil.

They kicked a stone to each other along the road: Billy Walker and Billy Kirton, deftly passing between defenders and dribbling around pot holes to shoot between the gate posts of Ivy House Farm, in front of the Holte End at Villa Park. A last minute winner: the goalie never saw it. They found another stone and started again.

"Stan. D'you think it's possible to fall in luv with someone you hardly know?"

Fred's deep question so wrong footed his fellow attacker that the stone bobbled uncontrolled into the ditch.

"Come again?"

"Well, you know. It's just that I can't stop thinking about her, that's all."

"About who?"

"About Kate, of course."

"You're having me on! Really? Kate?"

"Yeah. Kate. You know, her that gave you all that free ginger beer you didn't want."

"But, Fred. You hardly know her."

"I just said that, you cloth-eared get. That's what I just bloody well asked you."

Stan decided against verbal retaliation. His friend was clearly in an uncommon state of agitation. He played along. "In love? Me? Well, no. I don't think so. At least, not with someone I really know."

"But that's just what I'm bloomin' on about. I'm not talking about the pictures, Stan, where Fairbanks always gets the girl and she's glad to be got. I'm talking about something much more deep and complicated."

"Which is?"

"Unrequited love, Stan. Un-re-bloomin-quited love. Get it?"

"Yeh, of course I get it. But how do you know its unrequited?"

"Oh, come on! She's loads too beautiful and miles older than me. I don't stand a chance."

Stan knew Fred was right. Definitely right. "You never know," he said, kindly. "You just never know. I'm sort of hoping the same thing might be true for me with Emmy."

"The girl from the church? I thought you said she was out of your league."

"Well, she is. Of course she is. Same as your Kate really, except she's obviously much prettier." Stan smirked as his friend reddened and almost took the bait. "I see her every week at church and she even came over to talk to me a couple of weeks ago. She's at Cadbury's too - works in Assortments - and I think she's an orphan, brought up by her granny. Rather like you, in that respect, but obviously a hundred times better looking!"

Fred missed with an attempt at a dead-arm punch. Stan became more wistful.

"She has such beautiful skin, Fred. Olive complexion, they call it. Long dark hair that shows off her brown eyes. She's half Italian, you know. Father came from there. You can see it in her looks." He sighed deeply.

"Blimey, Stan. If it's not love you're in, then I'm not sure where you are!"

"Yeah, well. Maybe I am. But it's just the same hopeless mess as you, isn't it. She's seventeen and beautiful and I'm fifteen and spotty. Where's the justice in that?"

"There ain't none, mate. No god either, if you ask me."

They walked on in silent contemplation of the trials of love and the impossibilities of attracting the fairer sex. At the Warwick Road they met Duggan and Coley, coming from Rowington in fine good humour. The smell of ale hung about them.

"Or'ight, Parker? Johnson?"

The greeting was friendly and cheerful, unusual from boys so much older than Fred and Stan, particularly as it came from the normally thuggish Coley. Fred responded in kind.

"Afternoon, gentlemen. How's your stroll going?"

"Just grand, Parker. Lovely day for it an' all."

Duggan was smiling broadly. Coley lit a cigarette. They strolled on down the road together.

"How about you two, then?"

"Fine thanks," answered Fred. "We're having a fine old time."

"How far would you say we have to go?" asked Stan, seizing the moment. "We got a bit lost and missed collecting one of the facts on our itinerary."

"Oh no!" exclaimed Coley dramatically. "You've not gone and

missed a fact have you? Blimey, I wouldn't like to be in your shoes. Old Peg Leg will string you up by your bollocks when he finds out. He hates that sort of thing."

Stan's heart stopped. Fred turned grey. Duggan burst out laughing.

"He's only winding you up. Pay no heed to him. You'll be fine. Barker'll just be glad you made it back alive. What's the one you missed, anyway?"

Coley smirked as Fred and Stan regained their composure. Stan's heart, so recently stopped, now seemed to be making a terrible din in his chest.

"The words on the horse trough at Kingswood," replied Stan. "We never even got to Kingswood, yet alone found the horse trough." He looked ashamed.

"What booklet you on, then?" asked Coley. "We was never asked about no horse trough."

"C," said Stan. "We're in Brigade C."

"Ahhh. You're in a brigade now, are you?"

"Leave it out, Bert," said Duggan gently. "Give 'em a break, eh?"

Coley smirked again as he drew on his cigarette. Duggan turned back to Stan. "I've got a feeling that Barker might have set you a bit of a trick question there," he smiled. "I'm pretty sure that Kingswood doesn't even exist, at least not as a village. We were supposed to go through it on our way down to Rowington and didn't see anything but canal bridges. I reckon he made it up."

"Really?" Stan was aghast. "You think that Mister Barker would do a thing like that?"

"Absolutely. He's a bit of a bugger on the quiet, our Mister Barker. Likes a bit of a joke, now and then. Quite the lad, too, I shouldn't wonder."

"Top bloke," affirmed Coley from afar. He had fallen behind to relieve himself of two pints of Flowers' Best in the hedgerow. "Even for a teacher."

The conversation lulled. Stan silently reevaluated his teacher in the light of Coley's compliment and decided that Fred was probably right: they would share their discoveries with Mister Barker at the first possible opportunity.

Eventually the barge came into sight, tied up a few hundred yards beyond Shrewley tunnel. A group of a dozen or so boys were chattering excitedly amongst themselves, comparing notes and bragging about their Warwickshire adventures. Alongside the barge, a trestle table sported a quantity of cups and plates, piled up on either side of the tea urn. Fred spotted Edgington, sitting on Mr Barker's straight-backed chair, Mr Pickup ministering to an ugly looking black eye.

"Edgington, I still do not understand how you came to trip over a ploughshare and land on your face. What on earth were you doing in a ploughed field anyway?"

The bemused teacher applied a tincture of arnica to the side of Edgington's face with a cotton handkerchief, whilst Hendry and Bushell watched on nervously lest the horrible victim should forget his torture-extracted promise and reveal the true cause of his injury. Away to the right, four more hikers straggled in and dropped to the grass, exhausted.

Stan felt elated. What an adventure! Not only had he made it safely back to the barge, but he had done so with a pocketful of objects acquired in the most mysterious of circumstances. What could it all mean? Where would it lead them? So many questions crowded together in his brain. What on earth would happen next?

Mister Barker provided the immediate answer with a question of his own: "Right, lads. Who is ready for a spot of tea and cake?"

8

THE BEGINNING

S hrewley Tunnel was officially opened on December 19th, 1799. From the outset, the managers of The Warwick and Birmingham Canal Company had sought to reduce the cost of their enterprise by avoiding the construction of tunnels wherever possible, preferring to create deep cuttings, such as those at Rowington and Yardley. However, as the planned course of the canal passed directly under the village of Shrewley, the navvies were left with no choice but to tunnel beneath it. At 433 yards in length, it is the canal's only tunnel. The northern portal comes after more than six miles of flat running; all the way from the bottom lock at Knowle, the last of a flight of five locks that include the broad pound at Kingswood Junction. After the southern exit from the tunnel, the canal winds along its level course for a further two miles before it encounters Hatton top lock, the first of a tumbling flight of twenty one locks that drop the canal down almost 150 feet on its approach to Warwick.

Built of brick, the tunnel's interior is uncommonly damp. The continual dripping down of water over the course of many decades *has created a number of curious flowstone formations that hang from the roof. At sixteen feet, the tunnel is wide enough to allow two narrow boats to pass each other, but there is no towpath. Barges must be propelled in both directions by legging. Unusually for the region, a second, parallel tunnel was constructed for the passage of horses, thereby avoiding a time-consuming traipse up and over the hill. A ramp rises up from the towpath at the northern end to enter the horse tunnel, which is positioned above and to the right of the main opening, and continues to slant upwards until it reaches a road. Having crossed the road, the path re-enters the hillside, descending by way of a gentle slope to reunite horse and driver with the canal at the southern portal.*

For the geologically minded, the exposed sides of the deep cutting at the exit of the tunnel display clear evidence of the Triassic Mercia Mudstone sequence: layers of greenish shale, deposited upon some vast desert plain hundreds of millions of years ago, striped alongside the fine white Arden Sandstone like a prehistoric humbug. These sediments provide a natural decoration to a most unnatural cliff face, hemming in the tranquil waterway for several hundred yards on its left hand side.

By 17.45, the barge was underway once more, gliding towards the day's final port of call at Hatton. Mister Barker had positioned himself at the front of the class, leaning upon his cane with a look of benevolent generosity on his face. Or was it abject misery? It was simply so difficult to tell.

"Well, chaps. I must say that you all made pretty short work of Afternoon Tea!"

Smiles lit up the length of the barge, faces glowing with sunburn and happiness.

"I am pleased to see that you all made it safely back, even if one or two pairs did cut it rather fine on their arrival time. Was it an enjoyable experience for you all?"

"Yesssss, Sir!" they roared back in unison, Hendry and Bushell loudest of all. Edgington remained silent, applying pressure to the wet handkerchief that he held to his left eye.

"Good," responded Mister Barker. "Very good! So, perhaps we might reflect together upon some of the key learnings from our afternoon ramble." He scanned the benches and alighted upon the ruddy face of Coley at the back. "Ah, Coley! Just the chap. Would you care to share your own key learnings with the others?"

"Sir?"

"You know, Coley. Things that have made a particular impression upon you during the course of the afternoon. Watering holes, perhaps, and their relative situation along the course of your route?"

Coley hesitated. Could it be that Old Peg Leg knew that he and Duggan had taken refreshment at The Navigation, or was it that watering holes were actually part of the canal system? If so, were they one of the vital factual details he was lacking? Mister Barker's question felt loaded, but could it have been loaded by his own guilty conscience? Watering holes certainly sounded like they could be canal features. Perhaps he should have read the booklet. The murmuring of the boys around him was not helping his concentration. He played for time.

"Yes, Sir."

"Yes, Sir? What, Sir?"

"Yes, Sir. Watering holes were definitely a key learning, Sir."

Giggling broke out. Even Mister Barker was smiling. Possibly. He changed tack.

"Did your learnings about watering holes, Mr Coley, contribute to the completion of the factual requirements specified in your booklet?"

"Yes, Sir."

"Very good, Coley. Then I look forward to reading your insights when I mark the booklets this evening."

With a twinkle in his single eye, the teacher brought a temporary end to Coley's discomfort and a permanent end to the day's ramble.

"Would the scribe of each team please pass their booklets to the front? Armstrong, I should be grateful if you would make a neat pile of them and place them beside my briefcase over there."

A brief eruption of activity followed, precipitating the arrival of twelve creased and battered booklets into the care of young Armstrong. Mister Barker spoke again:

"As I said, I will look through your answers once we make camp. We will announce the results at supper time."

Several of the boys exchanged anxious glances. Results? This was more serious than they had thought; certainly more serious than the attention they had paid to the questionnaire.

"We now have a little more than twenty minutes to run, so I would invite you to capture a few of the more atmospheric reflections of your afternoon within the pages of your diary."

A further burst of activity ensued as boys scrabbled in bags and under desks to retrieve their diaries. Stan felt suddenly exhausted. The emotions and physical activity of the long day had caught up with him and he launched himself into a huge yawn.

"Are we keeping you up, Johnson?"

It was Mister Pickup, arriving from the galley with a morsel of fruit cake stuck to the corner of his mouth.

"Sorry, Sir," replied Stan, ears reddening, "It's rather warm in here, Sir."

"Indeed it is, Johnson. Indeed it is. And you lads have all had a strenuous afternoon. But I am sure that we would all much prefer to see your hand in front of your mouth, next time, rather than a full-on display of your tonsillary equipment."

"Yes, Sir. Sorry, Sir."

Stan ignored the sniggering of his comrades and focused his attention on the chart within his diary. There was so much to write about, but dare he write anything at all? So many things to recount, but which of them would bare the scrutiny of the teachers? And how should he separate the booklet's local history challenges from the mysterious clues that they had come across so accidentally? A terrible doubt chilled him. Could it be that the graveyard episode had actually been some kind of intelligence test set by the teachers? A part of the expedition booklet that they hadn't even read? Were Fred and he meant to find the cloth in the flower vase all along? If Barker had devised the whole thing, then how foolish would he and Fred look when they went to him for help translating the sacrament? Stan felt stressed and confused. He blew hard and glanced around in search of a comforting look from a neighbour. Instead, his eyes met those of Young Doran on the towpath. Stan let out a short, involuntary scream, which was followed by an instant of total silence in the barge, before everybody wheeled round noisily to look at Stan.

"Who was that? Who was that?" called out Mister Pickup. "Has there been an accident?"

"Johnson, Sir," reported Morris gleefully. "It was 'im, Sir." He was pointing at Stan.

"Ah, Johnson. You again! First a yawn, now a squeal. Is there no end to your personal repertory?"

Embarrassment burned into Stan's face.

"Have you been stung, Johnson? Bitten, perhaps? Are you bleeding?"

"No, Sir. Sorry, Sir. Just got my finger stuck, Sir."

Mister Pickup observed him quizzically. He fleetingly considered asking which finger and where it had become stuck, but thought better of it. The boys were rowdy enough already and he could well do without giving them any further reason to misbehave. He let the matter drop.

"Settle down, everyone. Settle down now. Let's not allow Johnson's unfortunate accident to disorientate us from the task in hand. Back to your diaries, please. Settle down."

Stan's heart was thumping.

"You alright?" whispered Fred. "What's up?"

"Fine. I'm fine," lied Stan. "I'll tell you later."

All thoughts of scooping the prize for best diary disappeared. It suddenly seemed so unimportant compared with everything else that was swirling around his brain. He bent low over his chart, entered 2pm in the appropriate column and then, in six short words, succinctly overlooked every ounce of the adventure and mystery of his unforgettable afternoon: *Went for a walk. Got lost.*

By half past six the weary adventurers had arrived at their destination. They were to pitch their tents on the grassy field that rose from the canal to the left of the first lock of the Hatton flight. The barge was moored at a safe distance from any passing traffic and the gangplank lowered. The cargo of camping equipment, kit bags and latrine shovels then passed swiftly along an orderly chain of volunteers straggled up the steep slope to level ground. It would be their home for the next three nights.

Mister Pickup took another stencilled sheet from his pocket and announced the occupants of each tent. The principle applied, he assured, was one of strict fairness: each tent would be a mix of ages with one leader, an older boy, to whom respect and obedience were due at all times. There would be six boys to a tent, except for Tent A which would have seven. Each team should put up its own tent ("This is not a race, mark you. No prizes will be awarded for finishing first") and every member should be responsible for cleanliness and order within. Boys should sleep on the ground sheets provided, with feet toward the tent pole. There should be no talking after lights-out.

"Have I been fully understood?"

"Yes, Mister Pickup, Sir."

"Good. Then I shall now disseminate the allocation of berths. Pay attention."

Stan and Fred were relieved to learn that they had both been billeted in Tent B, under Duggan's leadership, along with Hendry, Bushell and Morris. Ironmonger, Coley and Green were the other three tent leaders, with the luckless Ironmonger garnering not only the mischievous Bedlow, but also the horrible Edgington.

"I reckon that turned out pretty well," commented Fred as they sorted themselves into clumps before their respective piles of camping equipment. "We could have got Coley."

Within thirty minutes, four bell tents of heavy white canvas had sprouted on the edge of the field like a quartet of giant mushrooms, their triangular entrance flaps tied back to admit an airing breeze. To the left, a war surplus ridge tent of camouflage green had been erected for the teachers, each of whom benefitted from the use of a narrow camp bed and a pillow. To the right, the fatigue squad was busy with picks and shovels digging out the latrines, soon to be hidden from sight behind a canvas screen. Mister Reid and Mister Phipps had pitched their own tent canal-side, next to the barge. Young Doran seemed to have completely disappeared along with the donkeys. Nobody had seen them leave.

Stan and Fred laid out their groundsheets to the right of the tent entrance and placed their folded blankets and kit bags in a neat pile. The smell inside was of damp canvas and trampled grass: it filled Stan with a profound sense of happiness.

"Let's go and see what the others are up to," he enthused.

The camp site had already taken on the look of a tented holiday village. An assortment of clothing hung from the guy ropes of Tent C where, it transpired, Barnwell was attempting to dry out the contents of his kit bag, accidentally dropped into the canal during unloading. On the open ground behind the tents, four boys kicked around a football, whilst Bushell vainly attempted to sell them on the idea of a game of cricket instead. Smoke rose from the barge's chimney as Mister Phipps prepared the galley stove for supper. Beyond the barge, half a dozen swimmers dived and splashed around in the top lock, their cries of joy echoing up into the blue sky from the high stone walls of their noisome pool.

Mister Pickup sat on a grassy bank smoking a pipe. His eyelids were heavy and the newspaper he had been reading slipped slowly from his grip. Nearby, Armstrong and Bedlow played out a silent reenactment of The Relief of Mafeking, using twigs and pebbles and a handful of battered lead soldiers smuggled away from home in Armstrong's kitbag. Fred caught hold of Stan's sleeve and drew his attention to the figure of Mister Barker, sitting alone on the straight backed chair by his dingy tent. He had a pile of booklets on his knee and appeared to be reading through them with keen attention.

"Now's our chance, Stan. Have you got the rag on you?"

"It's not a rag," retorted Stan. "It's a piece of cloth that might even turn out to be a relic."

"Same difference. Have you got it?"

"Of course I've got it, you pudding. I wasn't going to leave it in the tent, now was I?"

Fred grinned. "Let's go then."

Stan looked unsure. "I'm not sure," he said, unsurprisingly. "I mean, old Barker might just flip his lid or something."

"Look, Stan. We agreed to do this, so let's just get on with it shall we. What's the worst that can happen, eh?"

Stan did not want to think about the worst that could happen. It would probably be very bad. "Alright," he sighed. "Let's get it over with."

He stalked off across the field towards the staff tent with Fred in stumbling pursuit. They arrived in front of Mister Barker almost without realising it; certainly without Stan having prepared anything coherent to say.

"Johnson. Parker. To what do I owe the pleasure of your company this evening?" The teacher almost looked as if he had been expecting them. "Perhaps an element of local knowledge that you neglected to write in your brochure?"

"No, Sir," replied Stan. "Well, that is, yes Sir. But that's not actually what we came for, Sir."

Mister Barker looked intrigued. At least, he *looked* intrigued. Whether he actually was or not was just so difficult to tell. "Go on," he invited.

"We've found something, Sir, on our expedition this afternoon, and we thought that you might be able to tell us what it is. Or rather, what it means." Stan paused for breath. "It's not from the brochure, Sir," he added. "At least, we don't think so." He felt a bead of sweat trickle down his neck and took a nervous pace backwards.

"How interesting, Johnson."

Silence ensued. Stan seemed to have frozen: his mouth had stopped working.

"Well?" asked Mister Barker presently. "Are you going to share your discovery with me now or when we get back to Bournville?"

Fred gave his partner a dig in the ribs with his elbow. Stan burst back into life.

"Now, Sir. Certainly, Sir." He pulled the tightly furled linen square from his pocket and held it out for Mister Barker's inspection.

"Would you mind unrolling it for me, Johnson? I'm afraid that I'm not quite as dexterous as I used to be."

The unfurled cloth was laid in the palm of the teacher's ungloved hand. He looked at it for two or three seconds, then raised it closer to his eye to examine the text at close quarters. He did so in silence. After thirty seconds or so, a period of time that felt more like an hour to the boys, Mister Barker made a low humming noise and turned his eye towards them.

"Would you care to tell me where you found this, Mister Johnson? Or Mister Parker, perhaps?"

"We just found it, Sir," Stan replied weakly.

"On the floor, Sir," added Fred, flustered. "On the road. Looked like it must have fallen out of somebody's pocket to me."

"Ah ha," purred Mister Barker. "I see. On the road, you say? Tell me, Parker, would this particular road by any chance have been within a graveyard?"

Now it was Fred's turn to freeze. Stan could stand the deceit no longer.

"Yes, Sir," he blurted out. "We got lost and found it in a graveyard, Sir."

"I see," came the teacher's measured response.

"We didn't steal it, mind," added Fred quickly, getting in his defence well ahead of any accusation. "Found it lying there, that's all."

"Quite so." Mister Barker looked at the boys with a twinkle of amusement in his eye, or something that looked like amusement.

"How did you know, Sir?" asked Stan, his courage buoyed by the twinkle, "that we were in a graveyard?"

"The text, Johnson. There is a clue in the text, although I do not profess to have been able to translate every word."

"Is it Greek, Sir?" asked Fred.

"No, Parker, it is not Greek. It is a much more recent language, although the calligraphy does give it a rather more antique look, don't you think?"

Fred and Stan did think, but they said nothing. Their teacher was revealing himself to be even more of a linguistic genius than they had thought. He proceeded uninterrupted.

"I am pretty sure that this is written in Esperanto."

"Ah," said Fred blankly. "Esperanto, eh." Neither he nor Stan had any idea what Esperanto might be.

"It is a constructed language, Parker: a new language, if you will, created by a fellow called Zamenhof. I came across it at university. It was something of a hot topic amongst us linguists, particularly those of a socialist persuasion who saw it as a passport to international peace and equality. Damned clever, too, if you like that sort of thing."

Fred and Stan followed wide-eyed, not sure if they liked, or even understood that sort of thing, but entranced nonetheless by their teacher's learning. When invited so to do, they sat down on the grass in front of him.

"Zamenhof came from Eastern Europe and spoke many languages, but his dream was to create an international language, spoken and understood by everyone. He argued that if there was no chance of misunderstandings between nations, there would be no reason for war. It is an idea that has seduced a lot of people over the years, especially since the Armistice."

"So, do you think that the Esperanto we found in the graveyard has got something to do with the war, Sir?" Stan was trying hard to tie together the loose ends.

"No, Johnson, I do not. Not directly. But the language has obviously become more widely known of late, particularly as there has been talk of adopting it at the League of Nations."

Mister Barker examined the cloth again. "What you have found appears to be a poem of sorts. A riddle, almost. The sense is obscure and I will need a little time to try and piece it all together. Why don't you two scoot off and enjoy yourselves with the others for a while and we can reconvene before supper. Shall we say, half past eight?"

"Yes, Sir," they replied together, scrambling to their feet.

"Oh, and Johnson: if by any chance you found a box on your travels, would you mind bringing that along, too?"

"Yes, Sir."

Stan and Fred beat a hasty retreat towards their tent.

"How'd he know about the blinking box, then?" asked Fred in a loud whisper.

"Search me. Same way he knew we didn't pick the cloth up off the road, I suppose. Same way he knew it was Esperanto. He just seems to know everything."

"Blinking clever clogs."

"And it's just as well for us that he is. We'd have never guessed it was Esperanto in a million years."

"Yeah, well, that's as may be. We've still got no idea if it's valuable or not, have we? Nor even what it means."

The two friends arrived back at the tent in full contemplation of this latest remarkable development in their day. The lanky Hendry was there, lying on his back, kitbag for a pillow, reading a book held at arm's length above his face. He glanced at Fred and Stan as they came in and grunted a greeting.

"Or'right, Norman?" replied Fred, on behalf of them both. "What're you reading then?"

"*The Black Mask*, if it's anything to you. By Hornung." He gave a short look at Fred that signalled the conversation to be at an end and resumed his reading. Fred shrugged his shoulders and stuck out his tongue. Stan pulled out his diary from the top of his kitbag.

"Got a pencil, Fred?"

"Sorry mate. Tryin' to give 'em up."

They both smiled. Stan feigned a right cross to Fred's chin and turned back to rummage once more in his bag. As he did so, a pencil hit his head, apparently falling from the roof of the tent.

"Don't break it, Johnson, or I'll throw you in the boggin' latrine."

"Thanks, Hendry. You're a sport."

Stan restricted his diary entries to a further two lines: *18.25, Reached Hatton; 19.30, Several boys are having a swim in the locks.* He closed the notebook and lobbed the pencil back towards its owner.

"Bloody hell, Parker. Was that you?"

Hendry's expostulation was accompanied by a terrible grimace, as if gassed, which, in a way, he just had been.

"Sorry, Norman. Must have been the ginger beer." Fred's pudgy features were creased by a wide smile. "Given me a case of the wind without the willows, I'm afraid. Bit of an SBD."

"Well keep your boggin' SBDs to yourself in future, you prick, or I'll duff your boggin' head in."

Fred was inordinately proud of his Silent But Deadly farts. "They sneak up on you unannounced," he had explained to Stan with great seriousness, soon after his friend's first exposure to their unpleasantness. "Even I don't know they're coming half the time."

Stan stowed away his diary and went outside for some fresh air, just as Duggan and the tiny Morris arrived back at the tent, dripping and panting from their exertions. Duggan nodded a short greeting to Stan as Morris launched into a chattering account of the tent leader's prowess:

"Jumped right over the canal, 'e did. Clean as a whistle. Yards to spare an' all."

"Lock, bird-brain," corrected Duggan. "I jumped the *lock*, right? Not the bloody canal." He stared down Morris's blabber and burst into the tent, showering its occupants with cold canal water as he entered.

"You boggin' idiot.....Oh, sorry: it's you, Duggan."

Stan marched towards the football match to let off steam for a few minutes until Fred came to find him, just before half past eight. On the far side of the field, Shaw and Pickles trudged back towards camp from the distant lock keeper's cottage, bearing pails of fresh water for the evening's ablutions. The rhythm of life under canvas seemed to have hit its swing.

Fred was tense as they walked once more towards the teachers' tent: he could not decide whether he and Stan were about to be in big trouble or in big money. He stared ahead and said nothing. Stan, on the other hand, bounced along with positive intent. The kick-about had cleared his mind and he was excited to hear what Mister Barker might have to say. In the first instance, this turned out to be:

"Ah, right on time, Gentlemen. I do hope that I am not keeping you both from fatigue duty."

Stan and Fred assured him that they had so far escaped the pleasure of fatigues, whereupon Mister Barker bade them sit down on the grass in front of his chair. A leather bound book lay in his lap, between the pages of which were inserted a piece of writing paper and the fragment of cloth from the graveyard, apparently as book marks. If Fred was still worried about being in trouble, Mister Barker's next statement swiftly put his mind at ease.

"I must say I am very glad that you thought to share your discovery with me. It really is most intriguing. Most intriguing. Thank you."

Stan and Fred mumbled an embarrassed reply, but so quietly that it died upon their lips.

"I have done my best to translate the Esperanto riddle that you left with me, but I must stress that some of it is pure guess work. Any text books that I ever had on the subject have long been misplaced and, in any case, it is almost ten years since I studied them at all. Nevertheless, as you yourselves may have noticed, there are certain similarities to contemporary Romance languages, so I have taken what one might call an educated stab at it!"

He looked pleased with his approach. Fred looked nonplussed. Mister Barker opened the book at the page marked by the cloth and continued.

"The first three lines should, I believe, be read as one: *You have found the grave outside the chapel, now find the chapel that bears my name, though I myself sleep not there.* Or something like that.

It could be church, rather than chapel. Do you now see why I asked if you had been in a graveyard, Parker?"

Fred nodded dumbly, his mouth open. Stan blinked wide-eyed behind his spectacles.

"I do have a number of questions about the graveyard, of course, including how exactly you came to be there, but let us pursue my translation for the moment, such as it is." He took out the writing paper from between the leaves of the book and consulted it carefully for a few seconds. The light of the day was beginning to fade into evening.

"The final couplet has proved to be rather tricky. I am struggling to make a lot of sense of the ending. I think it goes something like this: *the box you hold contains a clue. The next is at the feet of the thirteenth parent.* Or it might be kin - the thirteenth kin - but I can't quite see what that might mean."

Stan silently removed the metal box from his pocket, eyes still fixed on his teacher.

"Here it is, Sir. The box."

"Ah yes, Johnson. *La skatolo.* Would you mind opening it for me?"

Stan handed him the open box and watched as Mister Barker inspected the engraved detail therein. It clearly impressed him. Fred and Stan exchanged a glance. Both were now on their knees, bursting with anticipation, but not quite sure of what. Mister Barker asked them how they had come across the box, to which they both replied as honestly as they could without revealing the act of vandalism central to its discovery.

"Sat down on it for a rest, Sir," explained Fred, "and just sort of felt behind it with my hand, like." It seemed plausible enough.

Stan then revealed the sonnet clue that had guided them to Baddesley Clinton.

"Not out of the top literary drawer, Johnson, is it?" remarked Mister Barker, having read through the poem. "But an amusing ditty nonetheless. How strange that I should have been talking with you about this very Brome fellow, just this morning!"

"It was me that got that, Sir," chipped in Fred proudly. "I remembered your story about him shaaa..of him killing the priest, Sir."

"The value of education," smiled Mister Barker. At least, it looked like a smile. "Well, this is all most interesting, isn't it? Most interesting."

The daylight faded weakly across the field. Behind them, Mister Pickup was supervising the seating arrangements for supper around a newly lit bonfire. Boys were drifting in towards the body of the gathering from all corners of the camp site, chattering happily. Stan and Fred's audience with Mister Barker was coming to an end.

"What say we keep this to ourselves for the time being, chaps? We really do not yet understand what we are dealing with and we can't have too many noses in the trough, now can we?"

"Absolutely not, Sir," nodded Stan.

"It looks as though I have more reading to do, this evening." He tapped the heavy volume on his knee with his gloved hand. "If I can ascertain the owner of the coat of arms engraved within this box, then we may be able to pull together the various elements of the puzzle more easily, though exactly where that might lead is anybody's guess."

Stan's heart was thumping. What an adventure! And old Barker was right in it with them! They agreed to reconvene after breakfast and to get a good night's sleep in the meantime.

"Parker, be so good as to pass me my cane, would you? Thank you. Now, run along, boys, and join the others for supper. Mum's the word!"

Mister Reid's supper of sweet tea and meat paste sandwiches passed by in something of a blur for Stan and Fred. What an extraordinary day! Stan looked towards Mister Barker, seated on the other side of the fire. He was engaged in a jolly conversation with Bedlow and Armstrong. Could he be trusted? Of course he could be trusted, but why was he taking such an interest in their discovery? What was his angle? Maybe the cloth was not worthless after all. Or maybe it was just an elaborate game, devised by Mister Barker, in which Fred and Stan were being played like innocent fools. Stan was beginning to get a headache. It was getting late. Mister Pickup got to his feet.

"Er hem. Settle down, everyone. Shhhhhh. Thank you. Good. Well, here we all are then: the end of a very long day. Ordinarily, at this junction, we might think to entertain ourselves with a few jolly songs around the camp fire, but the hour is late and the legs are weak, as somebody once said. Or not. Anyway, I shall delay you for but a few seconds more; the time to let you know about tomorrow's itinerary."

Inexplicably, Morris fell off the end of the low bench on which he was sitting, his misfortune being greeted with howls of laughter.

"Right-ho, lads. Right-ho. Quiet down, won't you. Quiet please. You'll wake up the cows in the barn. Now, as I was about to say: tomorrow being Sunday, we shall attend morning service at Warwick church. Reveillé will be at seven o'clock, with breakfast at eight sharp."

Coley groaned in disappointment: Mister Pickup appeared not to hear him.

"Mister Barker has asked me to inform you that his feedback on the contents of your brochures has been postponed until tomorrow morning, immediately after breakfast." He consulted a scrap of paper in his left hand.

"Oh yes. Morning fatigues are to be carried out by today's squad until lunchtime. We will change rotations thereafter."

More groans rumbled around the circle of campers. Mister Pickup chose to ignore these, too.

"So, without further ado, it is time for us all to retire for the night. Tent leaders: please be careful with the hurricane lamps. No chattering after lights out, or you will feel the weight of my hand. Sleep well everyone."

Stan did not need a second invitation. He was asleep even before Duggan had fastened the tent flaps. Fred lay on his back beneath his threadbare blankets, listening to the sounds of the camp site. He had never felt more contented.

9

MORNING CALL

Reveillé came as a surprise to everyone. With no bugler in their midst, wake-up was sounded by Mister Phipps, squeezing the rubber bulb of a motor car horn as he shuffled past the line of tents. For a second or two, Stan thought that he was riding in Sid Biddle's lorry, so deeply had he been asleep. It took him a further three or four seconds to find his bearings, by which time Morris, having shot out of bed like a startled rabbit, had crashed head first into the tent pole and fallen across Hendry's legs.

"Oi! Get off me, will you? Bloody hell, Morris. What are you up to?"

Stunned, Morris could not remember what he was up to. Instead, he passed his hand over a fast emerging lump on his forehead and whimpered. Duggan roused himself with a yawn and asked what the blazes was going on. Bushell, who had been lying next to Hendry at the moment of impact, compounded the small boy's misery by kicking him in the shins.

"Get off us, Morris, will you?"

Morris whimpered louder. Duggan growled out a warning to all tent members to give him a bit of bloody peace and quiet and to be quick about it. Morris sniffed twice and the tent calmed down. Fred slept on, oblivious.

Outside, the sun was already strong enough to dispel the morning dew from the east facing slopes. Mister Pickup emerged from the latrines wearing a green dressing gown over his shorts and unlaced boots. He breathed in deeply of the morning air, throwing out his chest like a skinny cockerel before exhaling a tuneless hum of contentment. Seven o'clock and all was well. He marched off towards his tent, swinging a wash bag from his left hand and nodding a greeting to Mister Phipps as the wake-up artist sauntered back to the galley.

Within an hour, breakfast was underway. With only two or three exceptions, the boys had all partaken of the soap and water that had been laid out near the latrines. Teeth had been brushed, hair combed and clothes donned. The finished effect was variable. Bedlow's hair was sticking up at the back for fine weather, Armstrong appeared to have mislaid his socks and Barnwell had no footwear at all. Edgington's black eye had turned a rich purple. Mister Pickup strode to the centre of the arc of benches clutching a mug of tea in one hand and a blue stencilled sheet in the other. The boys raised their eyes towards him as they munched through their slices of bread and damson jam.

"Before Mister Barker shares his thoughts on your expeditionary work of yesterday, I thought that I would prevail myself of the opportunity to run through the day's key timings with you. Er hem."

In attempting to unfold the sheet of paper, he spilled tea down the right leg of his shorts. "Drat!" He put his mug down on the grass and wiped his shorts with a handkerchief.

"Right," he resumed at length, "As I was saying. The service at Saint Mary's church will begin at eleven o'clock, so we will need to be on our way from here by 10.15 at the latest. We shall all walk there together, following the canal and the lanes and returning by the same route. Thereafter, we shall have dinner in the field before enjoying a reading of Shakespeare's *Midsummer Night's Dream."*

None of that sounded too onerous. The boys munched on contentedly.

"Before all of that, at nine o'clock sharp, I shall conduct an inspection of your tents."

This was a bombshell. Munching came to a halt. Spoons lowered, spirits sagged.

"Please ensure that side flaps are up-furled to allow an airing breeze to circulate. Your blankets should be neatly stacked and placed next to your kit bags. I am afraid that any non conformists in this regard will not go to church."

He looked slowly around the semi circle of puzzled faces with what he hoped was a stern look. "But I am sure that it won't come to that, now will it?"

There was a brief pause. "Right-ho, lads. I shall see you all at nine then, lined up in front of your tents."

As Mister Pickup departed, so Mister Barker rose unsteadily from his chair at the end of the arc to lean forwards upon his cane. He appeared to smile warmly at the assembly.

"Good morning, boys."

"Good morning, Sir," they chorused with a certain relief. At least with Mister Barker you knew where you stood. Or sat, in this case.

"I discovered a bottle of green ink, the other day," he began obscurely, "at W.H. Smith in Moseley. A most attractive shade, as you will see, for I have used it to embellish your booklets with a number of corrections, completions and, indeed, congratulations." His twinkling eye scanned the arc of attentive faces.

"I must say that my knowledge of Warwickshire has been considerably enhanced by your efforts and I am most grateful to one or two of you in particular for your insights. I now know that the village of Rowington possesses a parish church honouring, not Saint Lawrence, as I had originally thought, but Buffalo Bill!"

Giggles rolled around the circle of campers.

"Packwood House Farm, it appears, boasts a fine collection of shoe trees and the school master at Lapworth is none other than Mr I.P. Knightly." Mister Barker paused to allow the next wave of laughter to die down.

"I have inserted my own version of the facts in your booklets, as and where appropriate. Now, Armstrong: would you be so kind as to hand me them from beneath my chair?"

Armstrong dropped to his knees and scrabbled about at the teacher's feet in order to retrieve the booklets.

"Oh dear, Armstrong," observed Mister Barker. "Do I discern an oversight in the footwear department?"

"You what, Sir?"

"Socks, Armstrong. You appear to have forgotten to put any on."

"Can't find none, Sir. Me Mom must have forgot to put 'em in me bag. And she knitted me a new pair specially an' all."

"Ah, I see," replied the teacher. "Then I had better check if I have a spare pair for you in my tent."

He turned his attention back to the main body of the camp. "As I call out your names, would you please come forward and retrieve your work? You should then wash your breakfast things in the bowl over there and proceed to your tents to prepare for inspection."

The arc thinned as names were called, the campers scurrying off to join the noisy scrum around the washing-up bowl. In the end, only Fred and Stan remained.

"I'm afraid that I appear to have left your booklet in my tent," apologised Mister Barker. Perhaps you could pop over to collect it once Mister Pickup has finished with you?"

Stan and Fred glanced at each other. Surely the ruse of the forgotten booklet was to allow them to continue their discussion of last evening. Which way that discussion might turn now was the subject of their low chatter as they made their way back across the field.

The members of B tent fared well at inspection. Duggan had taken organisational control, ensuring that the side flaps were evenly tied and that blankets were neatly folded and stacked. Kit bags were lined up outside the tent, as were the boys. Mister Pickup fussed about the guy ropes for a few seconds, and turned over one or two of the blankets as if they might be hiding something unmentionable, but it soon became clear that he could find no major fault with the turnout.

"Splendid, lads. Splendid effort. Well done, Duggan. Keep it up, boys."

He proceeded to C tent where display arrangements appeared to have run less smoothly. At Mister Pickup's approach, a length of side flap unfurled to flap in the breeze. Barnwell's boots remained tied around the tent pole, victims of Coley's knot, whilst the blankets and groundsheets lay in general disorder. With relish, Mister Pickup launched into an outpouring of admonishment.

Stan lugged his kitbag back into B tent and helped the others lower and peg down the side flaps. He awaited Duggan's nod of approval before setting off with Fred towards the teachers' ridge tent.

Mister Barker sat stiffly on his chair, right leg outstretched, smoking a pipe of Ogden's Asthma Mixture. Several sheets of foolscap lay on a low table at his left hand, scribbled upon in green ink and held down from the morning breeze by an enamel mug. Beside them lay the leather-bound tome and the missing booklet. His greeting to them was brisk.

"Good morning, boys. Take your booklet, please, and sit down on the grass where I can see you. Anyone nosing in our direction must think that we are talking about yesterday's excursion, do you see?"

Stan and Fred nodded obediently and settled cross-legged in front of Mister Barker with their booklet, waiting for what might come next.

"We do not have much time and there is much to relate. I will be as brief as I can."

Stan's mouth was dry: he suddenly found it hard to swallow.

Mister Barker laid down his pipe. "I am intrigued," he confessed. "You boys appear to have stumbled into the middle of a ripping good mystery, but I am dashed if I can see quite where it might lead. There are many layers and contradictions and the sense is still not entirely clear, but I do believe that fate may have dealt us a slice of good fortune. If you are in agreement, I propose to start with this element."

The boys were most definitely in agreement, if not yet on the same wave length.

"For reasons that I will explain later, I believe that the next piece to this puzzle lies in the very church that we will be visiting for morning service."

Stan's eyes widened.

"The coincidence is quite uncanny, but there we are. As far as I can tell, the Esperanto stanza suggests that the next element to the riddle is hidden in the Beauchamp Chapel of Saint Mary's church, somewhere in the vicinity of the tomb of one of Guy de Beauchamp's descendants."

"G.B." said Stan, half under his breath, "the initials on the box."

"Yes, Johnson. Precisely. With the help of a magnifying glass, I have studied the engravings on the box and compared them with those illustrated in the historical volume that I found in the barge's small library." He indicated the worn book on the table. "And I am pretty sure that your box once belonged to the Beauchamp family."

Fred leaned over and opened the cover of the book, revealing an engraved print of a pastoral scene and, on the opposite page, the title: *An Historical and Descriptive Account of the Town and Castle of Warwick.*

"These are the marks of Guy de Beauchamp, tenth Earl of Warwick and loyal servant to King Edward I," continued Mister Barker, slanting the box into the boys' line of sight. "His initials feature on the base of the box, here, and this is his coat of arms." He touched the heraldic shield with his index finger. The boys leaned forward, squinting into the sunlight as it reflected off the gold interior of the box.

"Who's the bloke with his head cut off, then?" asked Fred, pointing to the depiction of the knight on the other engraved panel. "I mean, who's the man?"

"He would appear to be Sir Piers Gaveston," answered Mister Barker, "a favourite knight of Edward II and sworn enemy of Guy de Beauchamp. The image depicts the moment, in 1312, when Beauchamp killed Gaveston following the latter's return to England from exile."

"1312?" gasped Stan. "Crikey O'Reilly!"

"Indeed, it is all rather a long time ago, isn't it? And that in itself adds another element to the mystery." The young teacher paused, turning this thought over in his mind for a while, before returning to the subject of the engravings.

"Notice that Beauchamp is holding a church in his right hand. At first, I thought that this might be the church of Saint Michael, at Baddesley Clinton, thereby tying the riddle to your discovery of yesterday, but, of course, the dates are wrong. This church clearly boasts a tower, whereas the tower of Saint Michael's - as you may recall - was not erected until the early fifteenth century, some two hundred years after Guy de Beauchamp's time on earth. The image is almost certainly meant to represent Christianity and the concept of right, rather than any particular church, although there does seem to be a certain resemblance to the church of Saint Mary at Warwick where we shall presently assemble."

This excursion into the realms of christian symbolism left Fred lost. Stan asked for clarification:

"Sir, if this box is so old, and Esperanto isn't so old, how come the two are linked?"

"That, Johnson, is a very good question."

Mister Barker picked up the book from the table, glancing around the field to assure himself that no uninvited eyes were trained upon them. He leaned in towards Fred and Stan. "The box is undoubtably very old, but not as old as Guy de Beauchamp himself. I have found a reproduction of the engraved images within the pages of this book and they would appear to come from a fifteenth century publication by John Rous who wrote many books on Warwickshire, including a detailed chronicle of the Beauchamp family known as the *Warwick Roll*."

He looked at Stan and Fred who were struggling to follow. "Bear with me," he encouraged them, "I *am* coming to the point." He took a sip of tea from the enamel mug.

"As you have rightly suggested, Johnson, the riddle is of a very different age to the box. And yet the two are closely connected. Whoever wrote it did so with the box in mind, clearly linking the Beauchamp family to the mystery. Or, more accurately, to the solving of the mystery. And the fact that your square of linen is written upon in Esperanto obviously means that whatever this mystery is, it can not be more than thirty or forty years old. Similarly, the sonnet that was in the box must also post date Guy de Beauchamp by several hundred years, not least because it is written in the vernacular of our own time. Or at least, in the vernacular of Mister Ferguson's time!"

He afforded himself a smile, though it was not easy for the boys to spot. "So, where does this all leave us?" he enquired, largely to himself.

"Nowhere?" ventured Fred. He had lost the sense of Mister Barker's exposé, as well as the will to sit through it, and was thinking that now would probably be a good time to head off to church and forget the whole thing. By contrast, Stan was fully engaged.

"The riddle talked of finding a grave within a chapel, didn't it, Sir?" he asked. "And you just said that the Beauchamp family had its own chapel in Warwick."

"I did, Johnson. Good."

"So, is that where the treasure is?"

Fred perked up again at the mention of treasure and craned in for the reply.

"Possibly. But I would venture to suggest that this will not be the end of our quest. If you recall, the riddle contained a line about the next clue being at the feet of the thirteenth of Beauchamp's kin. A 'next clue' would suggest that we may yet have to follow the trail further if we are to bring this to a resolution."

Stan scratched his head. "If I've got this right then, Sir," he pondered, "we have found a box that contained a poem that took us to a church where we found a clue, written in Esperanto, that now leads us to the chapel of the family whose crest is on the box." He exhaled deeply.

"Couldn't have put it better myself, Johnson. Wished I had, actually. Might have saved us some time!"

Stan and Fred looked at each other, then back at Mister Barker who was suddenly indicating, by way of an exaggerated flick of his head towards mid on, that somebody was coming. It was time to bring the interview to an end.

"I will get word to you in the church," whispered Mister Barker conspiratorially. "There is more to tell."

And with that he plunged his attention into the pages of the open book on his knee and ceased to acknowledge the boys' existence. Stan and Fred sprang to their feet, grabbed the corrected copy of their expedition booklet and turned straight into Mister Pickup.

"What ho, chaps! Been getting a roasting over the course work, have we?"

"Er yes, Sir. Sort of," answered Stan, thinking fast. "We got the first question wrong and missed another one altogether."

"Oh dear! Yes, well I see." Mister Pickup was smiling. "Terrible stickler for detail is Mister Barker, isn't he? Quite right, too, mind. Quite right!"

"Yes, Sir."

"The important thing is to learn from the experience. That's the main point, isn't it, Parker? Learning."

Fred nodded dumbly.

"Well, so long as that is the case, let's be off with you. We will be on our way in a matter of minutes and I don't want to have to be looking for anyone before we leave."

Fred and Stan made a dignified exit and ran off towards their tent.

"Crikey!" said Stan as they sat together on Fred's groundsheet, their breath regained, "We're in a right old adventure here! And it looks like it is leading us straight to morning service."

10.15 arrived and Mister Pickup was having difficulty rounding up his troops. The sky had clouded over and several boys had returned briefly to their tents to seek sweaters.

"Come along, lads. Come along. We can't have the vicar left waiting at the altar, can we? Bushell, no cricket bat! Armstrong, will you please stop picking your nose?"

Eventually, Mister Pickup was able to shepherd his flock across the sloping field to the towpath, along which they single-filed under a road bridge, past the derelict wharf and on to the flight of single locks that tumbled down towards Warwick.

The Hatton flight was opened by the owners of the Warwick and Birmingham canal in 1799. Spanning less than two miles, the 21 locks lift the waterway up 150 feet from the Avon valley, stepping through a series of gates that become ever more tightly spaced as it heads north. Boatmen have long referred to this flight as the "Stairway to Heaven", a reflection of the heavy labour involved in piloting a fully laden coal barge up the steep climb before arriving at the relatively flat run in to the company's wage office at Camp Hill.

In its pomp, the flight boasted a busy wharf and maintenance yard where skilled craftsmen manufactured and maintained the heavy oak and iron lock gates. For vessels arriving too late in the day to complete the flight before sunset, the wharf also proposed refreshment to the boatmen and stabling for the horses.

Fred and Stan stayed at the back as the boys straggled down the descent towards Warwick. They spoke together in hushed voices, analysing their discoveries over and over, testing each other's understanding of the facts with blunt questions. Fred challenged Mister Barker's deduction that there would be no treasure in the church: Stan kept asking himself why the metal box had been hidden under the milestone in the first place. Why hide it so comprehensively if its sole purpose was to lead to other clues?

"Easy," reflected Fred, suddenly brilliant. "Because it wasn't the first clue. I mean, there must have been another clue that led to it."

"Except that no one ever found it," completed Stan. "Yes, that's it! The trail went dead because nobody could work out where the next clue was. If it hadn't been for you uprooting the stone, the secret of whatever it is we are looking for might have been lost forever."

"Didn't uproot it," corrected Fred indignantly. "It just toppled over with me stood on it, that's all."

"Yes, well. Whatever. Our good fortune is down to you is what I'm saying. Thank goodness you're such a clumsy oaf!"

"But we still don't know hardly anything about what we're doing, do we? Not really, I mean."

Stan was forced to agree. There was certainly a clear link between the engravings on the metal box - their first discovery - and the name of the chapel where Mister Barker thought that they would find the next clue. But there were still more questions than answers. How important was this GB chap, for example? Could he be the key to unravelling the whole mystery? Or might the deceased Joseph Bray, unwitting protector of the second clue, yet have a bigger role to play? If so, how? And why was the clue written in Esperanto? Most intriguingly of all, what did Mister Barker mean when he said that there was more to tell? The tangled strands of the mystery felt daunting, but there could be no giving up. Mister Barker was right in there with them, counting on them to move things forward. There was no way that they would let him down now.

10

SUNDAY SERVICE

Warwick has been continuously inhabited for at least fifteen hundred years, although evidence of Neolithic human activity in the area suggests that man may actually have visited the place for the first time over five thousand years ago. The town's rise to prominence began almost exactly one thousand years ago, in AD 914. Back in those darker ages, the Kingdom of Mercia faced a serious threat of being overrun by Danish invaders, swarming in from the north and east. Warwick was one of ten sites chosen for the construction of Anglo Saxon fortifications, known as burhs, built around the Kingdom to defend its inhabitants against attack. The tiny group of houses that constituted Warwick (literally, "dwellings by the weir") was selected by the Lady of Mercia herself; Ethelfleda, sister of the Saxon King Edward the Elder and daughter of King Alfred the Great. Warwick owed this signal honour to its proximity to the river Avon and to the major transport route of the day, Fosse Way. The original fortifications were constructed atop an earth mound and succeeded *in preventing any serious Danish attack for over 130 years. As a burh, Warwick quietly prospered, expanding beside the Avon and developing, amongst other important buildings, a nunnery. However, the Danes were not to be held at bay for ever and, in 1050, they finally invaded Mercia. Almost everything in and about Warwick was burned to the ground.*

Serious reconstruction began in 1068, when William the Conqueror founded Warwick Castle within the burh and built a new wall around the dwellings. The Middle Ages brought stability and growth to the town under the control of the Earls of Warwick, most of whom belonged to the Beauchamp family. Of the ancient town walls, only the east and west gatehouses remain, the eastern gatehouse now forming part of the King's High School.

In fact, very few of the original medieval buildings within the walls survive. The Great Fire of Warwick in 1694 destroyed much of the fabric of the town and a good deal of the medieval church of Saint Mary. Only the crypt and the chancel survived, along with the Chapel of Our Lady, commonly known as the Beauchamp Chapel, which had been built in the fifteenth century in accordance with the wishes of Richard Beauchamp, Earl of Warwick, following his death in 1439. The rebuilt church, Gothic in design and with a tower standing 130 feet tall, was completed in 1704. Much of the reconstruction of Warwick was undertaken by Francis and William Smith, its builder architect sons, but the imposing church tower was the work of Sir William Wilson, appointed by the Crown Commissioners to oversee its construction.

As the campers turned into Northgate Street they caught their first sight of Wilson's Gothic tower, standing in the road on four bowed legs, pealing out its call to worship. Ahead of the boys, a platoon of the Warwickshire Yeomanry marched smartly to church; boots gleaming, puttees tightly bound, heads held high. A smattering of applause accompanied them to the front door where they removed their caps and filed in. The Camp School pupils followed them, led by Mister Pickup, to sit together on the last three rows of chairs on the right hand side of the aisle. The absence of pews in the church accentuated the spaciousness and light of its recently renovated interior.

Stan found himself on a narrow chair in the back row, wedged between Fred and Duggan, who sat to his right. The church was full, its congregation humming gossip and pious greetings along its serried ranks. In the choir, Allen Blackall, organist and church institution, pedalled his way towards the finale of a Bach prelude and fugue, the music bouncing off the high ceiling in waves. The church seemed enormous. Stan craned his neck to see around Hendry, planted in the seat in front, and tried to determine where and what a family chapel might be, but the church was so full of people, forever standing up and sitting down like dancers in some ancient ritual, that it was difficult to see anything beyond half way down the nave. He lifted his eyes to the vaulted ceiling and marvelled at the skill of the stone masons. How on earth did they build such a thing? How does it all stay up there? In response, he received a heavy dig in his ribs from Fred's right elbow.

"Stan. Stan!" whispered Fred urgently. "She's 'ere. Look: it's Kate!"

And so it was. Standing in the row of chairs to the front of the Warwickshire Yeomanry, Kate was gazing into the eyes of a young soldier whose two hands she held in hers, a radiant smile illuminating her face. They seemed so happy. Kate looked so pretty. Fred groaned softly.

"Should have known it, I suppose. Only walking out with a bloomin' Tommy."

Stan leaned over to console his friend and caught sight of Mister Barker making his stiff entrance through the main door behind them. The teacher briefly halted to adjust his eye to the light, then limped slowly past the Camp School assembly to rendezvous with a young lieutenant amongst the soldiers on the left. Their greeting was warm and friendly, Mister Barker's back patted several times by the lieutenant as they chatted in the aisle. A space was made by soldiers shuffling one chair along and Mister Barker took his seat next to the officer.

"I wonder how he got here?" wondered Stan.

"The Tommy?" Fred was still fixed on the love scene. "With the others, I suppose. They do tend to stick together, you know."

The organ music crescendoed to an end and conversation died down. It was 11.15. The Reverend Llewellyn Wood waited patiently for his congregation to fall into respectful silence, then shattered it with a loud, lusty greeting:

"Dearly Beloved," he boomed. "Welcome to Sunday worship."

"Came to the right place then," quipped Coley from the other side of Duggan.

The Reverend's opening remarks washed over Fred. His world had just taken a serious turn for the worse. Kate was the focus of his attention, but all he could now see of her was the back of her head, slightly tilted and perfectly still as she listened to the opening address. Perfectly was a good word, he thought. Perfectly perfect. Fred had an empty feeling in the pit of his stomach.

"I'm not hungry, Stan," he whispered.

"What?"

"Don't think I'll ever eat again."

"What are you on about, you numbskull? What's food got to do with it? Can't you shut up while the vicar's talking?"

Fred sighed deeply and gazed once more at the back of Kate's head. She was seated near the aisle, between a man with unfashionably long hair and a smartly dressed woman in a brown hat. Her soldier boyfriend sat two rows back, lost to all but Fred's eyes in a sea of uniform khaki. Fred looked longingly at Kate's hair and suddenly had an idea. He would pray for her. Pray for her to rush up and give him a kiss. After all, wouldn't this be the perfect place to do a bit of praying? The lines of communication must be direct in church and God always worked Sundays. Fred settled back in his seat and closed his eyes, placing his fingertips together between his knees.

"Our Father," he began to himself, "Please make Kathryn Moore - her with a Y - love me. I promise to be good, to work hard at Day Continuation School and to help old ladies cross the road. Yours sincerely, Amen." Fred opened his eyes and felt better.

At the front of the church, a choir of high voices shrilled into a hymn and everybody stood up. Such unexpected movement caused an outbreak of jostling in Hendry's row which resulted in Bedlow being ejected into the aisle on his backside. The soldiers nearby found this highly amusing. Bedlow clowned it up for an extra laugh by pulling a Ben Turpin face he had seen at the picture house, before a stare from Mister Pickup forced him back into line.

The hymn dragged on into a prayer. It was difficult to hear from the back, especially over Coley's incessant low chatter, but eventually Reverend Wood allowed everyone to sit down again and climbed the steps of the pulpit to preach the sermon. Fred briefly thought about letting go an SBD, then changed his mind. The congregation settled into dozy repose. Stan followed the Reverend's drift for less than a minute before his mind wandered back to the main task at hand. How would they find the next clue if they could not even find the chapel? He opened his hymn book to the fly leaf. Might there be a layout of the church inside? Sadly not. He closed the book and returned it to rack on the back of the chair in front of him, whereupon he received a sharp prod between the shoulder blades, swiftly followed by another.

"Oi!" he protested to Fred, only to become aware of a greasy cap adjacent to his left ear.

"With the compliments of Mister Barker," rasped Young Doran. "The reading."

An envelope was thrust into the space between Fred and Stan.

"Stay quiet. Bide your time."

Fred and Stan sat petrified, neither daring to turn around even though both knew that Young Doran had already departed. Stan glanced quickly towards Duggan, lost in a game of three card brag with Coley. He seemed not to have noticed the delivery. The service lumbered on. Reluctant even to touch the envelope in his lap, Stan instead produced a handkerchief from his pocket and proceeded to clean his spectacles. Fred stared at him.

"Have you quite finished?" he whispered. "Blimey, Stan, the suspense is killing me."

Stan fitted the wire arms of his spectacles behind his ears, stuffed the handkerchief back into his pocket and picked up the envelope. It was unmarked, save for an embossed manufacturer's mark on the back. Slipping his finger knife-like beneath the flap, he carefully tore open the envelope and pulled out one folded sheet of cream writing paper, liberally scrawled upon in green ink. There was also a small printed leaflet showing a plan of the church. He blinked behind his glasses and turned to Fred.

"Why Young Doran?" he whispered.

"What?"

"I mean, what's he doing in church? He gives me the creeps."

"Yeah, well, don't let it worry you too much. What's the letter say?"

"It's just that he's always there at the wrong time," pursued Stan. "You know, like yesterday, in the barge."

"D'you mean it was him who bit your finger?"

"What? No, of course not. For goodness sake! Nobody bit my blessed finger!"

"But I thought you told Old Pickup..."

"Leave it, Fred." Stan was cross. He turned his attention back to the contents of the envelope.

Fred glared at him. "I don't get you sometimes."

"Yeah, well. He just puts me on edge, that's all. My fault."

"Let's leave it then, eh?" Fred tapped his friend's forearm reassuringly. "What's it say?"

Stan held open the letter so that both boys could read it without being seen. Mister Barker's green writing was childlike and messy, its unnatural slant betraying the left hand expression of a right-handed man. All of the original first line had been crossed out. There followed one sentence, written in capital letters, which neither boy understood:

FRANKIE CAN BE TRUSTED AND WILL BE OF SERVICE

After this strange opening came a series of numbered statements of few words. Staccato phrases, written, it seemed, as if to be read in a hurry. The boys did just that.

1. Locate Beauchamp Chapel on the plan.
2. Go there immediately after the service.
3. Locate the tomb of Richard Beauchamp (great grandson of GB: box crest).
4. The clue should be at his feet (bear & griffin).
5. Look for the out-of-the-ordinary: search carefully.
6. Do not be seen!
7. Reconvene at the camp site. ACB.

"Blimey!" Fred's wide eyes turned to Stan. "What d'you make of it?"

Stan's heart was beating fast. He looked again at the green writing, then scrutinised the sheet of thin blue paper upon which was printed the church layout. The Beauchamp Chapel was clearly marked, situated off the south transept. It would be impossible to go there without being seen. Unless, of course, they waited until everyone was milling around at the end of the service, just as Mister Barker had instructed. Stan felt a surge of excitement, Fred's ears had turned red. They were both impatient to get on with the adventure, but were pinned to their chairs by the high pulpit rhetoric.

The sermon eventually droned to an end and the congregation rose to the opening bars of *Onward, Christian Soldiers!* It was one of Stan's favourite hymns, but he did not feel like joining in. Fred, on the other hand, hummed his way through each verse and belted out the refrain as though auditioning for the Salvation Army. At the end of the hymn came the invitation to take holy communion. Mister Pickup rose from his seat on the far end of his row, made his way along the outside of the congregation, passed in front of the altar and turned back up the central aisle to join the long queue of disciples waiting to receive the blood and body of Christ. The lady in the brown hat to the left of Kate also stood up and edged towards the aisle past her two neighbours. Kate stood up to let her through, turning her head as she did so, and caught sight of Fred, stretching his legs in the aisle behind her. Straight away she left her seat, pushing past the man with long hair, and skipped up to Fred.

"Well hello, Fred Parker! What a lovely surprise."

Fred, reflecting that his first serious attempt at prayer had hit the jackpot, greeted her with a beaming smile, but without words. He seemed to have lost the power of speech. Kate pursued the conversation.

"I never imagined that I might see you *here*. How lovely! Is Stanley with you, too?"

Fred nodded dumbly, indicating his accomplice with a jerk of the thumb. Stan stood up clumsily, made as if to doff his cap, realised that he wasn't wearing one and sat down again. As he did, so Duggan stood up. It was like musical chairs.

"Johnson," whispered Duggan, ventriloquist-like through closed lips, "who's the girl?"

"What?"

"You're gonna have to introduce me, Johnson," he continued. "Who's your friend?"

Kate came confidently towards Stan and held out her hand.

"Hello again, Stanley. How lovely to see you."

"Likewise, Miss," he managed to say, scrambling to his feet to shake her hand. "Er, this is our tent commander," he stuttered. "Duggan. Er... Sorry, Duggan, I don't think I know your first name."

"William, Miss. It's William, but my friends call me Bill. I am indeed very pleased to make your acquaintance." He held out his hand.

Fred looked at Duggan with undisguised loathing. Where did he learn to ponce out a phrase like "very pleased to make your acquaintance"? Kate was noticeably less sure of herself as she took Duggan's hand.

"Kathryn Moore," she said quietly. "Likewise, I'm sure."

"With a Y," blurted out Fred. He had suddenly rediscovered the power of speech and needed to make a point. Duggan ignored him. His eyes were glued on Kate.

"Do you live around here, Kathryn?"

"No, not really. I am staying with family in Warwickshire for the summer. In Rowington. It's about an hour's drive from here."

"Long way to come for a service," observed Duggan with a gentle smile.

Stan had definitely never seen this side of Duggan before. It made Fred feel sick.

"We came to see my brother," answered Kate softly, looking into Duggan's eyes. "He's in the Warwickshire Yeomanry. I haven't seen him since Christmas."

"Ah! I see," said Duggan, radiating empathy.

You had to hand it to him, thought Stan. This was a masterful performance. Fred wanted to hit him. The vicar came to the end of his communion queue and called the congregation to order for the blessing. Kate hurried back to her seat. The man with the long hair threw the campers a look of disgust as Kate pushed past him. Fred unclenched his fists and closed his eyes. It was time to have another word with God.

A few minutes later, the service was over. Organ music swelled up against the rising buzz of conversation. Fred stood in the aisle, breasting the exiting tide as he tried to catch Kate's eye. Stan grabbed his arm.

"Come on. Follow me. Quick as you like."

He raced off towards the south transept, plunging into the chattering throng around which he danced and sidestepped like a bullfighter. Fred ploughed a more direct course, barging people out of the way as he chased after his friend. Within seconds they had arrived at a flight of fourteen stone steps that descended beneath a carved doorway to the Beauchamp Chapel. The boys were down in a trice, pushing aside the unbolted wrought iron gate and skidding to a halt on the black and white tiled floor in amazement.

It was a place of staggering beauty, much bigger than Stan had imagined and bathed in the light of many windows, high up on all sides. The architectural forms were exquisite: the iron works filigreed like intricate brooches. Reflections of gilt and bronze and finely painted motifs flickered all about them. Stan felt as though he were inside a jewellery box.

Within touching distance of the boys' right hand stood the tomb of Ambrose Dudley, Earl of Warwick, his marble effigy lying in coloured finery, head towards them, hands held in prayer above his chest. A small muzzled bear lay at his feet, one front paw crossed over the other in loyal repose. To the left, in a columned recess behind a fretted ironwork screen, lay the effigies of Robert Dudley, 1st Earl of Leicester, and his beloved wife Lettice, sleeping upon an elaborate tomb. The effigy of their infant son, Robert, "The Noble Impe", lay on its own marble casket close by. But the grandest tomb of all was sited squarely in the centre of the chapel, its feet towards the altar and the beautiful stained glass window behind.

Stan and Fred approached Richard de Beauchamp in awe. He lay at eye level, in full armour save for his helmet, on top of an opulent tomb of Purbeck marble. The bronze was so beautifully worked, the sculpture and gilding of such fine quality, that the noble Earl looked ready to stand up at a moment's notice and head off to the battlefield. He lay within an arched cage, hands apart in supplication, his face at peace with the after world. The boys circled the tomb, one either side, meeting at the business end, as Fred called it. There they encountered the bear and the griffin, as foretold by Mister Barker, also exquisitely cast in bronze, sitting back-to-back at their master's feet.

"Blimey," breathed Fred. "Just look at the workmanship in this lot."

"We've got to move quickly, Fred," urged Stan. "Can you see anything unusual?"

"The whole blinking thing's unusual, Stan! I've never seen nothing like this in my whole life. Can you just imagine just how difficult it is to get a bend like that in metal?"

He was looking at Beauchamp's pointed boots. Stan could not imagine, but was prepared to take his friend's word for it. He ran his hand down the back of the bear, then over the pointed wings of the griffin. He minutely inspected the gaps between each foot and claw, beneath each boot and backside, within every nook and cranny of the whole sculpture, but in vain. He turned his attention to the gilded carvings on the marble tombstone and to the strange lettering that ran around it.

Fred looked around for something to stand on so that he could examine the end pieces of the cage bars that enclosed the figure of the Earl. He spied a heavy wooden chair to the right of the altar and dragged it noisily across the tiles, eliciting a loud shushing noise from Stan. Mouthing a silent "sorry", Fred climbed onto the polished seat and began his inspection. There were five round knobs at each end of the tomb, one for each horizontal rod of the cage. They were about four inches in diameter and featured a carved and enamelled coat of arms set within four concentric rings of brass. Wonderful workmanship: such symmetry, such perfection. Then he noticed something odd. The end piece in the middle was different from the other four. Barely noticeable, even at close quarters, the knob's central motif was slightly duller than the others and appeared to be surrounded by only three concentric rings. Fred swallowed and glanced towards Stan, now on all fours at the side of the tomb, face to face with one of the carved "weepers" that adorned the marble. He turned back to the end piece and extended his hand, fingers trembling. He touched the knob lightly, as though it might be hot, then took a more determined hold and tightened his grip. Outside, the organ music came to a sudden end. Stan looked up anxiously. Fred squeezed the brass knob and attempted to unscrew it to the left, but it did not move.

"Found something?" asked Stan.

"Not sure. Thought so, but it won't budge," grunted Fred, trying again.

"What makes you think it's supposed to turn?"

"Thought it might," grumbled Fred disappointedly. "It's different. See?"

Stan looked but saw nothing different. "Try turning it the other way."

Fred tried, but to no avail. Muttering, he leaned forward to examine the knob still closer. He could have sworn that it was different. He traced the three concentric rings with his index finger. The third sat an eighth of an inch proud of the recessed central motif, reminding him of something at work. He thought for a moment, then it came to him. The lifting apparatus in the tinplate warehouse. Of course....

"It's not a knob," he declared confidently. "It's a button. At least, the middle bit is."

He pushed his thumb gently against the heraldic motif and heard a gratifying click. As the centre depressed, so the outer casing lifted an eighth of an inch, like a lid on a saucepan. Fred held the top part in his fingertips and unscrewed it through five anticlockwise turns. It came away in his hand, revealing a small gilded chamber behind, within which lay a velvet pouch, pulled tight with a drawstring of golden braid.

"Blimey, Stan!"

Fred removed the bag and weighed it in his palm. There was something inside the bag; obviously small, but heavy enough to be a jewel or a piece of gold: a sovereign at least. It actually felt more like a thimble when Fred ran his thumb over it. A solid gold thimble? Fred pushed the bag into his pocket.

"Can you put it back together alright?" asked Stan. "We really need to be getting out of here. The others will be looking for us."

Fred screwed the top of the knob until it was tight and the central motif clicked back into place. The two parts again became one. Fred ran his finger around the knob, expecting to feel the join, but there was nothing; no line. It was as smooth as glass.

"What a bloomin' piece of work that is," he marvelled. "Never seen workmanship like that before. Never."

"Got to go, Fred," urged Stan.

Fred jumped down from the chair and dragged it noisily back to its place beside the altar.

"Quiet," hissed Stan. "For goodness sake. And get a move on."

They left the chapel as quickly as they had arrived, sprinting up the stairs and back through the empty church to the main doors. Outside, the air was warm and the scene animated. People milled about in all directions. Clumps of congregation had formed around a number of soldiers with whom they exchanged family hugs and stories, whilst the rump of the Warwickshire Yeomanry lounged about on the pavement opposite, smoking army cigarettes and reading the Sunday newspapers. A profusion of carriages, horses and motor cars littered the roadways, honking and snorting: individually determined in their purpose; collectively obstructive in their haste for Sunday dinner.

Stan spotted Mister Pickup addressing the vicar. He seemed animated, as if he had lost something. A hundred yards behind him, Bedlow clung to the top of a lamp post, brandishing Edgington's cap in his fist. A crowd of cheering campers encouraged him from the ground. Edgington threw a stone at Bedlow's head. Fred and Stan set off to join them.

"Hey there! You two. Ho! Johnson. Parker. Not so fast, if you don't mind." Mister Pickup strode up sporting a decidedly cross face. "Where on earth do you think you have been? I have looked everywhere for you. Heaven knows, I even engaged myself with the Reverend on your account."

"Sorry, Sir," ventured Fred. "We couldn't find our way out of the church, Sir."

"Parker, nobody was sitting nearer to the exit than you two. How on earth can you possibly construe to be last out?"

"We went looking for a plan of the church, Sir," invented Stan. "To stick into our diaries."

Mister Pickup seemed taken aback by this unexpected show of initiative. "And did you find one?" he asked, testily.

"Yes, Sir. Here, Sir." Stan wafted the printed blue sheet vaguely in his teacher's line of vision.

"Really difficult to find an all, Sir," confirmed Fred, picking up the thread. "Took us ages."

"I did notice that, Parker," harrumphed Mister Pickup, looking to the floor for his next move. "Well, just be sure that we are not all retarded by your antics again, do you understand?"

"Yes, Sir."

"Right, well come along then or we'll be late for Mister Reid's dinner." He marched off towards the others. "Bedlow, I'll give you three seconds to get down from there or you will feel the weight of my hand on your Derry Air!"

Fred and Stan exchanged a brief glance of relief and set off in pursuit of Mister Pickup, busy herding his charges into line for the return journey. After a further delay, when Bushell nipped into a newsagent's shop to buy a copy of *The Sports Argus*, they were finally underway.

Leaving Saint Mary's behind, they headed out of town by way of the long demolished North Gate. A mile or so further and their course would veer off across open countryside to rejoin the canal below the Hatton flight. Stan and Fred hung back. There was much to discuss and prying ears were not welcome.

"Let's wait until we get back to the tent to open it," suggested Fred, tapping his pocket in case Stan might not have followed his thought process. "It'll be safer."

Stan agreed. His mind was running through the series of events in the Beauchamp Chapel like a looped moving picture film, the images racing past each other ever faster.

"D'you reckon we found the right thing?"

"What? What d'you mean, the right thing?"

"Well, you know, we didn't miss anything, did we? Anything else, I mean. Are you sure that this was what we were supposed to find?"

"Of course, you blockhead! What are you on about? We followed every line Barker wrote to the letter. You know we did."

"I know. You're right. It's just that we had to work so quickly in there. We didn't really have time to think about what we were doing, did we?"

"Don't worry, Stan. This is definitely what we came for." He winked at his friend and smiled broadly. "And I'm pretty sure it'll turn out to be gold, too. Or jewels, at the very least. Certainly better than a piece of old cloth. Did you *see* how beautiful that ironwork was?"

As Fred drifted off into his metallurgical reverie an ancient gig surged by, pulled along by an old farm nag. Neither boy would have paid it much attention had it not been for the loud "giddy-up" shouted by the driver as the vehicle flew past. Could that have been the voice of Young Doran? Stan and Fred stopped in their tracks and turned as one to stare after the vehicle. Sure enough, there he was, cap pulled low, moleskin trousers rucked up around his shins, driving on the old horse as if racing for the Gold Cup at Cheltenham. Beside him, the epitome of composure, sat the upright figure of Mister Barker.

"Well I'll be jiggered!" exclaimed Stan. "At least that explains how he got to church."

"Got his own private coachman!"

The boys turned back to their path and were instantly met by Duggan, coming the other way.

"There you are, Parker," he said breathlessly. "Been looking for you everywhere."

"Well well! If it isn't our esteemed tent commander," growled Fred. "I am indeed very pleased to make your acquaintance."

Stan winced. Duggan thought briefly about knocking Fred's insolent block off, but recovered himself just in time. He pursued a more diplomatic line.

"Careful, Parker. Wouldn't want Johnson to have to dig you out of the latrines, now would we?"

Fred bit his lip and said nothing. Stan took a brave step of solidarity towards his friend, heart racing. He hated conflict. Duggan took one step forward, too, then grinned.

"Look, I'm sorry, Parker. I didn't mean to butt in on you in church. You know, with Kathryn and all that. It's just that, well, time was tight and I knew straight away that I absolutely had to speak to her."

Fred continued to glare at Duggan, but Stan noticed that his fists were now unclenched. "Her name's Kate, not Kathryn," he said petulantly. "She asked me to call her Kate."

"Really?" asked Duggan. "Kate? How lovely! Kate." His eyes seemed to have lost focus.

This was worse than Fred had thought. He knew then that the game was up. What could he offer against a bloke like Duggan anyway? He was strong, good looking and three years older. And now it turned out that he could do the posh talking as well. The fight was fast draining out of Fred.

"S'oright, Duggan," he managed to say. "No hard feelings. She's too old for me anyway." He held out his pudgy hand, rather as he had done to Stan all those months ago in the dining room. Duggan took it with a broad smile.

"You're a good bloke, Parker. Thanks."

They resumed their walk back to camp.

"I've got to find her again, you know," he enthused, smitten. "Just got to. You don't happen to know whereabouts in Rowington she lives, do you?"

Stan looked at Fred anxiously, but he need not have worried. His friend seemed to have fallen out of love just as quickly as he had fallen into it.

"Of course. She lives in a pub called the Punchbowl. What else d'you wanna know?"

"Er, where it is, for example?"

"Ah, now that one might cost you!"

Fred and Duggan pursued their banter about the delightful Kate all the way back to the camp site. Stan lagged behind, his mind otherwise engaged, replaying the extraordinary events and discoveries of the last twenty-four hours. Who would have guessed, as he left home yesterday morning, that his first experience of camp school would be so strange and wonderful? And what on earth might happen next?

11

GOLDEN REFLECTIONS

Stan was the last of the church-goers to trail back into camp and the place was already a hive of activity. Mister Pickup was in full flow.

"Over here, Ironmonger, where the ground is flatter. Come along, come along. Dinner will be as cold as the canal at this rate."

Ironmonger and his ragged fatigue squad lugged their trestle tables up to the identified spot where Mister Pickup awaited them, hands on hips and chest puffed out, like a man who had just reached the summit of Snowdon.

"Erect them here: in a U. That's right. Well done, lads. Splendid. Good show. Now, scoot off as quick as you like and bring the forms." He scanned the field. "Where on earth are Bedlow and Shaw?"

"Fetching plates, Sir," replied Ironmonger, bored.

Right on cue, the plate fetchers appeared over the brow of the slope, Shaw preceding his partner by a distance, swinging along with a single plate in each hand whilst Bedlow staggered along behind, creased at the waist and barely able to see over the pile of crockery clutched to his midriff. He was blowing hard.

"Really, Shaw!" observed Mister Pickup, frowning at Bedlow. "That's hardly equitable, now is it?"

Stan's attention was dragged away from the camp's domestic arrangements by the bustling arrival of Fred at his side.

"Old Bill's alright, you know, but he's completely bonkers for Kate," gabbled Fred, his ruddy face beaming with happiness. "Right in head first, if you ask me. Gone all soppy round the bloomin' edges."

"So its Bill now, is it?" asked Stan, peevishly.

"Oh come on, Stan," retorted Fred. "Don't tell me you're gonna do a strop just because I walked back with Duggan."

A sustained crash of broken crockery to the boys' left indicated that Bedlow's tortured journey towards the dining area had fallen short. Mister Pickup let out a wail. Stan pursued his sulk at Fred.

"I'm not stropping at all. But you might at least have waited for me instead of haring off like that. We had things to talk about."

The plaintive tone of the last few words extinguished Fred's fleeting sense of injustice. He playfully punched his friend's shoulder. "Come on, mate. I'm sorry. Got a bit carried away with the lovely Kate, I'm afraid." He jammed his fist into the pocket of his shorts and pulled out the small velvet bag. "This what you wanted to talk about?"

The royal blue material shimmered in the sunlight against Fred's grubby right palm. The bag measured no more than two inches from top to tail and was tied around the neck with a length of gold braid. Its discoverers inspected it minutely, neither of them daring to move it from where it lay. The bulge of its contents could have been the outline of a thimble, as Fred had suggested, but it seemed rather longer to Stan than the thimble his sister Elsie used for needlepoint.

"How heavy is it?" Stan asked.

"Featherweight," answered Fred, weighing the object with an exaggerated lowering of his hand. "Here, feel for yourself."

He tossed the bag over and waited for his partner to corroborate his judgement. Stan solemnly performed his own version of the hand-weighing ritual and nodded confirmation to Fred.

"Not much to it at all."

There was a brief pause for serious frowning on both sides before Fred ventured the next question:

"Gonna open it, then? Or d'you want to take it to Pegleg first?"

Stan glanced up at his accomplice, then back at the bag. "I'm gonna open it now."

The knot in the drawstring was tight and Stan had trouble undoing it. He adjusted the spectacles and fumbled at it again, cursing his mother for having insisted he cut his finger nails for the trip. No use asking Fred, though. He had fingers like sausages and nails bitten to the quick. Stan persevered: Fred craned in to see. Eventually, the knot came free and Stan pulled the two ends of braid apart before loosening the neck of the bag. He shot another glance at Fred, took a deep breath and emptied the contents into his left hand. Fred gasped as the bright sunlight bounced off the brilliant object. Stan swallowed hard.

"God Blimey, Stan," whispered Fred. "We've only gone and struck gold, you bugger."

Stan's heart thumped in his rib cage. In the light of this blessed Sunday the golden reflexions were dazzling. Stan moved his hand into shadow, the better to examine the precious jewel. As he did so, two facts became apparent: the thimble wasn't a thimble and it wasn't made of gold. Rather, it appeared to be a highly polished brass rifle cartridge, truncated by a saw cut and plugged by a white porcelain disc. As he turned the object over in his hand Stan could make out intricately engraved scrolls and letterings along the length of the casing. It was the work of a master craftsman, the like of which they had seen on the box from beneath the milestone.

"Don't tell me it's not what I thought it was," groaned Fred in a low voice.

"It's not," replied Stan tactlessly. "But it's beautiful anyway. Look."

He proffered his cupped hand to Fred who picked up the brass object in his clumsy, delicate fingers.

"Blimey, Stan. I really thought we'd made it big for a minute." He squinted closely into the reflections. "But you're right: just beautiful."

"Parker, Johnson! What in blazes are you dawdling over there for when the rest of us are presently assembled for dinner?"

Mister Pickup's bellowed command caused the boys to jump in surprise before scampering over to the dining area, Fred stuffing both cartridge and bag into his pocket as they squeezed in together on the end of one of the forms. Mister Pickup said grace before inviting the campers to form a queue for soup.

"Use your bowl for the soup and your plate for the main course," he advised wisely. "Those of you on fatigues can use your bowl for everything." He gazed forlornly at the broken crockery heaped beneath Mister Reid's serving table, upon which stood the steaming urn of mushroom soup.

"Don't like mushroom," whined Edgington to no one in particular.

"Well sit down again then, Edgington," rejoined Mister Pickup calmly. "You'll just have to make do with bread-and-pull-it for starters."

The soup was slurped down with relish and another tight-packed queue formed for a slice of veal pie. Drinking water was also on offer, served in stumpy glass beakers borrowed from the Boys' Dining Room at Bournville. All of the campers filled their glass to the brim from the earthenware jugs; none of them completed the return journey without upsetting at least some of the contents into the grass.

"For goodness sakes, lads," groaned Mister Pickup. "If you put less in you wouldn't spill so much, now would you? Try to be a bit more careful, eh? We're not made of water, you know."

"What's happened to old Pegleg, d'you think?" whispered Fred to Stan between mouthfuls of pie. "Wonder why he hasn't made it for dinner. You don't reckon he's still in the cart with Young Doran, do you?"

Stan shook his head and shrugged his shoulders at the same time. His mouth was so full of pie he couldn't speak. Delicious it was, too.

Stewed rhubarb and thick custard completed the feasting, washed down with a steaming mug of sweet tea. Mister Pickup made his way to the focal point of the U holding a battered old biscuit tin in his hands. He looked for all the world like one of the three wise men of the bible, except that this was Mister Pickup and they were not in Bethlehem.

"Lads," he solemnly began, "this being the Lord's day, Cadbury Brothers has decreed upon me the honour of presenting each of you with a small token of our appreciation of the firm's eternal support for the Camp School."

He paused to reflect upon the syntax of his utterance before, apparently satisfied, pursuing his oratory towards its spectacular climax. "I would ask each of you, therefore, to form a queue in front of me in order to receive one of these." He grappled with the bent lid of his tin box, almost dumping its contents onto the field before recovering its equilibrium.

"A penny bar of Dairy Milk!"

"Corrrr," sighed young Armstrong, promptly to be elbowed aside in the rush that ensued. Edgington was the first to skid to a halt in front of the teacher.

"Not turning your nose up at chocolate, I see," observed Mister Pickup, dispensing the foil wrapped communion. "Steady! Woah! Steady, boys. No need to push. Plenty for everyone. Stand up, Armstrong. For goodness sake, lads, give Armstrong a chance to get back to his feet will you? There's more than enough to go around."

Sometime during the scrummage for chocolate Mister Barker had reappeared, for he was standing behind the last row of benches as Stan turned back from the offering. He nodded briefly to Stan and raised his eyebrow questioningly. Stan nodded in reply and sat down, heart racing, next to the chomping Fred.

"He's clocked us and I let him know we'd got it," he whispered.

"What?"

"Pegleg. He's behind us," continued Stan, "and he knows we've got it."

"Got what?"

"The *thing*, you blockhead. The *bag*. For goodness sake."

"And?"

"Well, er... He knows. That's all." Stan sighed deeply. Sometimes Fred just seemed to live in a world of his own.

As the chocolate bars disappeared so chattering broke out amongst the boys, until Mister Pickup interceded once more.

"That'll do, lads. Simmer down now. Simmer down."

The assembly simmered down.

"In a moment, Mister Barker will outline to you this afternoon's main event, but first I have an announcement to make regarding fatigues. I am sure that you will have all noticed by now that our current fatigue squad is entirely comprised of the members of A tent - not least those tent members themselves, of course." He chuckled at his humour, allowing time for the boys to do likewise, though none did.

"Er hem," he pursued. "I am sure that we are all most grateful to those boys for their efforts, but their time is now up. Heretofore, fatigue duties will pass to B tent and will so remain until close of play tomorrow."

Fred's low groan was directed at Stan: "That's gonna put the mockers on our adventure, no mistake."

Mister Pickup carried on. "Duggan, Hendry, Bushell and Morris are to attend to clearing away and washing the serving dishes. They should report for duty to Mister Reid immediately after Mister

Barker's address. Parker and Johnson are assigned to potato preparation and will receive further instruction in due course."

"You've got to be joking," whispered Fred hoarsely. "Spud bashing? Two of us? We'll be at it all bloomin' night."

"Quiet in the ranks, Parker," admonished Mister Pickup. "Fair shares for everyone, now. No need to grumble."

The general consensus amongst the boys, however, was that Fred and Stan had drawn the short straw and jolly good luck to them! Mimed hilarity and gleeful winks were aimed in their direction by most of the campers causing Fred's ears to redden in indignation. Stan just felt deflated. Mister Pickup rambled on for a few more sentences before handing over the floor to his younger colleague, whose job it was to outline arrangements for the afternoon's reading of *A Midsummer Night's Dream* by members of the Hatton and Rowington Ladies Literary Circle.

"The play recital will begin at fifteen thirty sharp," began Mister Barker, "so do please make the effort to return to your seats at twenty-five minutes of the hour. Use the time until then to stow your eating irons, visit the latrines and tidy yourselves up for our guests. We can't have the good ladies of the literary circle frightened away by what they see before them, can we?"

Mister Barker paused to allow a ripple of laughter to run around the low benches.

"Those of you on fatigues must attend to your duties directly. Parker, Johnson: you need not make a start on the potatoes until the end of the reading, but I *would* like you to collect the books in which we will follow the text from my tent. That's all, boys. Class dismissed."

"Fred?" asked Stan amidst the hubbub of the mass withdrawal. "Have you got it? We should show it to Barker right away."

"Got it, Skip," replied Fred, tapping the top of his thigh with a grubby hand. "Shall we proceed?"

Mister Barker's laboured progress across the field meant that Stan and Fred had been waiting at the ridge tent for a full minute before their teacher arrived: Stan walking round in tiny circles, kicking at dandelions, whilst Fred gazed up at the clouds, hands thrust in his baggy pockets, legs apart, shoelaces untied. Eventually, Mister Barker limped into the scene and sat down gingerly upon his chair. He blew hard, pushed back a flop of hair from his forehead and levelled the gaze of his twinkling eye upon Fred and Stan, now standing together at attention before him.

"So, chaps? What did you find?" His voice was strangely boyish; sing-song and excited. He leaned in towards them. "Do tell."

The boys shuffled their feet, unsure of where or how to begin.

"And do sit down, please. Sit down, of course. Forgive me: I have quite forgotten my manners."

Mister Barker's obvious excitement rather took Stan aback and he almost toppled into Fred as he sat down on the grass in front of Mister Barker's chair.

"Oi!"

"Sorry."

"I understand that you were in safe receipt of my note," continued Mister Barker unfazed, "and I hope that you found the church plan to be of assistance."

"Yes, Sir. Thank you, Sir."

They both spoke together. Stan took the bull by the horns: "I think that we found what we were looking for, Sir. At least, we found *something*. Something really rather beautiful, in fact."

"But not really treasure, Sir," completed Fred.

Stan shot him a look of exasperation and then attempted clarification. "We followed the directions in your letter, Sir, to the, er, well, to the letter. It *has* to be the right thing, I'm sure. *We're* sure. It's just that we don't actually know what it is."

"Tell me about the chapel," enthused Mister Barker. "Did you see a bear as foretold by the note? How did you come by the object itself? Was it difficult to find?"

Mister Barker's excited questioning gushed forth. He was as animated as they had ever seen him. Stan and Fred described their quest in the chapel in as much detail as they could remember, culminating in Fred's discovery of the secret compartment within the end-stop of the gilded railings.

"Never seen nothing quite like that workmanship, Sir," he sighed. "There was not a mark on the thing once I'd closed it up again, you know. Not a line, nor nothing." He looked earnestly into Mister Barker's eye.

"And what did this secret chamber contain then, Parker?" he asked in a voice laden with anticipation.

Fred rummaged in his pocket and, after a period of unseen sorting and discarding, brought out first the blue velvet bag, then the truncated rifle cartridge, offering them up one by one to the teacher. Mister Barker's eyebrow jumped half an inch up his forehead as he beheld the brass cartridge.

"Well I'll be blessed," he exclaimed. "A point 303 Ball Cordite spitzer. British, I'm sure, but rather earlier than that with which I am familiar."

The boys gazed at him in silence. They had no idea what he was talking about. Mister Barker raised the cartridge to his eye and turned it through 180 degrees in order to study its base.

"Kings Norton head-stamp," he purred reverentially. "Looks like a mark four, but it's been so highly polished that some of the stamping has been worn away. See here." He tilted the base of the cartridge towards the peering boys. "The KN stands for Kings Norton Metal Company, the letter C is presumably a production code, and the IV marking indicates a series four."

The boys peered at the brass disc between their teacher's fingers, squinting in the reflections. As soon as it appeared to Mister Barker that they had absorbed the information stamped thereupon, he pursued his thread:

"If it is a four, then we will certainly gain some precision on dates. That's one of the areas upon which I've been pondering of late, as I'm sure you can imagine."

Fred found himself nodding, though with no idea why. Mister Barker levelled his eye once more at the boys and smiled - probably.

"Fascinating, isn't it? Quite fascinating."

Fred nodded fervently. Stan blinked.

"You see, chaps," continued their teacher, "if this really is a Mark IV, and I am pretty sure that it must be from the head-stamp, then we know that our mystery clue-setter can not have been active before the end of the first Boer War. That is to say, before 1899."

He clearly knew his stuff, they thought. Whatever stuff that was.

"The Mark IV was withdrawn, you see, before the second Boer War began in '99." He held the cartridge towards them between thumb and forefinger. "Munitions such as this expanded upon contact, inflicting grievous wounds and frequent loss of life, so the powers that be decreed them inhumane and *hors combat.*"

He paused a reflective pause.

"Given what was to follow, the word *inhumane* does sound rather ironic, don't you think?"

"Sir?"

"Ironic, I mean, that such *inhumanity* should be replaced for the Great War by the Mark VI, a weapon so poorly conceived that it actually inflicted even more horrendous injuries than this fellow. Too arse-heavy, you see? I do beg your pardon. Weight/balance deficient, is what I should have said. Span on impact. Mashed up the insides something rotten."

Stan gulped. This was all getting a bit gory.

"Sir," butted in Fred, "what exactly have we found then?"

"Ah, Parker. I do apologise. Been babbling. On one of my

hobby-horses again." He took a deep breath. "What you have retrieved from the church amounts to rather less than two thirds of a military rifle cartridge. A *point 3-0-3* to be specific, designed for use in a variety of weaponry, but principally as the charge for the *Lee-Enfield* rifle about which I am sure you have heard."

The *Lee-Enfield*? Of course they had! It was only the weapon that won Tommy the war, wasn't it? At least, that's what the press had said. That's what Stan's father had told him night after night, as the family gathered around his fireside chair to hear the evening reading of *The Manchester Guardian*.

"Crikey," breathed Stan, lost in memories.

"Yes, but what have we actually found?" pursued Fred stubbornly. "I mean, what's the bullet got to do with the church and the box and the rest of the clues?"

"Quite so, Parker. Very much *the* question." Mister Barker smiled a semblance of a smile. "Back to our sheep then, as the French say. Where were we?"

"Er..."

"Dates, Sir?" ventured Stan.

"Indeed, Johnson. Dates."

The boys gave an audible sigh of relief. They appeared to be back on track.

"We had already established, I think, that our fiendish brain-teaser must have been at work after the early eighties, on account of his mastery of Esperanto. Now we are able, with some precision, to bring forward that window to a date not earlier than 1898. This was the year in which this particular version of ordinance was first produced. It is another step in the right direction, wouldn't you say?"

"Yes, Sir. But are we any nearer to finding the treasure?"

It seemed to Fred that Mister Barker had been so taken up with the history of the cartridge that he had completely overlooked the important stuff; like the engravings on its body, or the possibility that there might be something of real value beneath its ceramic plug. Surely it was time to open the blessed thing, but Mister Barker was back studying the head-stamp again and time was marching on.

"Shall we open it, Sir?" Fred blurted out, louder than he had intended. "I mean, you never know…"

The teacher's attention snapped back into focus and his manner became brisker. "Quite so, Parker. Of course we shall, and right away. But time is pressing and I must first confess my part in a recent change to the camp school rota." He was looking at the pocket watch lying on the small table beside his chair. Fred shot Stan a glance, but Stan was staring hard at Mister Barker.

"It is I who arranged for you to be on potato duty this evening and for that task to be carried out in the scullery of the lock keeper's cottage." His eyebrow twitched as he turned back towards them. "It is a ruse by which we shall gain time to follow up on our leads without the potentially prying intervention of curious minds. I have made other arrangements, too, but these I will make plain to you when you report for your fatigue duty after the reading of the play." He cleared his throat. "Is everything clear so far?"

"Yes, Sir," responded Stan. "Absolutely, Sir."

"Good. Then I see that we have but six minutes to discover what new secrets await us within the cartridge." His tone had taken on its earlier sing-song quality and his mouth twisted itself into a passable smile. "See what you can make of the closure, would you Johnson? You are rather better equipped than I to open such a fiddly object."

He handed the cartridge to Stan who raised it to his spectacles and turned the plugged end towards his line of sight. The tiny disc was less than half an inch in diameter, convex in form and off-white in colour, its dull sheen giving it the look of a peppermint sweet. In fact, the closure's composition turned out to be enamelled brass. As Stan exerted pressure down onto the disc with his thumb, it began to turn anti-clockwise. He raised his eyes to Mr Barker and Fred, both now peering in at Stan's fingers.

"It turned," he breathed. "It's been screwed in."

"Can you get it out?" asked Fred.

"I think so."

The grooves of the screw thread were so precisely cut that the tip turned almost without effort. After a couple of rotations it was off, lying on its back in Stan's hand like an upturned beetle. The underbelly and edges were of polished brass, the spiralled ridges of the screw thread glinting in the sunshine. Exquisite. Stan closed his hand around the enamelled plug and peered into the cartridge. It had been sawn off at a length of about two inches and the screw thread had been cut into the inner surface of its truncated neck. Inside was a tightly furled roll of paper, clinging fast to the inner walls of the cartridge.

"We're going to need a pair of tweezers," asserted Stan. "I can't get it out with my fingers."

Mister Barker nodded to Fred. "Hop into the tent, Parker, would you and see if you can find the first aid box. Mister Pickup usually stores it behind the Primus stove. Can't miss it. Just to your left as you go in."

Fred sprang immediately to his errand, bursting through the tent flaps almost before Mister Barker had finished speaking. The air inside was heavy and the light gloomy, but Fred was able to discern the paraffin lamp, hanging from the roof pole, and the two neatly made beds, separated from each other by an army trunk now serving as communal bedside table. The Primus stove stood on an upturned wooden box in the corner of the tent. Behind it, on a shelf fashioned from a wooden chocolate case, stood a tea caddy, two mugs and the camp school first aid box, it's lid emblazoned with a red cross. Fred grabbed the box and was outside again in the brightness within a trice.

"Dive in and have a rummage, Parker," encouraged the teacher. "Mister Pickup had to take a splinter out of Armstrong's knee even before we left the wharf, so I am sure that what we are after is in there."

And so it proved. Fred handed the tweezers to Stan and closed the box, placing it on the grass behind him. Breath was bated. Stan got to work. Within seconds he was brandishing a tight roll of white paper between the tips of the tweezers, looking towards his teacher for approval.

"Go ahead, Johnson. Let's see what we've got."

He handed the cartridge and plug tip to Fred and carefully unfurled the tiny paper roll into a strip of about four inches long, upon which was hand inscribed in blue ink a single line of text:

Sir P initially maps forth seven times to end on nineteenth prime

That was all. Stan handed the paper to Mister Barker who read its message with incomprehension. Fred, meanwhile, was studying the engraved cartridge case, holding it close to his eyes, his lips working at silent pronunciations. Nobody had any idea. The disappointment was palpable.

"Jiggered, I'm afraid," confessed Mister Barker shortly. "How about you two?"

Stan shook his head. Fred handed the cartridge to Mister Barker along with a verbal summary of his findings: "Lovely engravings, Sir. Beautiful work. But I can't make head nor tail of what's written."

Mister Barker raised the object to his eye and adjusted its position. Turning it like a tiny mangle between his thumb and index finger, he read out the words engraved between their decorative borders:

Ne čio brilanta
estas dement

"Loves his Esperanto, doesn't he?" said Mister Barker. "This time, he has given us a proverb that my grandmother used to recite when I was a boy: *Not all is gold that glitters.*" He turned the cartridge again between his fingers, musing.

"Seems a bit of an obvious thing to write, doesn't it Sir?" asked Stan. "I mean, Fred and me thought it was gold at first, but it didn't take long to see that it wasn't."

"Worst luck," grumbled Fred.

"No, but you're right, Johnson," concurred Mister Barker. "Why go to the trouble of engraving something so blindingly obvious? Unless, of course, our prankster believed Esperanto to be untranslatable, which seems a little far-fetched when you consider the words themselves. *Brilanto* and *diamento* are hardly beyond the bounds of simple comprehension, are they?"

The boys remained silent. Stan fixed what he hoped to be a pensive look on his features: Fred just looked vacant.

"Right, well," pronounced Mister Barker, suddenly stirred into action again. "We are not going to solve the riddle in the few seconds that remain to us, now are we? I suggest that we reconvene later, over potato peeling."

Stan and Fred scrambled to their feet, brushing grass stalks from their clothes.

"The books for the play reading are in the cocoa crate over there. Would you mind taking them over to Mister Pickup right away? Tell him that I have been delayed somewhat by my leg and that he should get the proceedings underway without me. I will join you all presently."

Mister Barker tapped his metal leg with the brass rifle cartridge and gave a conspiratorial wink. "The plot thickens, eh boys? The plot most definitely thickens!"

12

CURIOUSLY GIFTED

The warm applause that greeted the end of the readings from *A Midsummer Night's Dream* was genuine and sustained. The performance delivered by the ladies of Hatton and Rowington had captured the imagination of most of the boys for the duration and elicited a loud "bravo" from Mister Pickup at its conclusion. True, attention to the great work had, for some, been patchy. Duggan, for example, transported to a different planet by the love theme, had escaped early into his besotted imagination to compose poetry to Kate on the inside of a Park Drive packet, whilst Armstrong, Puck-like on the front bench, had actually nodded off. Coley, too, had struggled to follow the twists of mistaken identity and was soon abandoning himself to a succession of head-back yawns which earned him a lopsided frown from Mister Barker. And Bushell, having neatly cut out *The Sports Argus* report on the Test Match and concealed it within his copy of the Bard's work, had failed to turn a single page of the text even though his nose pointed resolutely in the right direction throughout. But, for the majority of the boys, this first exposure to Shakespeare's genius had been a delight.

"Better than the pictures," was Morris's starry-eyed take, whilst Hendry declared the plot to be "right up there with Conan Doyle, even if the language needs a bit of work." Stan had thoroughly enjoyed the antics of Puck and Bottom and had laughed out loud at Queen Titania's amorous advances towards the *fair large ears* of the ass-headed Bottom. It was all performed with such wit and gusto! Fred found the idea of a special love-juice much to his liking and was quick to point out its potential: "If you could buy it in *Timothy Whites*," he reflected, "Kate wouldn't have stood a chance."

At 5 o'clock, tea and fruit cake were served to the deserving ladies amongst a babble of chatter. Campers and staff mingled freely within the literary circle and all manner of conversations criss-crossed the tea urn. Mrs Mountford, who had entered into the part of Bottom with rare verve, was trying to explain something to Mister Pickup about a character in Sheridan's *The Rivals*, but her efforts at seed planting were falling wide of the vacant plot. Bushell, fresh from his comprehensive briefing on the rain affected first day's play in the Test Match, was explaining to Morris how Woolley had been dismissed by a wonderful throw in from Bardsley at Deep Third Man.

"Cor," breathed the enthralled Morris. "What's deep third man, then?"

"It's a position, Dimwit. In the field. The one behind ordinary Third Man."

The idiocy of the question took the wind from Bushell's sails and prompted a lull in the narrative. The answer left the wide-eyed enquirer as much in the dark as before.

Mister Barker, having kept himself beyond the melée for a while, now edged cautiously towards its centre, anxious not to miss out on the fruit cake. His path brought him close enough to Stan to be able to whisper instruction from behind a gloved hand.

"Five forty-five at the lock keeper's cottage."

Stan nodded once in reply and Mister Barker was gone, limping through the crowd towards the cake plate.

In time, the amateur thespians bade farewell and headed towards the towpath. Mister Pickup waved until they were quite out of sight then brought the campers to order.

"Boys, Boys," he coaxed. "Hush now. Settle down."

The campers turned towards their teacher and calm descended upon the field.

"Well, wasn't that splendid!"

The assembly murmured in agreement.

"I hope that you will remember to capture the moment in your diaries." He smiled encouragement to all. "We now have a period of recreation to enjoy before supper. Your time until then is your own, but I would encourage all of you to use at least part of it to write up the day's events and to tidy your tent."

He scanned the throng of faces in front of him, alighting upon Fred's sunburned features near the back. "Parker, I'm afraid that you and Johnson will have to put your own domestics on hold for the time being. Fatigue duties beckon, dear chap, as I am sure you recall, but I guarantee that you will be back amongst us well before it is time to eat."

"Why does he do that?" fumed Fred in a whisper to no one in particular. "Why is he always on about food when he looks at me?"

No one in particular bothered to reply. Mister Pickup concluded his brief speech with a reminder about not diving into the canal from the lock gates and the gathering dispersed. Fred and Stan headed off across the field towards the towpath.

"Oi! You two. Hang on a minute, will you?"

It was Duggan, jogging towards them with an empty cigarette packet clutched in his hand and a look of mild desperation on his face. His manner, when he reached them, was earnest.

"I need you two blokes to help me out. Are you up for it?"

"Of course, Bill," answered Fred assuredly. "What's on your mind?"

"I'm gonna need you to cover for me after lights out."

"What do you mean, cover?" asked Stan nervously. He didn't like the sound of this.

"You know," responded Duggan with worrying intensity, "make like I'd been in the tent all night if anyone asks."

"But... Won't you be?" This time it was Fred's turn to be nervous.

"No. I'm off to see Kate tonight. Got it all planned, see?" He proffered the crumpled Park Drive pack. "Train leaves Hatton for Lapworth at twenty past ten. Reckon I'll be with her just after closing time."

Stan thought Duggan must have gone completely mad. "Er, does she know you're coming, by any chance?" he ventured.

"Course not, Johnson."

"Ah."

"That's the beauty of it."

"Yes, well, if you say so, Duggan."

"How d'ya know the train times?" enquired Fred.

"Asked one of the old birds from the literary circle," replied Duggan, rather pleased with himself. "Told her I was keen on train spotting. Piece of cake really. She knew all the times by heart. It's the 22.08 out of Warwick. Last train on a Sunday an' all."

"Ah."

"Then how're y' getting back?"

"Don't know: don't care. Walk it, I 'spect. Oh, Johnson, you've no idea how wonderful she is, have you?"

"Er..."

"Why should I care how I get back? Maybe I won't come back at all. Who knows?"

He really had gone mad. Stan tried a different tac. "Do the others know? In the tent, I mean?"

"Told Bushell I'd likely be going for a beer with Coley and that he'd be wise to keep it to himself, which he will. Hendry will have his head in a book all the time and won't even notice and Morris will do whatever you tell him."

"Which is?" enquired Fred.

"To keep his gob shut."

There was obviously no point in trying to talk Duggan out of this. His mind, or whatever remained of it, was made up. Fred and Stan promised to cover for him, wished him good luck and headed off towards top lock.

"Mad," said Fred.

"As a hatter," agreed Stan.

The lock keeper's cottage was a lopsided edifice of two storeys, with a large bay window either side of a solid door and a third bay window upstairs, to the left. The first floor tapered away to nothing on the right, giving the house a distinctly unfinished look. It sat within a small, neat garden a few paces back from the top lock, no more than three hundred yards from the camp site. Diagonally opposite the cottage, on the other side of the canal, stood a stable block, its half doors thrown open to the afternoon air to reveal a glimpse of the barge's donkeys chewing hay from a wall-mounted manger. An old canal shire stood quietly beside them. Outside, an ancient gig was parked in the shade, its shafts leaning against the wall in a gesture of suppliance. Fred and Stan halted on the towpath and exchanged a glance. From behind them came the whooping and splashing sounds of boys ignoring Mister Pickup's orders. Fred beckoned Stan to get on with it and the two marched together up the short path to the front door which they found to be standing ajar.

"Hello? Mister Barker? It's us," called out Stan, timidly. "The fatigue squad. May we come in?"

The door opened immediately, tugged inwards by a stout,

middle aged lady with greying hair drawn into a bun. Smile lines were etched into her weather-wrinkled features.

"Come in, boys. Do come in. We are expecting you."

Fred gulped. It was Young Doran's bit on the side. The lady at the Lapworth locks. The one who had brought him the food. What on earth...?

"Thank you, Missus," stammered Stan as they passed in front of her into the hall.

Fred followed closely behind and prodded his friend in the back. "Stan," he whispered, "it's..."

"I know. Shhhh."

"Ah, Johnson, Parker! Welcome! Welcome indeed. Do come in and join us."

Mister Barker's invitation was warm, even though he remained invisible to the boys behind the half-closed kitchen door. Stan pushed, but found the door stuck fast on the uneven floor tiles. His forward momentum thereby arrested, Fred bundled into the back of him, propelling both of them through the opening at unseemly pace.

It took them a second or two to adjust their eyes to the bright sunlight streaming in through the bay window to their right, but they soon discerned three figures sitting around the kitchen table. To their left, at the head, sat Mister Barker, straight-backed and smiling - possibly. To his left - unbelievably - sat Young Doran, a smouldering briar clamped in the middle of his face, blue eyes fixed on the intruders. The third member of the gathering sat with his back to the boys, opposite Young Doran, and did not turn to greet them. A powerfully built man, he wore a blue canvas cap atop a bush of grey hair.

"Come in. Do come in," insisted Mister Barker. "I am sure that you already know Young Doran here, from the works, and this is Mister Middleton, the lock keeper, who has graciously agreed to host us this evening."

The lock keeper grunted briefly and raised his right forefinger in greeting, but he did not turn his head to look at the boys.

"Oh, and you were let into this fine abode by Mrs Prescott," continued Mister Barker, as though introducing an act at the Variety Theatre. "Mrs Prescott has been generously applying herself to fatigue duties on your behalf." He indicated with a nod of his head a colourful pail of peeled potatoes beneath the grey stone sink.

Stan's jaw had dropped to such an extent that he could manage no comment.

"It will buy us a good deal of time," pursued Mister Barker intently, "and just as well, too. There is much to discuss."

"Thank you, Sir," whispered Fred for no apparent reason. "That is, er..."

"Quite so," soothed Mister Barker kindly. "Much to be getting on with. Do please sit." He waved towards the two wooden chairs facing him at the vacant end of the table and waited for them to sit.

"Well then," he said at length. "Let us begin."

Now that they were seated, Stan and Fred could see the bearded features of the lock keeper to their left, the flattened bulb of his nose extending no further from his face than the short peak of his cap. Mister Barker retrieved a wad of papers from the briefcase and began his scene setting with an apology:

"Johnson, Parker; I am sorry if this unexpected gathering appears rather, well, strange to you, but I firmly believe that our quest for an answer to your curious riddle will be greatly enhanced by the presence of Jacob and Frankie here this evening. I do hope that you will bear with me."

Sitting white-faced at the other end of the table, the best the boys could muster in response was a mute nod. Stan's mind flashed back to the green scrawl on Mister Barker's note to them of that morning: "Frankie can be trusted and will be of service". Could this be the same Frankie? And if so, which one was he? Stan did not have to wait long for the answer.

"Jacob has been a canal man all of his life and always on the Warwick stretch," continued Mister Barker. "Nobody knows the area and its history more intimately than he."

Stan heard Fred swallow next to him, despite the infernal thumping noise that his own heart was making.

"And Frankie here.... Well, Frankie just knows so much about most things."

Fred gawped. Young Doran drew slowly on his pipe, a smoke ring rising from the barrel.

"So, if I can take it that I have your support, may I review where we I believe we are?"

Mister Barker held the wad of papers fast to the table with his gloved hand and flicked them with the nimble fingers of the left. On the table stood the rifle cartridge, on its end, beside the small metal box. He drew the fifth sheet from the deck and laid it in the middle of the table.

"This is a summary of the clues so far recovered," he explained. "You will note that I have cross referenced the obvious historical links between members of the Beauchamp family, whilst underlining those aspects of our riddle which appear, so far, to be unconnected: the gravestone at Baddesley Clinton, for example, and the author's use of Esperanto."

Stan could make out a mass of green lines and squiggles on the paper but he could not actually read any of it from where he sat. He adjusted the spectacles on his nose to no effect.

"And then there is our latest clue," pursued Mister Barker, nipping out the rolled paper from within the rifle cartridge with a pinch of his thumb and forefinger. "Dear old Sir P going forth." He paused in thought. "All rather rum," he concluded, more to himself than to the others.

Jacob Middleton reached out his left hand and drew the paper towards him, exhaling loudly through his massive nose. He took an old magnifying glass from the top pocket of his jacket and leaned forward over the paper, scrutinising every aspect of the green scrawl line by line. Nobody spoke. A timepiece above the hearth clocked away the slow seconds. Stan felt hot. Eventually, the magnifying glass was laid gently on the table and the paper pushed away with a walrus like snort.

"See us the box 'ere, Frankie, will you?"

Young Doran flicked out an arm and sent the box skidding across the table towards the lock keeper who fielded it within his cupped right hand. With the other, he raised the glass once more from the table and held it over the object. The clock pounded on into the stuffy air. Jacob turned the box slowly beneath his magnified gaze. To his left, a chair creaked as Mister Barker leaned in stiffly on the act.

Eventually, the canal man offered up the fruit of his pondering: "It's Beechum, right enough." He exhaled heavily though the bulbous nose and slid the box back towards Young Doran. Then he folded his arms and appeared to doze off. There was a moment's silence as Mister Barker clung to the forlorn hope that something rather more incisive might yet issue forth from the lock keeper's deep local knowledge, but he was obliged to move on.

"Yes, well. Good, Jacob. Thank you. I am glad that we appear to be on the same page." He cleared his throat. Stan thought that he looked rather crestfallen. "All still to go at then, chaps," he said.

He sounded rather crestfallen, too. Fred glared at the lock keeper and decided to come to his teacher's aid. "Sir?" he enquired. "D'ye mind if I 'ave a look at your paper a bit?"

"Certainly, Parker. By all means."

Fred leaned across and dragged the paper back to a spot between Stan and himself, smoothing it flat with his forearm. Stan craned in.

Mister Barker had written a few lines about the various generations of the Beauchamp family, notably those of Richard and Guy, and had drawn an arrow to the word "chapel", around which he had sketched a lopsided box. He had listed a number of dates, underlining 1898, against which he had scrawled "1st Boer War", and written out the Esperanto proverb from the cartridge casing. There was more, but Fred stopped reading. He had not found what he was looking for.

"Sir?" he asked hesitatingly. "What about the bloke with his head cut off in the box? I mean, the bloke in the box whose head's cut off. You know: in the shield. Wasn't 'e a Sir, Sir? Piers, or something?"

Half of Mister Barker's face lit up. "Why, yes, Parker! Sir Piers Gaveston. Of course. Why on earth didn't I see it? How stupid you must think me!"

"Of course not, Sir," mumbled Fred, embarrassed. "It's just that I remember him because his 'ed had been chopped off."

"And I am very glad that you do remember, Parker," enthused Mister Barker reaching for the thin roll of paper with his left hand. "Excellent! Excellent! Let us take another look, shall we?"

Trapping the loose end beneath his glove, the teacher unrolled the paper with the fingers of his left hand and read out the clue:

"*Sir P initially maps forth seven times to end on nineteenth prime.*" He looked around the table. "Any thoughts?"

Young Doran drew on his briar and fixed his gaze a foot above Jacob Middleton's head before exhaling into utterance. "Sixty-seven."

"Sixty-seven?" queried Mister Barker gently. "What is sixty-seven, Frankie?"

"Nineteenth prime."

"Come again?"

"Sixty-seven: nineteenth prime." The barge boy paused. "Sixty-one; eighteenth. Sixty-seven; nineteenth. Seventy-one; twentieth, seventy-three; twenty-first..."

"Quite, Frankie. Yes. I see. I see. Well done. Very good."

Mister Barker's soothing tones held sway and Young Doran ceased his incantation. Stan simply could not believe his ears. Mister Barker took stock.

"Mathematics was never really my cup of tea," he admitted, glancing at the clue on the table. "I am much more a word game kind of chap myself, but it would appear that Frankie has given us an excellent start."

Stan had struggled to keep track of developments and was still reeling from the surprise of Young Doran's intervention, but he turned his mind back to the problem of the clue and how to decipher it.

"Sir? If Young Doran is right," he glanced nervously to his right, "and I am sure that he is, then what does the sentence mean now? What do you think *to end on 67* might mean?"

"Exactly the right question, Johnson. Where does this particular insight leave us with regard to the rest of the phrase?"

"Nowhere?" ventured Fred. "I mean, I don't get what *Sir P initially* means, even if we know that he's the headless bloke in the box. Still makes no sense."

Mister Barker seemed to receive a flash of inspiration, for he stood up and tapped his forehead vigorously with his gloved hand.

"Of course," he exclaimed. "It is not a single phrase at all, but a series of connected problems set for us to resolve." All eyes in the room were on him. "It's obvious to me that we need to cut up the sentence into sections, like *the nineteenth prime*, for example, which problem Frankie has already solved."

Fred scratched his head. The lock keeper unfolded his arms and leaned in towards the table.

"In which case," continued Mister Barker, "we might perhaps ascribe a different sense to the first three words of the sentence, rendering our *Sir P initially* as *initials of Sir Piers*. Do you follow?"

Fred did not, but he refrained from saying so because Stan was nodding vigorously.

"Yes, Sir," he enthused. "We'd get S.P."

"Precisely."

"So that just leaves us the bit in the middle. What exactly was that again, Sir?"

"*Maps forth seven times.* I think that we are left with just these four words." Mister Barker appeared very pleased with progress.

Once again, Young Doran's low tones rose above the silence: "Fourth seven's twenty-eight. Seven fours, twenty-eight. Four times seven's twenty-eight."

"Goodness, Frankie. You've done it again!"

Frankie's recital came to an end and Mister Barker sat down once more behind the furled clue. "SP-28-67," he breathed. "Well I'm blowed. I think we may just have uncovered a grid reference!"

This time it was the lock keeper's turn to stand up from the table. "Maps, perhaps, Mister Barker?"

"Absolutely, Jacob. Bring forth whatever maps you may have of the area."

The teacher turned to Young Doran and laid his hand on the barge boy's forearm. "Thank you, Frankie," he said gently. "You have saved the day again."

A curl of smoke drifted up from the bowl of the barge boy's briar, but that was all.

"And thanks are due to you, too, Parker," enthused the teacher with a ghastly sort of half smile. "Without your key insight, we might still be floundering."

Fred lowered his eyes and blushed from his ears. Stan gave him a thump of appreciation in the back. Jacob Middleton lumbered back bearing four rolled maps which he deposited carelessly onto the table and watched, curious, as they rolled away from their landing point in all directions. Young Doran raised the fingers of his left hand and halted the widest of them before it fell to the floor beside him. Mister Barker fielded two in the covers, whilst the fourth came to a halt in front of Fred's folded arms. Jacob surveyed the outcome and seemed pleased. He dragged his chair back to its place at the table and sat down heavily, snorting in satisfaction. Mister Barker's eyebrow twitched: the knuckles of his good hand shining white against the grey furl of map in his grasp. He cleared his throat.

"Do we…" His pitch betrayed a certain strain. "Do we know, by any chance, Jacob, which of these might be the Ordnance Survey map of Warwickshire?"

The lock keeper furrowed the brow beneath his cap and assessed the lie of the rolls. He nodded towards Young Doran. "Big 'un in front of Frankie, I shouldn't wonder."

"Very good," said Mister Barker softly. "Frankie? Would you mind?"

Young Doran eased back his chair and stood up, sucking the briar into the centre of his face. He unfurled the linen-backed map to the full three feet of its width, carefully smoothing out the creases across the table. He rotated the map through ninety degrees and pushed it beneath Mister Barker's monocled line of sight. Then he sat down.

"Thank you, Frankie."

Mister Barker lowered his face to the map and scanned the margins. He traced a line with his left index finger, west to east, about a third of the way down from the top edge, halting at a splash of pale green that fell in line with the numerical reference he had located on the top margin.

"There," he said, his hushed voice adding a note of tension to the room. "There we have it."

Stan, unable to see what was going on, stood up and circled the table to stand behind his teacher's left shoulder, stretching his neck towards the map. Mister Barker peered more closely at the printed text. "Gaveston's Cross," he read. "Well I'll be blowed. Look at that!"

Stan did just that, squinting into the shadow of Mister Barker's finger tip to make out the name and adjoining black cross in the centre of a splurge of pale green. Beneath ran a broad road, with scattered dwellings on either side, towards the thickening grey lines and shadings of Leamington Spa. He could see the river, winding between the contour lines, and the canal, which his eyes traced around its bend to Hatton and the site of their camp. By now, Fred was next to Stan, bending low over the map.

"Coventry," he said. "It's just off the Coventry Road, Stan. How far d'you reckon that is from here?"

"'Bout three mile, I should reckon," replied Jacob Middleton, his nasal pronouncement surprising everyone. It was the only vaguely useful thing he had so far uttered. "'Bout an hour's walk, give or take. Right by Guy's Cliffe."

Mister Barker slid his finger an inch south across the main road to where *Guy's Cliffe* was printed below Loes Farm.

"Estate used to stretch right to Blacklow Hill and beyond," continued the lock keeper, suddenly into his stride, "but that was back when the Greatheeds owned the place and there ain't been none of them for many a long year. Place was turned into an hospital in the war and they only cleared out the last of the beds eighteen month ago. Nobody been there since."

"So if Blacklow Hill is still part of the estate," mused Mister Barker, his index finger moving back across the map in a north-westerly direction, "would that mean that Gaveston's Cross is part of it, too?"

"Reckon so," confirmed Middleton. "Though, like I says, it's none too clear who owns what no more."

Mister Barker made a clicking noise with his tongue and tapped his finger against the map. "Tomorrow's Monday," he mused, "and

Mister Pickup has arranged a charabanc excursion. I'm not sure that we will find the time…." He drifted off into thought.

Fred dug his elbow into Stan's ribs and whispered his joy at the prospect of a charabanc ride. Stan glanced at Young Doran, immobile save for the occasional twitch of his pipe, then at Jacob Middleton, now slumped back on his chair, exhausted by his recent coherence. He was about to ask Mister Barker where he thought the charabanc might be taking them when the kitchen door scraped open and Mrs Prescott bustled in.

"There's a boy at the door asking after the potatoes," she said calmly. "Seems that Mister Reid is keen to get on with cooking them."

Mister Barker woke from his reverie with a start. "Yes? Oh, right! Quite so, Mrs Prescott. Thank you. There is never quite enough time, is there?" He moved away from the table and stood with his back to the window. "Would you please ask the boy to reassure Mister Reid that supplies will be with him in just a few minutes?"

Mrs Prescott nodded demurely to Mister Barker, curtsied almost, and turned her eyes towards Young Doran. "I'll be back in while, Frankie," she purred before exiting the kitchen and pulling the door shut behind her.

Young Doran sat unmoved. Fred gawped once more.

Mister Barker became brisk. "Yes. Well. No time like the present, as they say, and no time to lose either. We need to act right away. This evening, I mean. What do you think?"

The question was directed at Stan and Fred, although they both instinctively averted their teacher's one-eyed gaze as he levelled it towards them. Stan gulped back a mounting sense of apprehension and looked at his feet.

"Absolutely, Sir," chirped Fred in response. "No time like the present, as you say." He sounded remarkably positive.

Stan shot him a quick glance, just to make sure that he wasn't frothing at the mouth, before sheepishly giving his own assent. "Me too, Sir. That is, I'm with Parker, Sir," he stammered.

"Excellent, excellent. That's the spirit, boys. But let's not go flying off without a plan, eh?"

The teacher resumed his seat at the table and leaned stiffly in towards its centre. He lowered his voice as he addressed Young Doran. "Frankie, can you ready the gig for a 10pm departure from the road bridge?" The barge boy silently nodded that he could.

"And Jacob, would you ensure that the coast is clear down at the workshops? We can't afford to have anybody nosing in on what we are up to: it simply wouldn't do to have to explain things at this juncture."

"Mum's the word, Mister Barker," he replied, tapping a gnarled forefinger against his bulbous nose.

Mister Barker was not entirely sure that this constituted an appropriate answer, but he was prepared to take it as such nonetheless.

"And as for you two: are you sure that you are up for this?"

The boys stared dumbly back, unblinking.

"I can be of no help at all to you on this particular mission, I am afraid," he continued. "Scrambling over gates and fences is well beyond me nowadays, let alone scaling Blacklow Hill." He looked earnestly into the boys' eyes.

"I will, of course, do my best to cover for you at camp, but it is likely that you will be gone for well over an hour and there can be no telling what you might find at Gaveston's Cross. Whatever happens, you must promise me that you will not put yourselves into harm's way, do I make myself clear?"

Stan's mind was racing between excitement and abject fear. How on earth had he got himself into this and what might happen next? He once again became aware of the pounding clock on the mantelpiece, counting out the seconds to, well, what exactly? Disaster? Wealth unimaginable? He removed his glasses and cleaned them on the flap of his shirt. Fred breathed wheezily beside him. Some part of Mister Barker's anatomical structure creaked as he shifted his weight. Stan took a deep breath, then the plunge: "Very clear, Sir, and we - that is, me at least - are definitely up for the fray."

Stan had no idea what *being up for the fray* actually meant. His father had once read it from the newspaper during the war and the phrase had stuck in his mind. He rather liked the bravura of it and hoped that a little of the same might rub off. Mister Barker softly hummed his contentment, whereupon Fred burst out of his trance and cleared his throat.

"Me as well, Sir," he croaked. "I mean, I'm up to be frayed an' all, Sir."

"Good fellow," said Mister Barker softly. "Well done both of you. That's the spirit. We shall get to the end of this mystery yet."

Stan glanced at Young Doran, sitting impassively at the table, arms folded. Could he really be trusted? The barge boy had hardly said a word - at least, nothing to suggest that he had followed the plan - and here he was in charge of the gig ride to Gaveston's Cross. Mister Barker was quick to sense the apprehension.

"You will both be quite safe with Frankie," he assured them. "I would trust him with my own life - have done, indeed, on several occasions. There is nobody more dependable, believe me."

He smiled what he hoped would be a reassuring smile and patted Fred on the shoulder. "Are you both still sure?"

"Quite sure," asserted Stan.

"Then let's be off with you back to camp, shall we? Not a word to anyone outside this room, of course, and be sure that you are not seen as you leave the campsite this evening."

Stan and Fred nodded in unison and headed for the door.

"The rendezvous with Frankie is at twenty-two hundred hours on the road bridge, just above the main flight of locks," detailed the teacher, "but he will wait if you are delayed and will have with him lamps and the map. I will meet you here, at Jacob's place, when you return. Is everything clear?"

"Yes Sir. Perfectly clear," replied Stan, excitement once again coursing through him. "We will meet you here when it is all over."

"Then, good luck, boys! I will be thinking of you. And don't forget to take the potatoes to Mister Reid."

13

NIGHT MOVES

They carried the painted pail along the towpath towards the barge's smoking chimney, gripping the handle between them. Fred was bubbling with conversation.

"What about Young Doran then? Blimey; who'd 'ave thought it? Turns out to be a blinkin' mathematical genius. And 'is bit of stuff was there, too! I mean, the bloke's got more sides to him than a wotsit."

"A what?"

"You know. An octopus, or whatever they're called. Mister Ferguson taught us: remember?"

"Octagon," corrected Stan patiently. "Something with eight sides."

"Yeah, well. Who'd 'ave thought? Blimey!"

Stan was not feeling talkative. He was trying to order his thoughts and it was proving difficult with Fred crackling away in his ear like a phonograph. They were nearing the barge where Mister Reid's folded arms awaited them. Stan decided to head off the quartermaster's impending volley of criticism with a cheery apology.

"Really sorry about that, Mister Reid," he chirped, "but we just didn't realise how long it was going to take us."

"Never peeled a spud before then?" grumbled Mister Reid. "Overrun with servants at 'ome, are you?"

Stan was briefly tempted to riposte with a line about the current difficulties of hiring good staff, but instead played it safe: "Sorry again, Mister Reid," he smiled. "And sorry for Parker, too."

"What? What 'ave I done?" squeaked Fred, incredulous.

"You were a little slow with the potatoes, now weren't you?"

"Well, no actually…"

"And so you apologise to Mister Reid, don't you?"

Fred glared at Stan before mumbling a semblance of apology into the ground between his feet.

"Give us that bucket, you varmints," growled Mister Reid taking a menacing step towards them. "And be sure to make a better job of tomorrow's carrots an' all." He grabbed at the handle. "Now, be off."

Fred made as if to answer back but Stan yanked his elbow in the direction of the tents and marched him off the scene.

"Absolutely, Mister Reid," he affirmed over his shoulder. "You can count on us."

"Creep," yelped Fred as they crested the rise into the field, "What the 'ell are you up to, for God's sake? And let go of my blinking arm, will you? What's got into you all of a sudden?"

"Look. The last thing we need right now is to be in Mister Reid's bad books and end up having to do extra jankers. We can't be late for Young Doran tonight and we mustn't mess up in the meantime. Do you get it?"

Fred shrugged sulkily. "You didn't have to go and break my arm about it."

"It's not broken, you chump."

They walked back to the tent in silence, the tension between them melting away with each stride. The camp site was sprinkled with groups of boys engaged in various evening pursuits. Bushell had press-ganged four of the younger boys into a makeshift game of cricket behind the latrines where a couple of hefty twigs leaned as crooked wickets against the canvas.

"For God's sake, Morris," he moaned in profound exasperation. "At least *try* and get the thing to land where I can hit it!"

Behind the line of tents a dozen or so campers hurtled around the field in a boisterous game of British Bulldogs, whilst Coley and Ironmonger sat at a safe distance, locked together in Three Card Brag. Over to the left, near the boundary hedge, Mister Pickup appeared to be rehearsing three boys in a choral rendition, his arms waving stiffly above his head like an orchestra conductor. Stan and Fred breasted the tent flap and entered the dimness within. Hendry was lying on his groundsheet, Hornung under his nose as usual. He ignored them.

"Don't you *ever* get out?"

"Bog off, Parker."

"Charming."

"What time is it, Hendry," asked Stan.

"Time for you to bog off, like I said."

"Yeah, but really?"

"Dunno. About half seven I should think."

Stan rummaged in his kit bag and pulled out *Words on Warwickshire*.

Any facts about Guy's Cliffe are inextricably intertwined with the fiction that surrounds Guy of Warwick, the knight celebrated in Middle English verse for whom the place is named. Nobody can be absolutely sure if Guy really existed, but the legends that surround his romantic quests remain popular to this day. The best known centres upon our young hero falling in love with the fair Lady Felice; epitome, as her name suggests, of all things happy and joyful in a knight's life. Felice was of noble birth and ranked much higher than poor Guy, so in order to gain her love he was obliged to undertake a number of chivalric challenges, including the slaying of giants and boars, as well as the customary dragon. Most memorable of all in the annals of Warwickshire folklore was his combat with the fearsome Dun Cow, on Dunsmore Heath near Rugby.

The Dun Cow, so legend would have it, came to Dunsmore Heath from Shropshire whence an old woman had precipitated its flight by seeking to fill not only her pail with the cow's milk, but also her sieve. Quite why the Dun Cow chose to flee to Warwickshire is not recorded, but the huge and savage beast must have been in situ there by the time Guy de Warwick received the order to kill it, for Dunsmore is where the young knight headed in his quest for love.

Having despatched the Dun Cow, Guy returned to claim his prize and was duly betrothed to his beloved Felice. But soon after his marriage, our hero began to feel remorse for all of the violent actions of his past and left upon a pilgrimage to the Holy Land. When he privately returned from his travels some time later he was a changed man. Eschewing both the riches and the beauty of his wife, he chose instead to live out the rest of his days as a hermit, dwelling in a cave within cliffs overlooking the River Avon.

There has been a settlement at Guy's Cliffe since Saxon times and the chapel of Saint Mary Magdelene was built in 1423. All land and buildings passed into private hands upon the dissolution of the monasteries and, in time, a large country estate flourished there with lands extending as far as Leek Wootton and Blacklow Hill. The current house dates from 1751, built by the slave trader and Whig Member of Parliament for Coventry, Samuel Greatheed, whose descendants still owned the property at the end of the last century.

It was Bertie Greatheed, Samuel's son, who erected the memorial to Sir Piers Gaveston at Blacklow Hill in 1823, marking the spot where the former Earl of Cornwall was run through with a sword and beheaded in 1312, an act of murder decreed by Guy de Beauchamp, 10th Earl of Warwick, and Thomas Crouchback, 2nd Earl of Lancaster, whose lands then included Blacklow Hill. Sadly, the memorial to this barbaric act of revenge is inaccessible to visitors and rarely seen, sited as it is within the private grounds of the Guy's Cliffe estate.

Stan shoved the booklet back into his kitbag and took a deep breath. Inaccessible? How on earth were they going to get in then?

So many threads criss-crossed their mystery that Stan once more questioned whether the whole thing might not just be some elaborate exercise dreamed up by Mister Barker. But if that really was the case, then the teacher was playing his part with extraordinary realism. And it would mean that Young Doran must be acting, too. Surely not? He shook his head and brought his thoughts back to the constantly recurring theme of the Beauchamp family. Even here, in a text so obviously about somebody else, Sir Guy makes an appearance. They were dogged by Beauchamps. What did it all mean? He hauled himself from his musings and looked around for Fred.

"Where'd Parker go, Hendry?"

"No idea. Bog off."

For a literary chap, Hendry certainly had a remarkably concise vocabulary. Stan went outside into the gathering dusk and found Fred a few yards away, engaged in a heated exchange with the horrible Edgington.

"Get lost, Edgington. Or go and play in the latrines where you'll feel more at home." Fred's ears were red.

"Oooh," mimicked Edgington, his face contorted into an ugly lear. "Fat Fred has got his knickers in a twist. What're you trying to hide, Parker? Scared we'll find out that you and Johnson are sucking up to Pegleg like a pair of bum boys?"

"Mind your own business or I'll knock your stupid block off."

Edgington pulled another grimace in reply but, weighing up the possibility that Fred probably *would* knock his stupid block off, adjusted his tactics and took a step backwards.

"I'm gunna tell Pickup on you," he whinged. "There's something fishy going on here."

"That'll be you then won't it, Codface," snapped Fred in reply. "I thought there was a bad smell around 'ere." His fists were clenched. "Now get lost. And keep your gob shut or I'll fill it full of broken teeth."

Edgington turned on his heel with a final sneer and walked straight into Stan, who had been observing proceedings from behind. A brief pushing contest ensued before Edgington made his get-away, firing a parting shot over his shoulder: "Girlfriend's turned up, Parker."

"Leave it," advised Stan as Fred took a pace towards the horrible one. "We've got lots to do and he really isn't worth getting a black eye for."

"It's 'im as would be gettin' the black eye, Stan. I'm telling you. Another one, I mean." Fred exhaled loudly and unclenched his fists.

"What did he want anyway?" asked Stan

"Just poking about. Had some idea that we were spending too much time with old Barker and wanted to make something of it."

"Like what?"

"Like we were crawling for extra marks or something. You know. The bloke's hardly over-burdened with intelligence so it's hard to know exactly what he's on about most of the time."

Stan was nodding distractedly, his attention elsewhere. "Fancy having a crack at British Bulldogs?"

"Abso-flaming-lutely, Stanley," beamed Fred. "Now you're talkin'!"

And so, for the few minutes that remained before supper, Stan and Fred let off enough collective steam to power an iron foundry, charging back and forth across the field's ancient cow pats to upend and be upended with unbridled glee.

After such a burst of physical activity supper was wolfed down. Never had a slice of breaded ham and a scoop of mashed potato tasted so good. It was devoured by all in reverential silence. The forms and tables had been arranged around a small pile of firewood, collected by Duggan and Morris from the nearby hedgerows. Duggan had volunteered for this particular fatigue duty as a way of avoiding the washing-up shift later that evening. He was paving the way for an on-time departure to the station.

Mister Phipps shuffled into the arena to bend over the pile of wood with an ancient box of Vestas, his panting breath fanning the tiny flames like bellows. Twigs crackled into the fading evening: it was time for the camp fire sing-along.

Mister Pickup rose confidently from his bench and moved to the centre of the gathering, close to the fire.

"Well, boys! The long-awaited moment has arrived." He took a hasty step backwards, lest his left boot catch fire. The boys stifled their giggles. "Time for Sunday night communal singing," he announced. "One of the highlights of our annual camp, as I am sure those of you who were with us last year will confirm."

He beamed a knowing smile to the assembled choristers. Coley, with the pleasure of two previous camp sing-alongs behind him, raised his eyes to the stars in profound disinterest. Mister Pickup distributed stencilled song sheets ("you will have to make do with one between three, I'm afraid") and polished his tuning fork on the seat of his shorts. Most of the boys would have rather been somewhere else.

But in the end, the singing went down well with everyone. Even Coley joined in, leading the *Prom Prom Prom* refrain of *I Do Like to be Beside the Seaside* in a booming bass-baritone that made everybody laugh. Mister Pickup's ragged choir of Trotman, Clarke and Armstrong added syncopated harmony to their leader's bravura portrayal of Nanki-Poo's *A Wandering Minstral I*, whilst the ensemble's finale of *Keep The Home Fires Burning* left more than one camper brushing a tear from his eye in remembrance of a loved one lost to the war. Mister Pickup recited a short vesper before issuing his final instructions of the day.

"Bushell, Hendry: you are required at the barge forthwith to help with the washing-up. Duggan and Morris will take on the same job after breakfast tomorrow. Parker and Johnson are to fetch the milk from the farm at reveillé." Those not on fatigue duty smiled appreciatively.

"Mister Phipps has set lamps in your tents and in the latrines: please take care not to upset them." He took a step further back from the glowing embers of the fire. "Lights out at nine-thirty sharp and woe betide all of you if there is any chattering thereafter." He looked sternly around the tired faces.

"Reveillé will be at 6.45. Good night, boys. Sleep tight."

Stan and Fred repaired to B tent with young Morris in tow, babbling on about how he would stay awake until morning and see the sun rise over the canal.

"Very romantic, Morris," commended Fred. "Bet you can't, though."

Morris smirked in the absolute certainty that he would, before lying down on his blankets and falling sound asleep.

"Told you," said Fred, exchanging a smile with Stan.

Duggan arrived from the latrines, preceded by a pungent odour of sickly sweet lavender.

"Bloody hell, Bill!" exclaimed Fred, unable to check himself in time.

"What?" demanded Duggan. "What're you on about?"

"Nothing, Bill," he back-peddled. "Nothing at all. Honest."

"Liar."

"No, no. I assure you. Calm down, Bill. You're just a bit on edge." Fred tried to smooth things over.

"It's the perfume," said Stan, bravely. "Smells a bit, well, you know..."

"What? Smells a bit what?"

"Er... Floral?"

"Floral?"

"You know. Like my grandmother's Sunday shawl."

"Your grandmother?" Duggan managed to look both puzzled and distraught at the same time.

"Yes, well. Not that my grandmother smells bad, you understand." Stan tried a weak smile. "Just rather like, well, a grandmother."

"Might not be quite Kate's cup of tea?" suggested Fred.

Duggan was devastated.

"Where did you get it, anyway?" asked Stan gently. "You know, the lavender water?"

"The latrines. Off of the shelf by the mirror. Thought it'd be Pickup's cologne, but I couldn't see too well in there."

"Yes, well. I'd have a go at washing it off before lights-out if I were you."

Fred nodded a silent endorsement. Duggan turned on his heel and exited the tent in a hurry. He was back within a few minutes, scrubbed and perfumed with coal tar soap, his dark hair slicked back with water.

"Much better, Bill," reassured Fred. "Very Douglas Fairbanks."

Bushell and Hendry returned from washing-up duties, barely two minutes before lights-out. Duggan gave them a clear briefing. "Not one word out of you two to Pegleg or Pickup, d'you hear? I'm off out for a quick pint with Coley and I need you blokes to keep schtum about it. Alright?"

"Whatever you say, Duggan," answered the languid Hendry. "Just don't wake me up when you come back."

"Fine by me, too," affirmed Bushell. "Mum's the word."

From somewhere in the middle of the field came the sound of Mister Pickup's final warning: "One more minute to lights-out, boys. One more minute. Don't make me have to come in and put it out for you."

Duggan reached up towards the lamp.

"Just a sec, Duggan," pleaded Bushell. "I haven't got me pyjamas on yet."

In due course, the lamps of the camp were extinguished and the hubbub of chatter died away. In B tent, Duggan waited nervously on his blankets, straining to hear the sounds of the night, desperate to reassure himself that the coast would soon be clear. It would take a good fifteen minutes to walk to the station and time was ticking on. Eventually, he got to his feet and tiptoed to the tent flaps. Stan watched as the blurred figure tugged at the heavy canvas flap and slipped out into the dark field. Within seconds he was back, cursing under his breath.

"Bugger. Bugger. Bugger."

"What's up?" asked Stan in a hoarse whisper.

"It's Pegleg. He's only standing right in the middle of me way to the towpath!" He sounded desperate. "What's he doing there?"

Stan reflected on their joint dilemma for a moment. If Duggan stayed, then how could he and Fred leave the tent without being seen? And if he went, Mister Barker would surely see him and that might put an end to all of their plans. He came to a decision.

"Me and Fred'll go out and distract him."

"What d'you mean, distract him?"

"We'll go out and tell him some story about not being able to sleep or some such, then you can scoot round the back of tent when he's not looking. Make your way to the road through the farmyard."

"You'd do that?"

"Of course. Are you up for it?"

"Definitely. But we'll have to go right now, Johnson. I can't miss the train."

Stan stood up and pulled on his boots.

"You already dressed then?"

"Was a bit cold tonight: didn't fancy putting my pyjamas on."

"Just as well. You ready?"

"Hang on." Stan prodded Fred's leg with his boot. "Boots on, Fred. Time for the off." Fred was asleep.

"For goodness sake, Fred," hissed Stan and kicked him harder. "Get up, will you?"

After less than a minute that seemed an eternity to Duggan, Fred and Stan were dressed in double sweaters against the evening chill and ready to provide the required cover to their leader. All three glanced quickly around the tent where, as far as they could tell, the others were sound asleep.

"Wait 'til we get to Mister Barker first, before you come out," instructed Stan. "We'll draw his attention towards the canal and you slip out the back way and up to the farm."

"You're a pal, Johnson."

"Good luck, Bill," whispered Fred cheerfully. "Say hello to Kate for me."

Stan and Fred crept out into the field. A yellow light glowed dimly in the teachers' tent, but otherwise the camp appeared to be asleep. Clouds scudding across the sky obscured the moon. It was very dark. Mister Barker stood at the top of the bank above the towpath, directly in line with the barge. He had heard the boys coming and was waiting for them.

"Johnson, Parker?" he asked anxiously, "Is everything in order?"

"Yes, Sir."

"Only I thought heard you coming four or five minutes ago, but you turned back. Was there a problem? Did somebody see you leave the tent?"

Fred looked puzzled. Stan invented fast: "It was me, Sir. Sorry. I thought I heard someone snooping around outside so I went for a look."

"And?"

"It was no-one, Sir. Like I thought."

"Ah."

"So I went back and got Parker, Sir."

"I see. Well, so long as you were not observed."

"We weren't, Sir. I promise."

Fred looked over his shoulder towards the row of tents and verified his friend's assertion with a nod of the head.

Mister Barker became business-like. "Mr Middleton arrived at the barge five minutes ago and should now be distracting Messer's Reid and Phipps attention with canal yarns and vintage rum. The coast is clear for you to pass along the towpath to the bridge". He looked briefly into their eyes to be sure that they were following. "Frankie is already in place. Please be sure to do exactly as he tells you at all times, do you hear me?"

"Yes, Sir," answered Stan, wondering what on earth Young Doran could possibly say to them that might be of use. Wondering, in fact, if Young Doran could say much of anything, in fact.

"We will rendezvous back at Mister Middleton's cottage later, but I expect that you will be gone for at least an hour, so do take care."

The boys acknowledged the plea with a nod and prepared to set off down the worn path to the canal, but Mister Barker redirected them.

"Pass to the left of the barge, down the slope. That way you will not be seen or heard by Mister Reid. His ear is remarkably keen for a man of his age, notwithstanding the effects of Jacob's rum."

Soft laughter and tobacco smoke wafted up from the barge as Stan and Fred passed to the rear and headed off for the bridge.

When still two hundred yards distant, they caught sight of Young Doran standing by the horse, the barge boy and his charge casting dreadful parallel shadows by the glow of the coach lamps. Fred grasped Stan's forearm and they slowed to a halt. Stan shivered. His legs felt like jelly.

"Blimey!" breathed Fred.

Stan swallowed and they set off once more, the shadows growing taller with every step, crowding in on their progress. When they turned onto the bridge, they fell completely across Stan and Fred, blurring them into the night. They blinked into the glare of the suddenly bright coach lights.

"It's us, Mister, er, Young… That is, we're here.'

Young Doran did not move from his position by the horse's head, but spoke in a voice so calm that Stan at first thought it belonged to somebody else. "Climb up. Sit tight. Leave me the right."

The boys obeyed immediately, squashing up together on the left side of the wooden seat. At their feet, hard against the painted footboard, lay the rolled Ordnance Survey map and a pole topped with a boat hook. Young Doran clicked softly into the horse's ear and the gig lurched forward. He walked the horse down the slope and along the cobbles for several hundred yards, his hard hand soft on the bridle. When at last he considered them to be safely out the campers' earshot he climbed effortlessly aboard and snapped the reins tight. The old horse accelerated to a trot and they clattered off into the darkness.

They sat high above the road, over and between the ironclad wheels that whirred and crunched over the gravel on either side. It was a carriage as ancient as any that Stan had ever seen, thick with coats of paint that shone yellow in the glow of the gig lamps. Fred leaned heavily against Stan, pressing him painfully against the iron seat frame as Young Doran settled into his driving position. It was a tight squeeze for everyone. They were heading towards the glinting lights of Warwick, rattling along on a parallel course to the canal down an ever broader road. The smell of horse filled the void in conversation. Young Doran sat immobile, briar and unblinking eyes fixed on the road, reins held slack. Stan peered into the shadowy distance, heart thumping. They skirted the northern edge of Packmores before swinging left onto the Coventry Road at Cliff Hill and climbing back up towards Guy's Cliffe. The horse laboured, slowing to a walk.

"Get on, girl," encouraged Young Doran softly.

The gig passed the grand entrance to Guy's Cliffe House on the right and the road began to level off. Three minutes later they pulled to a halt alongside a five-bar gate several yards back from the road. The old horse was breathing hard. Young Doran climbed down to the verge and stood close to its head, murmuring reassurances and stroking its neck. He then led the horse to a nearby telegraph pole, around which he loosely tied the reins. Stan and Fred eased apart on the seat and stretched their limbs. An owl hooted. Young Doran removed one of the gig lamps from its mounting and placed it on the ground beside the vehicle. He then unrolled the map and held it close to his nose, tilted into the lamp's light. Satisfied that they were where they should be, he re-rolled the map and stowed it in the gig beside the footboard.

"Down," he said quietly to the boys. "This is it."

As they clambered down from the gig, Young Doran fixed the lamp to the boat hook and extinguished the other. He knocked the ashes from his briar on his boot heel, ground their glowing fragments into the grass and stowed the pipe in his pocket.

"Follow me. Stay close."

The latch lifted easily, but grass had grown so long around the lower bars that it required all of Young Doran's strength to force the gate open wide enough for them to pass through. The meadow beyond rose gently away from the road, its grass as high as their knees. Young Doran ploughed on at pace, holding the lamp pole low to the ground in front of him, swishing through the stalks and trampling a swathe for the boys to follow. Stan stumbled on behind, a few feet ahead of Fred, both boys panting in Young Doran's wake. The glow of the swinging lamp was almost invisible to Fred at the back who followed Stan by sound rather than sight, occasionally veering off their common furrow before instinctively correcting his course. On and on they went; the field interminably wide. Finally, they broke through the clinging grass stalks and came to a halt on a strip of bare earth at the edge of a copse. A wall of dark trees towered above them, leaves rustling sinister in the night breeze. Young Doran raised the lamp above his head and peered into the coal black thicket, scanning for a path.

"Can't be far," he muttered and headed off along the edge of the wood to the boys' left.

They followed dumbly, not even sure what they were looking for. Presently, he stopped searching and beckoned the boys with the jerk of his thumb.

"Track," he stated. "Stay close."

He plunged into thicket behind the lamp, Stan and Fred hard behind. The path climbed steeply up into the copse, winding clockwise around the densely wooded knoll until it issued onto a small plateau bereft of trees. Young Doran advanced several paces, holding high the lamp pole. Fred stationed himself to his left, Stan to the right. Before them, veiled in the deathly gloom of the strange place stood the monument that was Gaveston's Cross.

The cross itself was mounted at the highest point of the edifice, carved from a single block of stone and positioned on top of a pyramid of four stone slabs which, in turn, rested upon four square stone columns. Beneath the columns, a plinth, firmly planted on a second pyramid of five stone-built steps, brought the overall height of the monument to close on twenty feet. Its presence and sombre majesty in such a lonely place left the boys speechless. At least, for a while.

"Blimey," breathed Fred. "Who'd 'ave thought to put such a thing in the middle of nowhere?"

"A bloke called Greatheed," answered the reverential Stan. "'bout a hundred years ago. Just read about it in our booklet."

"1823," Young Doran informed the boys in a growling whisper. "Old Bertie Greatheed. More money 'n sense."

It did indeed appear to Stan that such an extravagant folly might have represented better value for money had it been sited in a market square, or at the side of a busy road. At least there it would be seen by people who might appreciate the commemorative gesture, not to mention the many hours of work involved in building it. But here, at this hidden spot, it seemed that only birds and wild animals would ever get to see it, or the oppressive trees through which they had arrived.

"See anything?" enquired Young Doran holding his lamp aloft.

Stan scrambled up the moss clad steps and peered at the lower plinth where an iron plaque was set within the stonework.

"There's something here."

Young Doran lowered the lamp close to the plaque as Fred bundled up the steps to join them. Stan pushed his spectacles up the bridge of his nose and read the inscription cast within the ironwork.

In the hollow of this rock
Was beheaded
On the 1st day of July 1312
By Barons lawless as himself
PIERS GAVESTON, Earl of Cornwall
The minion of a hateful King:
In life and death
A memorable Instance of Misrule

"Write it down," suggested Young Doran pulling a small book from a trouser pocket and handing it to Stan. "Every word."

He unhooked the lamp, set it down on the top step and withdrew into the blackness. Stan studied the book in his hand. Measuring no more than four inches by three, it was bound in covers of calf skin that years of handling had worn to a smooth patina. A pencil, held in place against the spine by two loops of tired leather, had been shortened to less than two inches by repeated sharpening. Stan opened the book to the title page: it was a pocket diary for 1883. He licked the tip of his forefinger and began to turn the pages. Each was densely packed with numbers, calculations, formulae, random letters and mathematical symbols beyond meaning, pencil-drawn in a tiny and precise manuscript, apparently unconnected to the days and dates around which they were written. The use of space was astonishing: lines of figures criss-crossed each other in apparently arbitrary fashion and formulae bent into every available space on the paper. Not one eighth of an inch was wasted - and there were pages and pages of the stuff. Stan was well into July before he came to the first unwritten page, shining suddenly bright in the lamplight, and its appearance made him decidedly uneasy about writing anything at all to spoil the strange beauty of what had gone before. He hesitated, looking around for Young Doran's permission, but the book's owner was invisible to him. He removed the tiny pencil from its holster and began to copy, as neatly as he could, the inscription that flickered before him.

Meanwhile, Fred had joined Young Doran at the other side of the monument, the two scanning the monolith for any kind of clue that might present itself. Surely there must be something more than just the words on the iron plaque. Every clue until now had been contained in an object - the silver box, the gravestone pot, the rifle cartridge - so what might it be this time? Or *could* it just be words, hidden within the inscription itself? Young Doran moved around the four sides of the base, searching as he went, and ending up back where he had started, on the trampled ground below Stan's perch. The light on this side gave him a better view of the upper reaches.

"There," he stated at length, head back and right arm outstretched. "Just there."

Fred rushed around from the other side. Stan, who had still not finished copying the text, stayed put, but raised his eyes to the indicated spot above his head. Fred arrived beside Young Doran and peered up the line the arm to where the widest of the four blocks beneath the cross met the top of the columns. There, where the geometric lines should have been perfectly straight, bulged the dusky outline of a bell.

"Blimey!"

"What?"

"Looks like a bell or somethin'. Hard to see."

"A bell? D'you reckon that's it?"

"S'pose so."

There was a pause, all three studying the shadowy shape.

"How we gonna get it then?" asked Stan at last.

Another pause ensued, before Young Doran came up with the solution.

"The lightest of you stand on me shoulders, top of the steps. Should 'ave four or five inches to spare."

Fred glanced at Stan who appeared unconvinced. "It could work you know, Stanley," he said, attempting reassurance. "And he 'as got big shoulders."

"It's gotta be twelve foot up, at least," complained Stan, "and that's on top of six foot of steps." He was decidedly unsure.

In the end, with no other option forthcoming, Young Doran's plan was adopted. Stan replaced the pencil in its holder and handed the book back to its owner before squaring up to Gaveston's Cross and preparing for the climb. Young Doran positioned himself at the top of the steps, straight-backed against the left-hand column, and presented his huge hands, cupped together in front of his stomach as a step by which Stan might begin his ascent. Fred stood close by, ready to help. Stan gripped Young Doran's shoulders and placed his right boot in the makeshift stirrup. Breathing hard, he heaved himself up to grab hold of the column above Young Doran's head. He pressed his left cheek against the stone and took a few more deep breaths.

"On three," he whispered shortly, not daring to move his head. "One, two …. three!"

Propelled upwards by Young Doran's muscular lift and by a hefty shove on the backside from Fred, Stan scrambled untidily up onto the barge boy's shoulders and stood with one foot either side of Young Doran's head, his face pressed against the chill stone column to which he clung for dear life. Fred moved down two steps in order to take stock.

"Almost there, Stan, me old mate. It's just a foot or so above yer 'ead, to the right. Easy from 'ere on in."

The moon suddenly appeared, flooding the scene with a ghoulish light, casting weird shadows across the human tower. Above them, the bell glowed surreally at the base of the cross. Fred swallowed hard.

"Let's get on with it quick," he advised in a strangled whisper. "While we can actually see the bloomin' thing."

Stan was not convinced. "Don't think I'll be able to reach it, Fred." His voice was as shaky as his knees. "Can't see how I'm gonna let go of the pillar."

"You can do it, Stan," encouraged his friend. "Honest you can. It's less than two foot away, give or take."

Stan's trembling increased. He tightened his grip. "Can't, Fred."

"Pole." Young Doran's voice boomed reassuringly calm beneath his feet. "Pass him the pole."

Fred scuttled back up the steps to where the pole was leaning against the plinth.

"Give it here," commanded Young Doran.

Fred handed over the pole and watched as Young Doran fed it upwards through his mighty hands. The hook now lay against the stone next to Stan's face.

"In your own time," continued Young Doran gently. "Take hold and move the hook to the bell."

Gingerly, Stan loosened one hand from the pillar and grasped the pole just below the hook. Then, feeding it through his trembling grip, he moved it closer and closer to the bell, finally hearing a dull chime as the two metals came into contact. Fred watched intently from the foot of the stairs and began guiding Stan in on the target.

"There's a loophole, or whatever you call it, on the top. Go up six inches."

Stan moved the pole again, feeling the hook trace the curve of the bell.

"You're right on it, Stan. Right on it."

He was, but it proved a frustratingly difficult catch to make. Ten or twelve times the hook skated over or under the loophole, leaving Stan in ever increasing agony from the contracting muscles in his right arm, but eventually the desired connection was made and the prey snared. Stan paused to draw breath. Then, clasping the end of the pole for all he was worth, he tugged at the bell and felt its full weight topple ground-wards, almost snatching the pole from his hand as it arced to a thudding halt against the moleskin trousers on Young Doran's thigh. If the impact had been painful to him, Young Doran betrayed it not at all. Unmoved, he stood erect, the bell suspended at his side from the pole at the end of

Stan's arm. Abruptly, the moon departed behind a cloud, rendering the feeble gig lamp suddenly bright against the dark plinth. Fred approached the bell and unhooked it.

"Get me down, will you Fred?" implored Stan. "Me arm's just about falling off 'ere."

Gently, Young Doran lowered the weight of his burden through a knee-bend crouch to the ground, where Stan was able to hop down as if from a stool.

"Thanks," he breathed quietly.

Young Doran nodded in response and stood up, stretching and flexing his shoulders and briefly rubbing his thigh. Fred was already inspecting the bell by the light of the gig lamp.

"Thought it was strange that it never rang when it hit 'im," he pronounced. "Look. Got no clapper. Somebody's stuffed an old bag inside instead."

The bell was about seven inches high and appeared to be of the type seen on fire engines or police vehicles. Even in the gloom of the night they could see that it retained at least some of its original sheen. The bag to which Fred had referred was of jute and hung below the bell, suspended from the absent clanger's anchorage by a length of wire. There was clearly an object of some weight within the bag, for the wire was as tight as a violin string, but its form remained indistinct in the gloom.

"We'll be away back to Mister Middleton's," stated Young Doran. "Time to go."

He took the pole from Stan and reaffixed the gig lamp. Fred took charge of the bell, stuffing it up his outer jumper and clamping it in place with his left arm. The three then silently retraced their steps down the winding path to the edge of the thicket and out across the flattened grass path in the field. Young Doran tugged the gate shut behind them, untied the patient horse from the telegraph pole and climbed up to join the boys on the vehicle's narrow seat. He clicked his tongue and pulled on the reins.

Stan and Fred, squashed in hard against each other, cradled the bell between them as the gig lurched forwards down the road towards the Avon. Within three minutes they were clattering past the regal gateway to Guy's Cliffe House once more, but by then the boys were both fast asleep.

14

COCOA AND COUNTING

Young Doran steered the gig over the humped bridge and onto the grassland beside the stables, coming to a gentle halt. Stan and Fred slept on, warmly pressed together on the hard seat. It was a quarter past eleven. The barge boy nudged his elbow into Stan's upper arm.

"Let's be 'avin' you," he coaxed. "Give the old girl a rest."

Young Doran hopped down and headed for the horse. Stan and Fred clambered sleepily after him and watched as he unhitched the heavy shafts and removed the harness. The gig tilted forward to rest upon its outstretched arms and the horse was led quietly into the vacant box for water, hay and a night's rest.

"Give us an 'and 'ere," grunted Young Doran, grabbing hold of one of the carriage shafts.

Stan and Fred took up the other and the three of them turned the gig through ninety degrees to park it beside the stable block. They then made their way to the top lock and over its single gate. A puny light showed behind the kitchen curtains of Middleton's cottage, but all other windows were dark. The front door stood ajar in expectation, so in they went.

Mister Barker sat at the head of the table as before, an oil lamp close at hand and his collection of green-ink-scribbled papers spread before him. Jacob Middleton lay slumped in a carving chair by the empty hearth, slumbering in the warmth of his rum. He barely twitched as the teacher greeted the returning adventurers.

"Welcome. Welcome. Are you all in one piece?"

"Of course, Sir," grinned Fred, rubbing sleep from his left eye. "Right as ninepence."

Young Doran resumed his place to Mister Barker's left and pulled out his briar. Stan and Fred stood together by the door.

"And did you find anything of interest?" probed Mister Barker.

"We did, Sir," affirmed Fred proudly. "A bell, Sir." He marched forward to place their find upon the table. "And with something stuffed up it, an' all," he added rather unnecessarily, retreating to Stan's side.

"Indeed," responded the teacher, leaning his face towards the bell. "I see, I see. Do please sit down, boys. We shall all have some cocoa. Jacob?"

The lock keeper jolted back into consciousness at the mention of his name. "M-M-Mister Barker?" he stuttered, momentarily unsure of his bearings. "Can I help you, Sir?"

"Cocoa, Jacob. Would you be so good as to make us all a cup of your splendid cocoa?"

Jacob staggered to his feet and weaved unsteadily towards the range on the far side of the kitchen. The boys settled into their places opposite Mister Barker and focused on the bell. Young Doran struck a match on the sole of his boot.

"Time for the Apocalypse of John," declared Mister Barker brightly to his blank audience. "Or Revelations, if you will."

The boys were lost. The teacher modified his approach. "Let's see what we have here, shall we?"

"Definitely," responded Fred, leaning in further towards the centre of their attention. "Can't wait, Sir!"

Stan felt strangely apprehensive, as if disappointment would presently befall them and that it would be his fault. He almost dared not look as Mister Barker detached the hessian bag and laid it on the table, pulling the lamp closer by which to inspect the bell itself, shining gold in the yellow light.

"Well, well," he declared, lightly passing his forefinger over an engraved motif. "If it isn't another Beauchamp family crest." He held the bell towards Stan and Fred. "See? Beautifully engraved, too."

It certainly was. Stan inspected the workmanship at close quarters, imagining the skilled hand of the unknown engraver and thinking of his grandfather, the glass cutter he had never known, whose apprentice pieces ornamented the sideboard at home and whose beautifully engraved mug his mother now used for celery. How strange that a similarly gifted hand should have laboured long over this bell, only for some idiot to hide it on top of a lonely monument. Good job nobody ever tried that with Grandpa Yeoman's tankard!

"Give it 'ere a bit, will you Stan? Let the dog see the rabbit."

The bell was passed to Fred who, in due course, returned it to Mister Barker.

"We are not short of common threads, are we?" reflected the teacher. "But we do rather need to start pulling one or two of them together."

Mister Barker's attention turned to the hessian bag, tied at the neck with an old piece of string and looking for all the world as if it would disintegrate before their very eyes if they were to wait any longer before opening it. "May I borrow your penknife, Frankie?" he asked quietly.

Jacob Middleton returned to the table for a better view as Young Doran drew a knife from the depths of his pocket, opened it and passed it handle-first to Mister Barker who straightaway slit open the bag. There was a moment of silence, a collective intake of breath and then a palpable sense of common disappointment. Gleaming proudly white amidst the remnants of jute was a small ceramic pot of dental cleansing powder.

"Hmmphh," exhaled Middleton and returned to the range.

"Well," exclaimed Mister Barker at length. "He never does cease to amaze me."

"Who, Sir?" asked Fred, in something of a daze.

"Whoever it is who is leading us on in this way."

Stan pulled the object across the table towards him and turned it so that the words on the lid were the right way up, gasping as they came into focus.

"What is it, Johnson?"

"The name, Sir. I mean, the brand name."

"Well?"

"It's Beauchamp, Sir. Beauchamp again. Here: have a look, Sir."

He pushed the pot back across the table and watched attentively as the teacher read the graphic text to himself before proclaiming its legend to the assembly:

BEAUCHAMP'S
CLEANSING, CHALK-INFUSED
RESTORATIVE AND PROTECTING
DENTAL EMULSION
Specially prepared in sizes for every trousseau

"Well, well!"

"So Guy de Beauchamp made toothpaste, then?"

"Probably not, Parker. I believe that dental powders had yet to feature in personal hygiene during his time. However, who's to say that the purveyor of such emulsions might not be descended from the very same line? There is certainly more than mere coincidence afoot here."

"But what's the point, Sir?" asked Stan plaintively. "I mean, what's a tub of dental powder got to do with anything?" He suddenly felt deflated: tired and disappointed.

Fred was more buoyant. "Maybe there's somethin' in it. You know: somethin' other than tooth powder."

Mister Barker tried the lid with his good hand but it was stuck fast. "Frankie, would you mind having a go at opening this for me?"

Young Doran tried and failed. He turned the jar onto its edge in order to gain a better purchase and tried again. Still it would not open. Then he noticed a small paper label stuck to the base of the jar. He pulled the oil lamp a little nearer. After a brief inspection he raised his eyes to Mister Barker.

"What have you got, Frankie?" enquired the teacher softly.

"Numbers."

Young Doran peered again at the base of the jar, eyes flicking left and right, processing data. The teacher and the boys gathered behind him and gazed into the pool of lamplight. Jacob Middleton arrived too, placing five steaming mugs of cocoa at the head of the table, before circling around on the window side to take up a position next to Fred. They all stared at the label on which they could make out, in a tiny but immaculate hand, a series of numbers:

12, 2, 2, 4, 5, 13, 1, 3, 6, 7, 3, 9, 3, 1, 1, 8, 3, 5, 3, 18
kovrilo

"What do you make of it?" enquired the teacher.

"Random," replied Young Doran, his eyes still scanning the label. "Not logical. Just numbers."

Mister Barker mumbled through the string of numbers himself, trying to find a pattern.

"And a word," added Young Doran. "If the numbers are a cipher, the word could be a key."

"Do you mean that the numbers could be some sort of code?"

"Algorithm, maybe," murmured the barge boy. "Decryption key." Mister Barker closed his eye in concentration.

"And the word, Frankie? What does the word mean? Is it the key or the code?"

"Can't say."

Stan was trying hard to follow, but losing the thread. He attempted to steer them back to more familiar territory. "Is it another map reference, d'you think, Sir? Like the last one."

"I'm not sure, Johnson. Perhaps, but there appear to be too many numbers. All rather flummoxing." He did, indeed, appear flummoxed.

"What's kovrilo mean then, Sir?" asked Fred bluntly.

"That's just it, Parker. I'm damned - sorry, dashed - if I can remember."

"Esperanto again?"

"Almost certainly, but my mind's a blank. *Cove*, perhaps, but I can't see how that gets us very far." He tried out a few pronunciations of the first syllable to himself: *kov, cove, cuvv*…

"Covering?" essayed Fred. "I mean like covering up, Sir? Or covering a biscuit box?"

"Or a pot of tooth powder! By jingo, Parker: the lid! It's the lid! Kovrilo is a cover and I bet it's referring to the lid. Well done, boy!"

Fred blushed. "Er..."

Stan gave a quick glance of approval to his friend, but had no idea what was going on. "So, how? I mean, where does this leave us now, Sir?"

"Counting," pronounced Young Doran.

"Counting, Frankie?"

"Counting." He pulled out the ancient diary from his pocket and allowed it to fall open at the last page used, where Stan's spidery hand had copied the inscription from the monument. For a moment he scanned the writing, as if trying to reconcile its unexpected presence within such a familiar object, then flicked to the next page. Leaning in close, he painstakingly noted down the list of numbers from the base of the jar with the tiny sharpened pencil. The others remained silent. When at last the numbers had all been transcribed, Young Doran pushed the jar towards Mister Barker.

"When I read 'em, Master Barker, would you count out the letters on the lid? Left, right; top, bottom." He spoke slowly and clearly, his deep voice rolling like a mill stone over the kitchen table. "B is one. Count twelve: write it down."

Mister Barker grabbed his pen and slid a piece of green-inked foolscap within range. Then he counted.

"It's an L," he stated. "The L of cleansing." He counted back again to make sure that he had not made a mistake then wrote it down in green ink.

"Now, two."

"A."

"And two more."

"S."

"Four."

"C."

And so it went on. Mister Barker knew what he was decrypting long before the last number was called out, but he continued to count the letters and to write them down, as if the mechanical act of so doing might prove his deduction wrong. But he was not wrong. A chill ran down his back: a sense of foreboding quickened his pulse. He inscribed the last letter and laid his pen upon the table, just as the clock chimed the three-quarter hour. He raised his blue eye from the green scrawled phrase and turned to face the dark window behind Stan.

"What is it, Sir?" asked Stan nervously. "Is it bad?"

"It's Dante."

"Come again, Sir?"

"Durante degli Alighieri: Dante." It was as if he was reading from a screen somewhere beyond the window pane. "Perhaps the greatest medieval poet of them all."

"Dante, Sir? I don't quite...."

"The cipher reveals a famous line of Dante - or half of the line, to be precise, from *Inferno*: the first part of *The Divine Comedy*."

Fred looked bemused. "What's he on about?" he mouthed to Stan.

Mister Barker hauled his gaze back from somewhere out in the garden and addressed his co-detectives in a serious tone. "*Lasciate ogni speranza,*" he pronounced. "*Abandon all hope.* In Dante's work the phrase was written in Italian above the gates to hell. *Lasciate ogni speranza, voi ch'entrate*: abandon all hope, ye who enter here. Our trickster friend has somehow managed to dissimulate it - or the first part of it, at least - upon the lid of a toothpaste jar!"

"And... so, is that bad, Sir?" Stan was reacting more to his teacher's expression than to his words, but Mister Barker stared right through him into some unknown distance and did not reply.

"Er..." Fred attempted clarification. "Is 'e asking us to give up then? You know, like it's no use us hoping for treasure anymore?"

The question brought Mister Barker momentarily back amongst them. "It is possible, Parker. Yes. Of course it is." He limped slowly around the kitchen table towards the window. "Or it could be that he is warning us about what we might find. That we might find something that causes us to abandon hope and give up, or that defeats us entirely. Either way, I find the tone disturbing, to say the least."

Now it was Stan's turn to feel a shiver of apprehension. "Do you mean, Sir, that this has all been some wild goose chase leading us nowhere?"

The fact was that Mister Barker had no idea. The lid's diabolical revelation - how strange that he should have used the very word "revelation" not fifteen minutes ago - had brought to mind the hell-and-damnation rhetoric of his university professor, with its symbolism and suffering and death without redemption. But could the innocent questions of his pupils actually be nearer the truth? Could this trickster simply have plucked the phrase from the air and used it to signal an end to their quest? A dead end, as it were: metaphorically morbid, signifying defeat? It was late. He was tired. He might have missed something…

"There's summat in it," declared Middleton brusquely. "In the pot." He was holding the ceramic jar to his ear like a sea shell. "Felt it. 'Eard it an' all." He put the jar back firmly on the table. "And don't forget your cocoa neither. It'll be stone cold at this rate."

"Excellent suggestion, Mister Middleton." A mug of cocoa suddenly seemed like a very good next step. Mister Barker summoned his troops and was briskly back to his old self. "Come now, everyone. Let's take stock of where we are with a draft of Cadbury's finest."

As they supped at their cocoa, each weighed the jar in hand and shook it to verify Middleton's discovery. Sure enough, there was something inside, moving minutely from side to side when shaken, not quite a perfect fit. It could have been almost anything, but it was definitely not dental emulsion. Fred had a go at opening the jar in the established manner, but met with the same result as Young Doran. Stan undertook a closer inspection, holding the jar to his spectacles and peering at the join between lid and base.

"It's been stuck shut," he announced. "Cemented. Look, you can just see some kind of deposit in the join."

Mister Barker held the jar close to his good eye, then laid it upon the table. "What next?"

"'Ammer," came Young Doran's considered response. "Jacob?"

"Right away, Frankie," replied the lock keeper, scuttling off to the tool shed.

When he returned, the cocoa mugs had been removed and the green inked pages spread out in front of Mister Barker, now reseated at his customary place and back in the frame of mind to solve the mystery. Jacob plonked himself down and prepared to smash the ceramic jar into a thousand pieces.

"Hold fire, Jacob," commanded Young Doran. "See us 'em over 'ere."

Reluctantly, Middleton aborted his assault and handed the hammer and its intended target to Young Doran who, holding the jar in his left hand, delicately tapped around the seal until the bonds of the cement gave way and the lid freed. He did not attempt to open the jar, but laid it intact on the table in front of Stan and leaned back in his chair. Mister Barker craned in and beckoned him to proceed, whereupon Stan lifted the lid and pulled out a small parcel, neatly wrapped in cream coloured writing paper. It looked for all the world like a tiny, cube-shaped Christmas present, tied with blue cotton thread and fastened by a tight knot. It was heavier than Stan had foreseen and almost slipped from his grasp as he lifted it towards his spectacles for closer inspection. The origami folds to the paper were precise, symmetrical and knife-sharp, as though creased with a flattening iron. A thing of great beauty, he thought. It would be a pity to spoil the effect by opening it.

"You gunna open it, then?" asked Fred. "Or are you tryin' to see through the bloomin' thing?"

"It's so beautifully wrapped, Fred," responded Stan reverentially. "Just look at the geometry of it." He offered up the object in the palm of his hand for inspection.

"I rather think," suggested Mister Barker in a strained tone, "that we would be better informed about the contents were you to open it, Johnson."

"Of course, Sir."

He cut through the blue thread with Young Doran's knife and unfolded the petals. Inside, the paper was covered with indigo handwriting - a letter, it seemed - whilst the object it enveloped appeared to be a solid brass cube, bereft of decoration and dulled by time to a greenish brown. Stan picked it up in his finger tips and passed it to Fred. He then smoothed out the folds of the paper and turned the letter towards him. It was written in a bold and confident hand, with neither flourishes nor crossings-out.

"Would you mind reading it out, Sir?" he asked.

"By all means, Johnson."

Stan pushed the letter over the table to Mister Barker who raised it to his good eye and cleared his throat:

My dear Bray,

So, you have come at last to Gaveston's Cross: memorial to the corruption of justice. I must confess that I am impressed. I can only assume that you relied more upon your own detective abilities (well hidden to me though they are) than defer to the quack posturing of that idiot Ellerby. Bravo.

What I can not know, of course, is precisely how long you have taken to unravel and retie the threads of mischief that I have woven into your quest. How much time has elapsed since that fatal day? No matter. My steamer has long since sailed. Your reward must wait.

I do hope that you enjoyed the coincidental gravestone and the fatality of the date upon the cross. But I digress. Your race is not yet run. There remains one knot to unpick - unlock - before redemption.

Begin with Hamlet 3, 1, 114-121, and end there. The ruins of similar lie hard by the Great Western line. Through heaven's hidden door may ye at last descend unto Hades.

ADIEU JC

Mister Barker's reading of the letter ended, but his lips continued to chew on the meaning. He knew Hamlet well and had attended Bridge-Adams's production of the play at Stratford just the previous year, but he was struggling to remember exactly what happened at the beginning of Act 3. It must be when Ophelia tries to return Hamlet's love letters, he thought, but what was the wording of those lines? Stan stifled a yawn and ventured to interrupt.

"Who do you think he's writing to, Sir?"

"I'm sorry, Johnson?" Mister Barker was still miles away.

"Who's Bray in the letter? Who's it really to?"

"I have no idea I'm afraid, Johnson. But it would appear that the hapless recipient lost the scent well before the end of the crusade. Goodness knows if he was ever on it, in fact."

Fred had been playing with the brass cube, negligently turning it in his hand whilst his mind wondered. "It's the gravestone," he declared. "The name on the gravestone. I knew I'd seen it somewhere. Remember, Stan? The church warden, or whatever he was."

"Joseph Bray," breathed Stan. "At Baddesley Clinton."

"*Coincidental gravestone*," recited Mister Barker, raising the letter back to his eye line. "Well, I'll be…. Not coincidental at all. He must have planned it all along and chosen the stone quite deliberately."

"But Bray never found it," surmised Fred.

"Perhaps we should take stock," pronounced the teacher, his mind racing. If only he had brought his *Shakespeare* with him. "Jacob, do you know whereabouts I might make use of a telephone tomorrow morning?" He had an idea that he might call his mother.

The lock keeper roused himself noisily and thought deeply, scratching at his beard. "They'll have one at the maintenance yard," he eventually announced. "But I've no idea how to use it meself."

"Thank you, Jacob. I am sure that somebody there will be able to instruct me in its usage. I am most obliged."

Middleton's nose emitted a bulbous snort of satisfaction and he folded his arms. Mister Barker resumed his stock take.

"It is clear that our correspondent has set clues for this Bray chap to follow. We have no way of knowing just how many clues, but Bray must have missed one, or failed to interpret one, before coming to the box concealed behind the milestone. And it would now appear that we, in Bray's stead, are coming to the end of our pursuit." Mister Barker paused for emphasis. "The bell and its fascinating contents apparently represent the penultimate riddle of this strange series."

The mantel clock struck the first of twelve soft chimes.

"But goodness, time has flown! You must be tired out. It is high time that we let you get off and have some rest."

Fred gave in to a huge yawn, eliciting a smile from his teacher. Well, it looked like a smile. "Off you trot, boys, and without further ado. Do take care on the towpath and try not to wake up the whole camp by tumbling over the guy ropes. You will be on milk duty tomorrow, so let us meet outside the farm's milking parlour at 7 o'clock. I hope to have more news for you both then."

Stan and Fred rose together and headed for the door. Mister Barker was clearly not done for the night and Stan would have loved to have stayed with him to work through the clues towards an answer, but he knew that he was too tired to be of any use.

"Run along now."

With a nod towards the others, the boys shuffled out into the night.

The towpath was poorly lit, but at least the moon had made a reappearance and the camp was less than 400 yards away. Fred took the lead and they stumbled off in single file towards the shadowy barge that marked the way up to their tent.

"What d'you make of all that, then?" enquired Stan when they were out of earshot of the cottage. "The Beauchamp name just seems to be everywhere, don't you think? On the bell, on the dental paste jar, even on the cross - sort of. And then there's Shakespeare and Dante and Mister Barker looking scared. The whole thing just keeps on getting more and more mysterious."

"Barmy, more like. The 'ole thing's weirder than a fish."

"What?"

"A fish - you know. Somethin' weird."

Stan had no idea what his friend was talking about, but neither did he have the energy to pursue the matter. Instead, he concentrated on planting his feet carefully on the rutted path. A few seconds later, Fred thought of something else to say:

"I reckon it's a mistake for 'im to have blown 'is cover like that."

"Who?"

"The bloke who wrote the letter to Bray, you know. Writing the letter has exposed his incredibility."

Fred was clearly over-tired: Stan could hardly follow a word. "How's that then, Fred?"

"Stands to reason. Before, he was an unknown quantity: an invisible hand, if you like. But 'is letter's gone and given us an insight, see?"

Stan groaned. He wondered how he could tell Fred to shut up without offending him when, abruptly, he crashed straight into the back of him. Fred had stopped in his tracks and stiffened like a pointer.

"Crikey, Fred. What're you..."

"Shhhhhh. There's somebody coming."

"Where?"

"Down there. Other side of the barge. Look."

Sure enough, a hundred yards down the towpath, a weaving light was heading their way.

"Have they seen us, d'you think?" asked Stan.

"Who?"

"Whoever's coming, you idiot." Really; there were times….

"Can't 'ave. We've got no light."

"D'you reckon its a policeman?"

"What? Why d'you say that?" Fred was suddenly worried.

"Because of the lamp. Who else has torch lamps?" The whispering between them was becoming louder.

"Loads of people. Me Uncle Harry's got one. Now shut up for a sec. 'Es coming."

The lamp progressed to the barge, stopped and turned towards the camp site. Fred and Stan held their breath. Then it swung back, winking at them as it cut through their line of sight and arced out over the canal. Stan moved a step closer to Fred. The beam began its return journey, flickering once more into their eyes. Then a metallic crash, the lamplight disappeared and a strangled cry bounced off the high banking to their left.

"Bollocks!"

"Bill?" breathed Fred.

"Duggan?" echoed Stan.

"Stick close, Stan. I think 'e's got a problem."

Fred led his friend cautiously along the path towards the source of the expletive where they soon identified, amongst the tangle of arms, legs and bicycle, the dishevelled features of their esteemed tent commander, William Duggan.

"Bollocks!" announced Commander Duggan once more, his whisper hoarse and pained. "Give us an 'and to get this bloody thing off of me, will you?"

Stan grabbed the handlebars whilst Fred attended to the back wheel. Duggan's legs had somehow ended up laced through the frame, with the chain digging into his left ankle and the dynamo squashed against his thigh.

"Careful, for God's sake," he hissed as Fred took hold. "Me foot's caught."

"Had a pleasant evening, Bill?" Fred yanked at the wheel, eliciting a wince and a further expletive from Duggan.

"Parker, you prick. I told you to be careful."

"Just taking care of Kate's bike, Bill. Wouldn't want you to damage it, now would we?"

He tugged at the wheel again, tilting the machine and freeing Duggan with a yelp and an oily graze to his left calf, before quickly retreating three steps and positioning the bicycle between himself and his tent commander.

"You moron, Parker. Could 'ave 'ad me bloody leg off."

"Tricky thing, a bicycle, don't you think? Does she know you've got it?"

"What? Of course she knows, you…"

"Why don't we just calm down a bit, eh?" intervened Stan, "or you'll wake up the whole blessed camp."

The bickering died down, but the tension between the love rivals persisted. Stan strained to hear if anyone was stirring on the barge, but all was quiet in that direction. A water rat plopped into the canal behind him and they span around to see its semi-circular ripples chase across the dark water.

"What are you two doing up at this time of night anyway?" asked Duggan.

There was hesitation; neither could think of a good answer.

"Night fishing, perhaps?" suggested Duggan.

"No knights to catch."

"Seriously. Why aren't you in bed? It must be after midnight."

"Had some fatigue duties to catch up on." It was the best that Stan could come up with.

"Oh yeah? Like what?"

"Thing was," began Stan, "d'you remember when we came out to distract Barker for you? Well, he asked us for a bit of help to get him along the towpath to Middleton's cottage. See?"

"Who's Middleton?"

Stan sighed. He was getting in too deep. "Lock keeper. Lives in the cottage back there at the top lock. Barker goes up there for an evening cocoa."

"So?"

"Er, so we went with him. Helped him along the path, you know."

"For two hours?"

"Yes, well. Time slips by when you're having fun."

"Ahh!"

"Stayed for a few hands of whist," contributed Fred.

Stan cleared his throat. "And how was your evening, Duggan?"

"Wonderful," he sighed, suddenly transported. "Oh, Johnson, if you only knew..." He was instantly a different man; lost in his romantic reverie, lyrical in every pronouncement, poetic in the eye-shut evocation of his soirée of love. "And her eyes are so clear, you know Johnson? Deep blue. Trusting. And when she looks at you with that look...."

"Er?"

"*My night shall be remembered for a star,*" he crooned, "*That outshone all the suns of all men's days.*" He paused, dreamily. "It's Brooke, you know. She loves Rupert Brooke."

"Really? We'd never 'ave guessed."

"She has his collected works, you know, and can recite them all by heart, nearly."

"And she lent you 'er bike an' all."

"What?"

"It's a bloomin' Raleigh Ranger!"

"So?"

"Is that 'ow you got back then? On 'er bike?" Fred seemed awfully interested in the bicycle.

"Of course, Parker. What d'you think I'd be doin' with the bike otherwise? Taking it for a stroll?"

"She must like you a lot then. I mean, to lend you 'er bike."

"D'you think so, Parker?" Duggan leapt at the flimsy proof of her affection. "Do you really think she likes me a lot? I mean, you're not just saying so?"

"Steady on, Bill. I only said that she must like you for lending you 'er bike, that's all. I didn't say she was gunna bloomin' marry you."

"Excuse me butting in here," interrupted Stan, "but don't you think we ought to be making a move towards bed? We've got fatigues in the morning and I really don't want to stand and listen to this twaddle all night. I'm off. Anyone else coming?"

They made their ragged way together up to the field, pushing the bicycle between them and skirting the guy ropes. They decided to lay Kate's machine down in the grass behind their tent, out of Pickup's morning line of sight but close enough at hand to be able to conceal it within the farmyard in the morning.

Hendry was snoring on his back when they entered the tent, but the others made no noise. Morris was curled like a dormouse beneath his untidy covers, chin resting on the back of his hand. Bushell lay face down, socked feet sticking out six inches beyond his blanket, oblivious to their entrance. Stan removed his boots and supplementary jumper and slipped beneath his best summer blanket. Fred did likewise but without removing his boots, fist closed tight around the small brass cube. Both were sound asleep within seconds. To their right, love's young dream lay on its back, smiling at the faint moon through the heavy canvas.

Stands the church clock at ten to three and is there honey still for tea....?

15

MORNING, AFTER
THE NIGHT BEFORE

Mister Phipps stretched himself to the full five feet one and a half inches of his straight-backed height and belched a sizeable quantity of *Old Navy* fumes into the morning air. Nostrils tingling, he scrutinised the steaming canal with deep suspicion, as if its murky waters might at any moment bring forth a German U-Boat. A coot scampered for cover on the far bank. Mister Phipps wheezed into a bend and gathered up a log for the fire from the pile beside the barge. It was half past six in the morning.

In B tent, Duggan had been awake for hours. Had he slept at all? How could he sleep? His bounding heart would never allow him to waste precious minutes not thinking about Kate. His mind had flitted through the night, projecting and re-projecting the images of that one stolen hour beneath the pear tree; replaying the sound of her harp-song laughter, innocent as her thoughts of love, enchanting as the depths into which he had fallen. Was this the feeling that poems seek to evoke? Was this what it was all about? Was this what *Brooke* was all about? Perhaps not such a prick after all. It now seemed obvious why Kate should revere his rhymes. Could she be feeling it too? Had she fallen with him into this delicious torture of want and longing?

From beneath his rough blanket, Fred's sleeping form let go a burbling fart.

Bloody Parker. Duggan heaved a sigh. What was eating him about the bike last night, anyway? He sat up with a jolt. The bicycle! It had completely slipped his mind. He would have to make a better job of hiding it before the others were up and about. But where on earth…? He had given absolutely no thought to returning the machine during that precious moment when Kate had entrusted it to him for the journey home. No thought to anything at all, in fact, save for her lips (how extraordinarily soft) and her fragrant chestnut hair and her smiling eyes and her manicured nails and …. Well, just about all of her really.

He decided upon a course of action and reached for his boots. Tiptoeing between sleeping tent mates, he tottered to the flaps before slipping into his shorts, pulling on a jumper and shoeing his bare feet, then escaping to the dewy grass. He scanned the field for observers and moved swiftly around the tent to where his beloved's bicycle rested moistly where it had been laid. Reverentially righting it, he caressed its sublime handlebars and headed off across the field on a diagonal course towards the farm. If he could just find some suitable barn in which to hide it for the rest of the day, he would be perfectly placed for a speedy getaway after lights-out that evening.

Behind him, Mister Barker made an undignified exit from the staff tent, his good foot skidding on the trampled turf and flinging his trailing artificial limb into a low orbit parallel to the ground which pirouetted him around like a clockwork soldier to end up facing the tent from which he had barely emerged. Teetering back into equilibrium, he glimpsed Duggan, exiting the field with a bicycle, and planted his two feet back on terra firma to contemplate the sight with a quizzical frown. Well, well.

Along the towpath in the lock keeper's cottage, Jacob Middleton slept before the cheerless hearth, draped across his armchair just as Mister Barker had left him barely four hours earlier. The mantle clock tocked its steady pulse into the chill room in counterpoint to Middleton's snoring.

One hundred yards away, in the stable block on the opposite bank, Young Doran brushed the night's road dirt from the horse's coat with sweeping strokes of his brawny arms. The dust hung thick in the grime-filtered sunlight, twinkling like a tiny universe. The old nag stood still, ears pricked, savouring every pass of the bristles over her flanks until the grooming came to an end, whereupon the barge boy turned his attention to the donkeys in the next stall, the rhythmic sweeping commencing anew.

Duggan crested the rise and followed the cartwheel ruts into the farmyard. The machine's vibrations calmed to a tremble on the worn stones and he loosened his hold on the handgrips. A chicken flapped across his path. To his left crouched the brick stable block, roof sagging under its moss wig, half-doors flung open for airing. To his right, a wooden cowshed, creosote dark and flecked with knot holes, lowing and chomping with the collective voice of cows at milking. Everyone must be in there at work, thought Duggan, imagining a factory-like army of milkmaids and farmhands seated beneath the udders of their charges. It was Duggan's first ever visit to a farm - there were no such things in Bordesley - and the whole place fascinated him. He lingered long over the bicycle to take in the smells and sounds of this entirely novel place: the occasional clop of a hoof on stone, the swishing of tails, a moo - of protest or of contentment, he could not tell - and the slopping of milk in galvanised pails. From away beyond the farmyard came the low parping of Mr Phipps's motor horn, rousing the slumberers from their blankets. It was time to find a hiding place.

He settled on a narrow alley between the wooden fence of the kitchen garden and the silage pen wall, against which he solemnly leaned his charge. The sweet sorrow of the night's parting welled up as his hand passed softly over the twin mounds of the leather saddle. He turned on his heel to head back into the farmyard and marched straight into the piercing, one-eyed stare of Mister Barker.

Skidding to a halt on the cobbles and blinking like an Aldis lamp, Duggan's mouth lolled open. The teacher was standing in the shadow of the stable block, his good arm clutching a manila folder of papers. He studied Duggan's struggle for comprehension with the composure of a bridge player about to finesse an ace, then bowed his head in polite greeting.

"Mister Duggan," he hailed, his tone as light as goose down, "how delightful to see you up and about at this hour. A very good morning to you."

"Yessir. Mornin' to you an' all, Sir," gabbled Duggan.

"Fatigues, is it?"

"Beg pardon, Sir?"

"Is it your fatigue duty that brings you up to the farmyard so bright and early?"

"Er, yessir. Fatigues. Exactly, Sir."

"I see. Hmmm. Well, I must say that it's jolly good of you to make such an early start. I am sure that Johnson and Parker will be most grateful for the assistance."

Duggan made a ghastly attempt at a smile. "Well, you know me, Sir," he began, dry mouthed, "always one to lend an 'and where I can, Sir."

"Of course, Duggan. Excellent show." Mister Barker nodded slowly in order to occupy a lengthy pause. "And may I ask if you have managed to conceal the bicycle?"

Duggan blanched and appeared to grab at an invisible handrail for support. "Sir? Bicycle, Sir?"

"Yes, Duggan. Bicycle. The pedal-driven, twin-wheeled contraption that you were marching across the field just now."

"Ah, er - yes, Sir. That bicycle."

"Exactly."

There was another pause.

"Well?"

"Sir?"

"Have you managed to hide it away in a place where it will not be discovered?"

"I, er, well yes, Sir. I believe so, Sir."

"Good, Duggan, for I would hate for it to go missing; inadvertently, as it were."

Duggan had once again lost the thread.

"For I may have need of it," continued the teacher, "and, given my own unsuitability, need of your good self as a rider, too. Shall we call it a fair exchange for my silence regarding your absence last evening?"

Duggan's jaw dropped still further. Mister Barker decided that enough was enough and brought the teasing to an end. "Please do not be alarmed, Duggan. I do not intend to report you or the bicycle to any higher authority; provided, of course, that you have the owner's permission for it to be in your custody?"

Duggan nodded dumbly.

"Howsoever the machine came into your possession - and I have no wish to be informed - I consider its presence here this morning to be most serendipitous."

Duggan would rather liked to have been able to sit down at this point. His emotions, already jellied by the lovely Kate, now felt as though they had been fed through a mincer. He seriously wondered whether he might be dreaming. Perhaps he was actually sound asleep in bed. He raised his eyes to the blue sky and exhaled heavily.

"Might I explain?" proffered Mister Barker.

Back in B tent, Duggan's absence had been noted by all except Fred, who slept soundly on, oblivious to the general kerfuffle that followed Mister Phipps's clarion call.

"D'you reckon he's bin gone all night?" asked Morris, star-struck. "Like Marco Polo?"

"Who cares?" replied Hendry. "Now, bog off to the latrines, Morris, and give a bloke some breathing space."

"Probably in the cells at Warwick Police Station," suggested Bushell cheerfully. "Drunk and disorderly, I shouldn't wonder." Hendry snorted his concurrence.

"He was here last night," said Stan quietly. "Saw him myself."

"Oh, so you was on guard duty, were you?"

Stan let the matter drop. He kicked Fred's leg to rouse him. "Fatigues, Fred," he called out loudly. "Rise and shine. We've got the milk to get."

"Yeah, Parker," sneered Hendry, "and don't be too slow about it neither. I could murder a boggin' tea."

Within five minutes, Fred and Stan were headed across the field, bleary eyed and unwashed, their boot laces and shirt tails flapping in the morning air. Fred yawned for what Stan took to be the fiftieth time and received a punch on the arm for his trouble.

"Look lively, Fred, for goodness sake. We're gonna have to be alert if Barker's there waiting for us."

"Be a Lert," recited Fred. "Cadbury needs Lerts. And don't punch my bloomin' arm, right?"

"How much sleep d'you get then?" asked Stan as Fred gave in to yet another huge yawn.

"'Bout ten minutes by the feel of it. Can't stop yawning."

"I hadn't noticed."

"How 'bout you?"

"No idea. Slept like a log, but woke up thinking about that cube. Remember? Any idea what happened to it?"

"Got it right 'ere, matey," beamed Fred, pulling the object from the depths of his pocket. "Found it in me 'and when I woke up, though I'm buggered if I can remember taking it to bed."

"Must have," pronounced Stan wisely. "Here, give us a look."

Fred handed over the dull cube and the pair slowed to a halt.

"It's heavier than it looks," observed Stan, placing the cube into the outstretched palm of his right hand and holding it under Fred's nose. "Cold, too." The boys peered at the object.

"What do you suppose it does, exactly? I mean, what d'you reckon it's for?"

"Dunno," yawned Fred. "Never seen one like it before."

Stan raised the cube to his spectacles and examined it closely. It was as dull as an old penny, save for a small area in the centre of one of the faces that shone burnished yellow, as if polished. He knew the colour well. It was the colour of the driver's handle on his father's tram, worn to a lustre by a million touches of coarse hands and leather gauntlets. It was the colour of use. But what possible use could there be for a brass cube? He held it to his ear and shook it, as one would shake a matchbox to check its contents, but it made no sound. He rotated the cube between his fingers, like a spin bowler preparing to run to the wicket, but the smooth sides revealed no secret design. Why was it worn just there, and nowhere else? And whose hand might last have held such a curious object? The metal was as smooth as glass. Stan moved his thumb to cover the worn spot, wondering if there might be an indentation there, but he could feel no difference.

"What ya got?" asked Fred.

"Nothing," replied Stan, absentmindedly rubbing the burnished metal with his thumb. "Can't work it out."

He looked up at the clouds for inspiration, continuing to rub the brass cube as he did so, an unconscious gesture that briefly gave rise to a sensation of warmth in his thumb but not to the breakthrough insight as to what the thing might actually be for. He levelled his gaze towards Fred, just as a faint "click" emanated from the cube. A musical sound; percussive, sonorous, barely audible. Stan stared in disbelief. The cube had split in half, connected - apparently hinged - along the middle.

"What the…?"

Fred bent in for a closer view. Stan eased the two halves apart with thumb and index finger until they lay flat in his palm, feeling them lock together as if drawn to one another by a powerful magnet. His palm now held something resembling a brass domino, about four inches long, two inches wide and an inch deep. The newly revealed face was as highly polished as a mirror, but etched and pitted by a labyrinthine pattern of grooves, lines and indentations, centred within a lacy frieze of swirls and serifs. Beautiful to behold, yet as unfathomable in its conception as in its possible use. The finery of the border seemed at odds with the geometrically precise incisions within, as though a Corporation Tramways technical drawing had been executed on a paper doily. Or at least, that's how it looked to Stan.

"Is it moving?" asked Fred in a whisper.

"What?! What are you on about, is it moving? For goodness sake, Fred. Does it look like its moving?"

"Well, no. I thought *you* thought it was moving, Stan. I mean, before it opened, like."

Struggling to find an adequate reply to such idiocy, Stan was interrupted by a bellow from the tent line.

"What in the name of Reilly are you two varmints dawdling over up there?" It was a seething Quartermaster Reid, journeying beyond the confines of his galley to establish the whereabouts of the morning milk. "We've got tea and porridge to prepare down here, so get a move on or you'll both be for it."

"Right away, Mister Reid," yelled Fred. "On our way."

Stan stuffed the flattened cube into his pocket and they charged off towards the farmyard. They arrived to find Mister Barker engaged in conversation with Duggan, a gallon jug of milk on the ground between their feet. Duggan shot them a startled look. It had been rather a bewildering few minutes for the tent commander.

"Ah, Johnson, Parker: there you are," hailed Mister Barker, cheerfully. "I thought that you might have missed the morning hooter." He seemed pleased with himself.

"We was up on time, but got a bit delayed," answered Fred warily. "On the way, like." He looked at Duggan. "What's he doin' 'ere, Sir?"

"I believe that he came to give you a hand with the milk. Isn't that so, Duggan?"

"Yessir," answered Duggan quietly, his jaw slack with incomprehension.

"In fact," pursued the teacher, "he was just about to take this jug down to the barge before you arrived. Right, Duggan?"

"Er? Right, Sir."

Now it was Stan and Fred's turn for bewilderment, watching silently as their leader gathered up the heavy jug and strode off towards the camp field.

"Remember, Duggan. Not a word to anyone until we reconvene after breakfast."

Duggan slowed to mumble a further "Yessir" over his shoulder and was gone. Stan could barely contain himself.

"Sir? What does he know? I mean, with respect, Sir, I hope you didn't tell him about the clues or anything."

Fred rallied to his friend's concern. "'Specially not 'im, Sir. You know - he's not really one of us."

"Calm down, boys," soothed Mister Barker. "Do not be alarmed. Duggan might just prove a timely addition to our band, but I assure you that I have shared with him only the barest of detail. By some fortuitous occurrence, it would appear that he has come into the stewardship of a bicycle. His timing in this regard could not be better."

"So you know about the bike, Sir?" asked Stan cautiously.

"It's a Raleigh Ranger," chipped in Fred, to no obvious purpose.

"Yes, I know of the bicycle," replied the teacher unperturbed, "but I chose not to enquire as to how it came to be in Duggan's care. There is more than enough to be getting on with without having to worry about the provenance of a Raleigh Ranger. I did, however, find myself well placed to exact a certain *quid pro quo* from Duggan for having turned a blind eye to the matter - in my case, quite literally." He emitted a strange, low chuckle.

Stan decided to bring matters back into focus. "Have you found out more about last night's clues then, Sir?" He was looking at the sheaf of papers clasped to the teacher's chest.

"I have indeed, Johnson; a good deal more. There is much to recount and I will endeavour to bring you both completely up to speed before the charabanc arrives at nine o'clock, but first let me deal with a few essential practicalities."

Stan and Fred instinctively shuffled a step closer to their teacher.

"I intend to inform Mister Pickup that you two - now along with Duggan - are required to perform extra fatigue duties this morning and that you will not be able to join the excursion until midday. This, I shall tell him, is because you failed to perform yesterday's duties to my satisfaction. I apologise, of course, particularly for the ribbing that you are likely to receive from the others, but it is the only plausible way of having the three of you miss the bus, so to speak. And I *do* need you to miss the bus."

Stan felt his mouth fall open. Mister Barker continued at speed. "I will obviously depart promptly with the others on the charabanc.

Much as I would love to be with you at the *dénouement,* my first responsibility is to the other pupils in my charge. But you will be well looked after. Frankie is fully briefed on what is required and he will take you both to the Priory in the gig. Duggan will travel by bicycle and will meet you there."

Stan's head was spinning. "Priory, Sir? What priory? I don't…. I mean, where did you get that from, Sir?"

"From Shakespeare," answered the teacher enigmatically. "But I shall come to that in due course." He looked around the farmyard and spied the equipment storage shed to their left, its double doors also flung open. "Let us scoot indoors for a few minutes before you head off to your ablutions. There may be seating within and there is much for me to tell."

They trooped into the dimness of the shed which they found to be a repository for rusting agricultural equipment, jumbled together in apparently random order. Ploughshares, scythes, cartwheels, hoes, harnesses, lidless milk churns and the deconstructed workings of a threshing machine were amongst the ancient building's occupants. Fred spotted the wooden tailgate of a hay wagon leaning against a wall and laid it flat upon two battered milk pails. They had their assembly bench. The boys sat to their teacher's left, on his "good" side, as he called it, with Stan squashed in the middle. Mister Barker struggled for a second or two with his papers before establishing order amongst the green scrawls that he now held before him. He cleared his throat.

"Yesterday evening, the pieces finally began to fall into place. At last, I found some logic to the sequence of clues and indices that you have discovered over the past two days. The picture is much clearer, although I confess that I am still no wiser as to exactly what you might find at the end of the trail. Neither, I am afraid, can I shed much light on the precise identity of the architect of our mystery."

Fred toyed with the idea of questioning just what it actually was that the teacher *had* discovered, but thought better of it. He allowed the monologue to proceed uninterrupted.

"We now know that the trail of clues was laid for a certain Mister Bray. We also know that said Bray either lost the trail or never found the trail or just plain gave up on it, somewhere before the point at which you two stumbled upon the silver box behind the milepost. Thereafter, the clues have been ours - yours - to discover and I must say that you have proved to be extremely capable in this regard." He paused to draw breath.

"But who is Mister Bray?" he continued. "And why did our protagonist take such apparent pleasure in defeating him, as witnessed by his letter? The only good answer that I could come up with is that Mister Bray must have been some kind of detective."

"A policeman?" asked Fred nervously.

"Indeed, Parker. A policeman. I hypothesised that our cunning clue-setter, perhaps the author of some act of burglary, may have taken pleasure in teasing his pursuer with a series of clues as to his identity or whereabouts, only to dash all hopes with the final clue at Gaveston's Cross and the revelation that he had sailed to freedom."

"But if that were true, Sir," pondered Stan, "then why did he leave more clues? I mean, the Shakespeare poem and those words on the toothpaste jar?"

"Exactly," rejoined Mister Barker. "The fact is that our quest is not at an end, even if the clue writer has apparently made his escape."

"Which means," reflected Stan, "that if it wasn't himself that he wanted Bray to find, then it must be his booty. Is that it?"

"That or some other cunning twist, Johnson. And I am sure that we are close."

"So where do we look next, Sir?" asked Fred plaintively. "I mean, we've been all over the blinking place already and we just keep getting told to go somewhere else."

"You go to the Priory: to the ruins of the Priory of Saint Sepulchre in Warwick. It is the closest thing to a nunnery that we came across on the local maps, and it is to a nunnery that Shakespeare invites us to repair."

"You remembered the line then, Sir?"

"Not exactly, Johnson. I remembered that Mister Ferguson had included the works of Shakespeare in the barge's library and Frankie was kind enough to retrieve it for me last night."

"So...?" Fred was too baffled to even try to finish his sentence.

"So, Parker, we turn to Dante and to the cunning use of the toothpaste jar. You will recall that the short quotation hidden thereupon is taken from *The Inferno*, Dante's extraordinary description of Hades, or hell as we more commonly refer to it. Or, indeed, the underworld." He paused for effect.

"I must have murmured that particular word out loud last night," he went on, "for suddenly, against all expectations to the contrary, Mister Middleton made a decisive and most brilliant contribution."

"Middleton?" enquired Stan, amazed.

"Indeed, yes. As soon as I uttered the word *underground*," explained the teacher, "Mister Middleton gave forth a most interesting monologue on the legend of Warwick's tunnels; of an ancient network of subterranean passageways, supposedly linking the medieval castle to a number of key sites around the town. It transpires that local people have talked of such tunnels for centuries, but few have ever actually visited them. Luckily for us, one of those few turns out to be Jacob Middleton, who not only came across an entrance to the tunnels as a child, but was able to locate it upon a map last night."

The teacher's discourse halted and he drew breath, his good eye glinting in the gloom of the shed. "It is not a nunnery that guards the entrance to the underworld, boys, but a priory! Or at least, what remains of a priory."

A clattering of hooves and iron-shod wheels traversed the farmyard and the exposé came to a temporary end. It was the ancient pairing of horse and gig from the previous night.

"Ah. Excellent," exclaimed Mister Barker rising stiffly from the makeshift bench. "Right on time."

The boys followed their teacher out into the yard to stand a few paces behind him. The horse stamped at the cobbles, snorting. Young Doran softly clicked his tongue. Mister Barker approached the gig and placed his good hand on the armrest of the seat, close to the patched elbow of Young Doran's coat.

"The boys will be ready to join you here at 9.15, Frankie, and you should go at once to The Priory. Duggan, one of the older boys, will join you there by bicycle, though he knows nothing of the tunnels nor the trail of clues that have led us to this point. I have simply told him that we may need him to run an errand for us. Therefore, if circumstances warrant - as we discussed last evening - you are to instruct him to go straight to the police station and summon help. I have informed him of its location."

Young Doran nodded his acknowledgement. Stan could hardly believe his ears. Police station? Circumstances? What on earth could Mister Barker have in mind? The teacher turned towards the boys as if reading Stan's mind.

"Nothing to alarm you, of course: merely a precautionary measure on my part."

Stan gulped. Mister Barker proceeded with his instructions.

"Upon arrival at The Priory, your first task will be to locate an entrance to the tunnel system. This is bound to be well hidden, although Jacob clearly remembers it being in a hollow beneath a grassy mound, topped by a large stone or boulder. Whatever you do, try not to be observed. It would be unhelpful, to say the least, were you to attract the attention of onlookers at this juncture."

Stan glanced at Fred. Mister Barker took a deep breath and addressed the barge boy in a serious tone. "Frankie, you must do your level best to keep these young men safe. Take no unnecessary risks and be sure to leave somebody on guard at the entrance should the tunnel system be found."

Young Doran fixed his pale eyes upon the teacher. "I will not let you down, Master Barker."

"I know that you will not, Frankie. Thank you." He patted the barge boy's arm then handed him the file of papers. "Here are the maps and documents that I hope will be of assistance to you. I have marked the possible location of Jacob's hollow on the Warwick town plan. Separately, I have listed out all of the clues and written down the main conclusions that may be drawn thus far."

Young Doran nodded once and stowed the file beneath the seat cushion.

"Now," continued Mister Barker, "you had best look sharp about collecting Mrs Prescott or you will be late back. Rendezvous here with Johnson and Parker at 09.15 hours."

Young Doran bowed his head once more, clicked his tongue and flicked the reins. The gig creaked slowly around and clattered out of the yard onto the road to Hatton. Mister Barker turned back to the wide-eyed Stan and Fred.

"Are you two sure that you are happy to pursue our quest?" he asked quietly. "There may be dangers ahead that I am quite unable to foresee and I would certainly not wish for you to act against your will in this affair."

"'Course we are, Sir," answered Fred calmly. "Haven't come this far to stop now, 'ave we Stanley? We're in for the whole show."

"Absolutely," confirmed Stan, his courage buoyed by Fred's confidence. "We're not pulling out now, Sir; not now we're so close."

"Very good. Then you must straightaway get back to camp and prepare for further adventures!" The gleam had returned to his eye. "Remember, Mister Pickup may be a little strict with you and the other boys will likely rib you, but I feel sure that it will be worth it in the end. Mrs Prescott has kindly agreed to help with my imagined extra fatigue duties, so we will be well covered in that department. Once the other boys have left to meet up with the charabanc at the road bridge, you should repair here and await Young Doran. The charabanc will visit the outlying sites of interest and is expected to deposit its cargo at 12.30 in the grounds of Warwick Castle. You would do well to be there ahead of times. I shall meet you there for a debrief."

Mister Barker was firmly back in officer mode and the boys were thrilled to be a part of his brigade. Or platoon, or whatever it was that a Captain commanded. They felt as elated as at any time on their quest.

"So," continued their leader, "if everything is clear...?"

"Absolutely, Sir," chimed Fred. "Crystal clear."

Stan's mind was in positive mode, too, but there was still one aspect of the whole affair that mystified him. Now would be a good time to ask...

"Sir? Where, I mean, how does Young Doran fit in?" He took a breath. "It's just that he seems to be, well, a big part of all this - and trusted by you, if you know what I mean - but we don't hardly know anything about him and, to be honest, Sir, he gives me the, er, that is to say he makes me a bit uncomfortable."

He paused, his heart beating fast from the unburdening. Mister Barker seemed to be smiling; perhaps. Stan glanced at Fred for support, but received only a stare in return. He lowered his eyes to his boot caps.

"A very fair question, Johnson," replied Mister Barker gently. "And one that you are perfectly entitled to ask." He paused. "I recognise that my relationship with Frankie may appear strange - surprising, even - and I do apologise if I have inadvertently sown seeds of doubt in your mind."

Stan raised his eyes to see the teacher looking earnestly back at him, eye patch and all.

"I have known Frankie all my life and I trust and respect him implicitly. My family has always looked out for him, in a manner of speaking, and taken care of him. It was my grandfather who secured employment for him with Cadbury Brothers, back in '79, when they moved their enterprise to Bournville. It was also the year that Frankie's sister entered service in my grandfather's household. She was still in my mother's service as recently as 1918, having been Housekeeper for more than twenty years, so you can see that family ties run deep. Now that his sister is retired she is able to spend more time with her brother which makes everything a good deal easier."

"Young Doran has a sister?" asked Fred incredulously. He had never imagined that such a thing could be possible.

"Indeed he has, Parker," replied the teacher with a knowing nod, "and I dare say that you were both very grateful to her for peeling the potatoes last evening!"

Fred was momentarily flummoxed. "Mrs Prescott?"

"Indeed."

"Well I'll be beggared," exclaimed Fred softly. "Who'd 'ave thought it?"

Stan was as amazed as his friend at the revelation. Not a bit of stuff after all then, but a caring sister, feeding and watering her brother even at work on the canal. He suddenly felt ashamed at having questioned his teacher at all. "I'm sorry, Sir," he apologised. "I really didn't mean to pry, but this does make everything so much clearer."

"Nonsense, Johnson. Entirely my fault." He smiled something that looked like a reassuring smile. "Now, be off with you both to breakfast. And be sure to return to the camp site with something that might usefully explain your protracted absence. Like a couple of pails of water, for example: for the latrines and the washing-up?" He indicated the tall pump behind the cow shed. "You have a most interesting morning ahead of you, but I shall not attempt to speak with you further of our adventure until you have safely returned from your mission. Good luck, boys, and God speed."

With that, he pivoted on his straight leg and limped off towards the camp site, leaving Stan and Fred to find two serviceable buckets and to reflect together upon the latest twist to their adventure.

Back at camp, Duggan was in the latrines, ostensibly shaving, but frozen in thought before the tarnished mirror. Chops lathered, razor in hand, he was struggling to comprehend just how Pegleg knew so much about everything. Coley burst in on his rumination.

"Or-right, Bill?" he greeted cheerfully. "How'd your night go, then? D'ya give 'er one?"

"What?"

"Yer bird. Did you give 'er one?"

"Leave it out, will you? It's not like that. *She's* not like that. Not at all."

"Oh, really? What *is* she like then?"

"None of your business what she's like. But she's not like that. Oright?"

"Blimey! Sorry I spoke. What's got you so rattled this morning?"

"Nothing. Just tryin' to 'ave a shave."

"Ahh."

"And Peg-Leg's gone an' given us extra fatigues." This seemed to Duggan the best way to change the subject whilst at the same time explaining his grumpiness. Coley bought the line.

"Bastard! What's 'e gone and done that for?"

"Something about slackin' yesterday."

"Bastard."

Down at the barge, Mister Phipps was spooning tea from a caddy into the urn when Bushell and Hendry arrived to collect the trestle tables.

"Mornin' Mister Phipps," boomed Bushell with exaggerated bonhomie. "All good?"

"Blast," wheezed the assistant quartermaster, "You've gone an' made me lose me place countin'."

"Won't make any difference," reassured Hendry impassively, reaching for one end of a trestle table. "Tea can't taste any worse than it usually does, Mister Phipps. Nobody'll notice."

Bushell grabbed the other end and they meandered off up the bank together in Indian file. Mister Phipps resumed his teaspoon count, grumbling expletives.

Mister Pickup was directing operations in the breakfast area but having to make do with the tiny Morris as his only helper.

"Really. This just won't do. Where on earth *are* they all?"

"Dunno, Sir," panted Morris, his slight frame buckled around the bench he was dragging into place. "Perhaps they've bin kidnapped by Injuns."

"Kidnapped by Indians? What on earth are you talking about, Morris? For goodness sake."

"Well, you never know, Sir."

Reinforcements, if not the cavalry, arrived in the shape of Bushell and Hendry, cresting the rise at either end of a trestle table with all the energy of a dormant mouse.

"Get a move on, for goodness sake! Come on! Come on!" Mister Pickup was increasingly agitated by the thought of the charabanc arriving before breakfast had been cleared away. "We really do have to be getting on. Where *are* the others?"

Two of the others were at that precise moment staggering beneath the weight of their sloshing water buckets, closing in on the latrines:

"But I still don't get why he was talking about the police," gasped Fred. "D'you reckon we've done somethin' wrong and he's gonna shop us?"

"Don't be daft, Fred. He's not going to shop us. Not when he could have done it ten times already. And definitely not by asking Duggan to do his dirty work."

"Not happy about 'im being involved neither," complained the panting Fred. "He's gonna want a share of the booty, I'm tellin' you."

Hardly had Fred finished his gripe than Duggan exited the latrines ahead of them, striding off towards the tent without offering a glance in their direction.

"He's gone a bit doolally since yesterday," observed Stan as they headed for the canvas screen. "Don't you think?"

"He's in love, isn't he. Bloody lump. Fallen right in up to 'is neck."

"And over," chortled Stan. "Listen, why don't you take your bucket down to the barge for the washing-up and I'll drop mine off here? You're getting on so well with Old Reid, after all."

Fred grinned as the two separated, circling the latrines and passing to the left of the breakfast preparations on his way down to the canal. Stan headed for the canvas flaps, bursting in and almost swinging his pail into Edgington, whom he found at the mirror, combing his horrible hair.

"Well, well," simpered His Awfulness, "If it isn't the camp school's number one crawler. Our very own teacher's pet." He pulled a fearful grimace. "Come to wash the shit off you nose have you, Johnson?"

"Get lost, Edgington."

"Ooooo! 'Get lost' it says. Is that the best you can manage, Bender?"

Stan was puce with rage. "You…you…bum, Edgington!!"

"Ouch! Oo! Oh that hurt! Arghhh!. Bum, eh!! Ha! Is that really the best you can do?" Edgington advanced a step and pushed Stan in the chest, circling around to his back. Stan wheeled around to face the yellowing black eye, fist clenched tight around the bucket handle.

"You really are a bum-boy in every respect, aren't you Johnson?" sneered the hideous one. "Can't even swear properly can you, you stupid……ahhh…." He broke off abruptly.

Stan felt a hand on his shoulder. "Allow me, Johnson?"

Coley deftly skipped around Stan and grabbed the fast retreating Edgington firmly by the throat. "Now, Edgington," he snarled, "you 'orrible little shite. Looking to pick a fight, are we?"

Edgington squirmed, half strangled.

"Any particular point you'd like to make right now?"

The spluttering victim was turning puce. "Let me go, Coley" it gasped. "You're stranglin' me! I'm, I'm sorry!"

Coley let go, ejecting Edgington from the latrine with a two handed shove that sent him yelping and cartwheeling a dozen yards into the field.

"And don't bother 'im no more, Edgington, or I'll have yer balls for window ornaments."

"Thanks, Coley," breathed Stan as Edgington slithered off towards the breakfast area. "But where on earth did you come from?"

"'Aving a crap, wasn't I. Heard him blathering. Good job I'd finished, an' all or 'e'd 'ave 'ad more than just me hands to deal with."

"Yes, well." Stan preferred not to imagine. "Really good of you, Coley. Thanks."

"'S'oright, mate. 'E won't bother you again."

Coley proffered a friendly slap on the shoulder and left for his tea and porridge. Stan exhaled hard and placed the water pail beneath the wash stand. Straightening up, he caught sight of his own sunburned features and tousled blond hair in the mirror and almost failed to recognise himself. He took a step closer and peered into the silvery glass.

"Crikey!" he said aloud. "What a blinkin' adventure this is!"

16

INTO THE UNKNOWN

Excitement permeated breakfast, the impending charabanc ride fuelling conversation around the trestle tables. Bedlow was almost beside himself with joy at the prospect.

"Imagine," he bubbled. "A whole day on the road!"

"Let's get the back seat," implored Armstrong. "Me Uncle Tommy says its the best place for pulling birds."

"Wow, yeah," purred Bedlow, entranced.

Mister Pickup waited for the last spoonful of porridge and jam to be scraped from the enamel bowls before rising to speak. He cleared his throat.

"Ahem. Pay attention, boys. Settle down." His tone was grim. "On this fine expeditionary morning, it grieves me to have to report that a number of our number have failed to live up to the work mantra that Cadbury Brothers has sought to install in each and every one of us."

The background hum dissipated. Had somebody run away? Died, perhaps?

"Fatigues duty must always be taken with the utmost seriousness," he continued, "and to be performed diligently by everyone concerned. All hands to the deck, so to speak." He paused a grave pause.

"Unfortunately, Mister Barker has reported to me that three of our number, whom I will not name, have seen fit to shrug their responsibilities in this regard and to underperform their duties." A collective intake of breath punctuated the teacher's recital. "Duggan, Johnson and Parker, therefore, will not be joining us on the charabanc this morning."

Heads span around to stare at the guilty parties. Edgington snorted his glee. Stan fixed his eyes on the grass between his boots. Fred's ears glowed red in the ensuing ruckus of collective disbelief.

"Settle down, boys. Hey, hey: come along now. Settle down. Settle down. What's done is done. Let us not sink to derogative behaviour. We all have a full morning ahead of us and we need to press on quickly with tent inspection before departure. If the three unmentionables make up for wasted time in time, they will join us for dinner at Warwick Castle, but I'm afraid that we need to press on without them. For now, let us concentrate on tent inspection followed by a punctilious departure from camp."

The boys clattered off to tidy their belongings, Edgington keeping well to Coley's blind side in order to launch a volley of foul hand gestures towards Stan, who ignored them. Duggan trudged back to B tent with none of his customary leadership swagger. His body and mind were in turmoil: his heart aching for the beautiful Kate, his stomach tied in a knot. And now that idiot Parker and his mate had landed him in it with Pegleg. How the blazes did he know about the bike?

"Oi, Bill. Get your arse in gear, will you, or your lot are gonna drop you in the shit on inspection an' all." It was the cheerful Coley, passing him at a lollop on his way to shake up C tent. "They're all over the place, mate. Only the shrimp's turned up."

Duggan lifted his eyes to see Morris grappling with the heavy side flaps, valiantly attempting to secure their unfurling length with a canvas tie. He was bathed in perspiration.

"Where's the others?" growled Duggan.

"Jankers, Duggan," panted the shrimp. "At least, s'posed to be."

Duggan wheeled round to check the field behind him and caught sight of Hendry and Bushell, one at either end of a table, descending the slope to the barge at snail's pace.

"Get a bloody move on, will you," shouted Duggan across the field, "or you'll cock this up for us an' all."

"Language, Duggan," implored Mister Pickup from close by. "Language, please! I have every intention of making B tent my last inspection of the morning, what with so many of your number being on extra fatigues and the like, so you will have plenty of time to make everything spick and span for me, now won't you?"

In the end, B tent performed poorly at inspection, garnering several "tuts" and a plaintive "this will not do" from Mister Pickup, but the ordeal passed off soon enough and departure hour was upon them. The excited throng tumbled down to the towpath and raced towards the road bridge. Pandemonium briefly erupted as Bedlow, performing an unheralded u-turn, hurtled back along the path into the onrushing crowd to retrieve something from his tent, but order was swiftly restored.

At precisely nine o'clock, twenty-two campers and two staff members lined up before the shuddering, belching Thornycroft motorised conveyance, its curved coachwork resembling a painted boat on wheels, with seven doors along the sides - one for each row of wooden seats - and a snout-like bonnet protruding beyond the windshield to the front. The high rear of the vehicle housed a canvas hood in case of rain and was emblazoned with the legend "Ivan Hayes Tours". Mister Pickup had no doubt that he did.

"Climb aboard, chaps," he yelled above the din of the motor, "and sit where you will. Keep your feet off the seats and refrain your fingers from grubby marks on the paintwork. Mister Barker and I will sit up front with the coachman."

In the ensuing scramble for places, Armstrong was ejected clear out of the far side of the vehicle and onto the road. Somebody trod on Morris's thumb and a boy called North broke his glasses and started to bleed from the bridge of his nose. Coley elbowed his way through the rearmost door to sit beside Ironmonger and Clarke at the back and there was briefly a pushing contest towards the middle where five boys were trying to fit into four spaces.

"Order! Order!" shouted Mister Pickup. "We're not Fred Karno's Circus, you know. A little order, please."

Order, indeed, was resumed, with boys slotting into place like dominoes in a box. By the time the hapless Armstrong made it back to the kerb, only two spare seats remained and both of them were next to Edgington.

Stan and Fred watched their departure from the barge, scrubbing at the porridge pot with wire wool and scouring powder before swilling with sud-less water from the tub. Only when Mister Reid was entirely content that their work was up to scratch were they allowed to race off to the farmyard and their imaginary extra fatigues.

Young Doran was already there, standing erect beside the horse's head, clothed in his heavy smock coat though the sun's heat bounced off the cobblestones. Duggan was waiting, too.

"Would either of you two dollies mind telling me what's going on?" His tone was aggressive. He rose from an upturned milk pail and advanced menacingly towards them, meeting them beside the gig.

Fred squared up to the oncoming tent commander, fists clenched. "I might ask you the same question, Duggan," he said bravely. "Nobody asked you to join in anyway."

"Barker asked me," snarled Duggan, toe to toe with Fred but four inches taller. "An' who d'you reckon told him about me bike then?"

"'S'not your bike, Duggan. Belongs to Kate. An' what are you incinerating anyway?"

"That you told him, Parker, you fat snitch. Who else would?"

Fred took half a step back and launched a haymaking right fist in the general direction of Duggan's left ear just as his opponent made a grab for Fred's throat, but neither blow landed. Instead, extraordinarily, Young Doran caught Fred's wrist mid-flight with one hand, whilst depositing Duggan on his backside with a shove to the thorax from the other.

"Enough," he growled at the astounded combatants.

Fred stifled a yelp of pain and flexed his wrist to check that it was still connected to his arm. Duggan, winded, gulped for air like a beached fish. Stan decided that now would be a good time to speak:

"Pack it in the both of you, will you?" he implored. "We've got too much going on to waste time bashing the living daylights out of each other." He took a deep breath. "Duggan, I'm sorry if all this seems a bit strange, but if Mister Barker wants you involved then you're going to have to trust him. We're none of us too sure what's going to happen: we just know we've got to follow it through to the end. Right?"

Duggan shook his head. "But follow what to the end, Johnson?" he panted. "I've no idea what you're on about. Why aren't you on the charabanc with the others? And why've I got to go to the police station if he says so?" He indicated Young Doran with a nod of his head.

"Because Mister Barker says so. Listen, you're part of it now, so just do as they say and it'll all be over by dinner time."

Duggan made as if to speak but no words came out. He suddenly felt very tired. Fred filled the void with a sideswipe:

"If you hadn't stolen her bike, this would never have happened and we'd 'ave all been better off without you."

Duggan scrambled to his feet, fuming. "I've told you, Parker, I didn't steal..."

"Enough!"

"Let's go, Fred," said Stan quietly, climbing into the gig. "We really don't have time for this."

He waited until Fred had settled in beside him before addressing Duggan once more. "Follow behind on the bike and I promise I'll tell you more when we get there."

Young Doran led the horse around to the farmyard gate and sprang up into his seat. He flicked the reins and the gig lurched forwards, pausing at the road before setting off at a clip down the hill towards Warwick. Duggan slouched off to retrieve the bicycle from the silage pen, scratching his head. His day was getting worse by the minute.

After a mile, the road levelled out and Young Doran let go his left hand from the reins to yank the file of papers from beneath the seat cushion, passing it to Stan. Amongst the maps and scrawled sheets was an extract from O'Brien's *Words On Warwickshire*, neatly torn from the camp booklet. The words "priory" and "outcrops" had been underlined several times in green ink. Stan nudged Fred and held the paper towards him so that they could both read the extract:

As the Great Western Railway line approaches Warwick station from the north it traverses an embankment at the north-eastern edge of what was once the garden of the ancient priory of Order of Saint Sepulchre. The priory stood as a place of reflection and prayer in Warwick for over 400 years, but was surrendered and forcibly closed down in 1536 during Henry VIII's dissolution of the monasteries. The grounds then became a private estate wherein Thomas Fisher built a splendid house in 1566, siting it on the low sandstone hill once occupied by the priory. Henry Wise, Royal Gardener to no less than three monarchs, purchased the estate from the Puckering family in

1709, but in 1851 it was sold by his descendants to the Oxford Junction Railway Company. Today, ownership is unclear and the estate is run down. The great house still stands, but nothing remains of the ancient priory save for a few remnants of masonry, scattered about like rocky outcrops, preserved by successive owners as testament to the estate's medieval origins.

"See that?" groaned Fred to his friend. "Private. We've got no chance of getting in, yet alone finding anything. And that would be assuming the priory's still standing. Which it isn't."

"Why d'you reckon Barker's underlined 'outcrops'?" asked Stan. "D'you reckon he means the stone he was talking about just now? You know, the one from Middleton's stunning revelation." He was still finding it hard to believe the lock keeper capable of anything approaching coherent thought.

"Has to be," affirmed Fred enthusiastically. "A hollow under a mound topped by a stone."

"Might be. Seems as good a place to start as any."

They swayed left as the gig swerved right and passed beneath the railway bridge. Three hundred yards behind them and closing fast, Duggan dipped his head into the breeze and clung tight to the shuddering handlebars. Whatever plot these clowns were hatching, he was damned sure he was going to be part of it.

Young Doran steered into Priory Road and brought the horse to a walk. To their left, a stone wall topped by iron railings separated the good burghers of Warwick from the scruffy grounds of the priory and the house on the hill, itself dilapidated and run-down. Whoever owned the place had clearly invested little in its upkeep.

"Woah, girl."

The gig halted by the low kerb and Stan stowed the papers back in the manila folder. Ten seconds later, Duggan dismounted beside them breathing hard.

"Blimey! You were goin' a bit, weren't you? You better not 'ave bust 'er bike."

"I'm warning you, Parker," gasped the perspiring cyclist. "And it won't be 'er bike I'm busting neither."

Young Doran descended from the gig and the bickering ceased. He headed off up the road towards a sign marked *Priory Nursery*. Stan turned to Duggan.

"The thing is, see: we've been following a series of clues for two days and we think we're nearing the end. You know, like we might be close to finding something: treasure, maybe. Whatever it is, Mister Barker has helped us unravel it all and we trust him to know what he's doing. If he's got you involved, there must be a good reason, so let's not keep falling out about it, alright?"

Duggan dragged his stare away from Fred's glare. "To be honest, Johnson, I'd 'ave miles preferred to be having a smoke on the back seat of the charabanc with me mates instead of acting out some stupid kids' game with you and your irritating twat of a friend. But seein' as how I'm 'ere - and I still 'aven't quite worked out how I *am* 'ere - will you for Christ's sake give me somethin' more useful to do than 'ave me hang around like a spare prick at a wedding on the off chance you might need the coppers?"

Stan saw both earnestness and fatigue in the tent commander's taut features. "Of course, Duggan," he replied kindly. "You can be one of us."

Stan glanced at Fred who appeared to be about to pop a blood vessel. "Put a lid on it for now, Fred, eh?" he suggested gently. "There's nothing to be gained from fighting with him and, who knows, we might even end up being glad he's 'ere."

Fred snorted a semblance of hateful contempt, but he was actually grateful for a reason not to enter into fisticuffs with Duggan. After all, he might get his blooming head kicked in, or worse. He took a deep breath.

"Oright. If you say so, Stan." He stuck out a grubby hand. "You're in, Bill."

The tension subsided and handshakes were exchanged all round. Young Doran returned with news.

"There's a gate at the back of the nursery," he announced. "Best way in."

Stan slapped Fred's shoulder, Duggan leaned the bicycle on its pedal against the kerb and Young Doran patted the horse's head.

"Wait on, girl," he whispered.

The four set off for the nursery and its rickety wooden stands of brassica plants, cut flowers, watering cans, garden trowels and hoes. An onion shaped man in a brown overall pushed a wheelbarrow full of marrows onto the pavement and positioned it carefully besides a stack of tomato boxes, its chalked sign pricing the contents at 2d each. He glanced towards the approaching delegation and nodded to Young Doran, signalling safe passage through the gate. Once inside the garden, the four spread out in detective fashion, each investigating the rocky outcrops within their own designated area. After barely five minutes, Fred's excited voice piped out a discovery:

"Over 'ere. I think I'm on it."

He had found an ancient lintel, lying on its side, embedded within a patch of briars atop a low rise. Picking his way carefully through the thorns, Fred had climbed the slope and was approaching the stone as the others hurried in from their various positions. When he reached it, he could see that the ground beyond dropped steeply away, bottoming out in a hollow some ten feet beneath his perch.

"Come round this side," he called to Stan, pointing down. "There's a cliff or somethin'."

Stan skirted the mound and arrived beneath Fred to face a crumbling sandstone bluff, fifteen feet wide, flecked with tufts of weeds and tiny flowers. He was standing in shade on the slope of an ancient sink hole. The air was cool. To the right, behind a patch of desiccated thistles, he spied a small, dark opening in the cliff, at ground level, like a tiny cave showing black against the ochre of the rock.

He swallowed hard. "You'd better get down here."

Duggan arrived first, swiftly followed by Young Doran, and together they stamped flat the dead thistles. Slowed by his prickly descent through the brambles, Fred was the last to arrive, but they were soon all huddled together on their knees, staring into a narrow tunnel that slanted downwards into darkness.

"Blimey! I'll never get down there."

"'Course you will, Parker. It opens up after a couple of yards. Look."

Fred peered into the dim opening and saw that Duggan was right.

"We'll need the lamp," announced Young Doran abruptly. "You: with me." He jerked his thumb at Duggan and set off on a direct course towards the gig. Duggan trotted obediently behind.

At the railings, the barge boy took off his heavy coat, folded it into a wad and draped it over the sharp tips of the bars. He then cupped his hands, as he had done at Gaveston's Cross, and propelled Duggan up his body and over the protected summit to drop down onto the pavement beside the horse.

"Chuck the lamp over the fence," he commanded, "then come back by the nursery gate."

Within five minutes they were all reunited at the tunnel entrance where Stan and Fred had been contemplating their imminent descent with growing apprehension. Young Doran loomed over them to stare into the hole. He knew at once that he would never be able to squeeze down.

"I'll 'ave to stay put," he stated, lighting the lamp with a match. "Duggan, look after them in there, will you?"

"Of course." Duggan sounded more confident than he really was.

"I'll lead," said Stan, unexpectedly. A strange sense of calm had come upon him and he suddenly felt no fear. "Hold the lamp so I can see in," he commanded, cleaning his glasses with a grubby handkerchief, "and as soon as I can turn around in there, pass it down to me."

Crouching before the tunnel, he fixed his spectacles on his nose, took a deep breath and slithered in head first. Fred gazed open mouthed at the space where he had just been. Duggan took the lamp and held it at arm's length inside the tunnel entrance. All three listened intently - for a crash, or a cry or, well, anything - but they heard no sound.

As foreseen, the tunnel quickly broadened, but it also steepened dramatically. Before he knew it, Stan was accelerating headlong down a precipitous slope into the blackness, bumping along on his belly, eyes shut, arms outstretched like the antennae of a centipede. For a second or two he was almost vertical, heart in boots, wishing it would end, incapable of crying out, anticipating death in the bloody crash of flesh and bone against the unforgiving rock below. Strange how clearly he was thinking; how slow his rapid descent suddenly seemed; how his mother would grieve…. And then, just as quickly as his fall had begun, the sheer gradient levelled out and he came to a halt.

For several seconds he lay motionless in the invisible dust that enveloped him. His mind, so recently blessed with clarity, was now jumbled in confusion. How far had he fallen? How long had it taken? How would he get out?

Back at the surface, concern was becoming panic. Fred was white. Duggan's outstretched arm trembled. "Still can't 'ear nothing," he affirmed.

"See us the lamp," demanded Young Doran approaching the tunnel. Duggan moved aside and the barge boy peered into the gloomy shaft.

"I'm gunna go after 'im," decided Fred abruptly, his voice unusually high.

"Not likely," replied Duggan. "I'll go. I'm the one whose s'posed to be lookin' after the pair of you. Ask 'im."

Young Doran withdrew his head from the tunnel and looked from one to other. "Neither of you's goin' down," he said slowly. "We're all going to the police. Just like Master Barker would want."

"Hallooooaaa." Stan's voice echoed eerily from deep below their feet. Fred wheeled round and grabbed Duggan's arm.

"Stan? Stan? Is that you, mate?"

"No, you dimwit. It's Marley's ghost. Who'd you think it is?"

Fred beamed a Fred beam. "Blimey, Stan," he hollered down the hole. "You frightened the living shit out of us up 'ere. Where are you?"

"Down here, you lump. Where else would I be?" There were times when Fred's utterances were almost beyond belief. "Are you coming down or aren't you?"

"Of course I am. Was just waitin' for you to invite me!"

"Well come down feet first, then; and on your back, or you'll skin your knees like I 'ave."

Fred sat on the grass and swung his feet into the tunnel entrance.

"And bring the lamp down, will you? Can't see a blessed thing down here."

"Hang on, Parker," interrupted Duggan. "Not so fast. I'll take the lamp, if you don't mind; you follow."

"Why you?"

"Because I'm older 'an you."

Fred thought about arguing but he caught Young Doran's stare and changed his mind. "I'll be right behind you, Bill, so don't hang about. I'm clostafobier enough as it is."

Duggan took the lamp and clasped it against his chest, then launched himself feet first into the opening. Below, Stan could see the lamplight racing towards him in plenty of time to clear the landing area. He could also hear Fred's scream, growing in intensity and pitch as he hurtled after Duggan's light into the void. They arrived in a heap: Duggan, the gig lamp, Fred and approximately three hundredweight of sandstone shale. The tunnel roof had collapsed behind them, half way down.

The dust took a long time to clear; long enough for Fred to check that all his limbs were still attached and to attest to a sharp pain in the coccyx.

"Me arse," he wailed softly. "Me bloomin' arse!"

Gradually - eerily - the lamplight permeated the sandy air to reveal a narrow, high-ceilinged cave in which they were now entombed. Stan picked his way through the debris to peer up the shaft by which they had arrived, but any hope of spying daylight beyond the fall of earth was quickly extinguished. They were trapped.

"We're trapped," he confirmed. "Blocked in." He felt strangely unafraid.

Duggan scrambled to his feet, still clutching the flickering lamp, and took a look for himself. "Bollocks," he corroborated.

Fred sniffed back a whimper of panic and stood up, gingerly. "What we gunna do then?"

Stan was gazing to the far end of the cave, into the murk beyond the range of their light. He was thinking about what Jacob Middleton had said to Mister Barker about tunnels and was wondering why they might exist at all. If they really were in a tunnel, he mused, rather than just a big hole in the ground, then wouldn't it have to lead somewhere? Somewhere else? He swallowed hard and turned back to the others.

"We're going to find what we came for," he informed them quietly, "and then we're going to find our way out. Right?"

"Right!" Fred's relief was palpable.

Duggan was less sure. "Hang on, Johnson. The roof's fallen in, we're blocked in down a soddin' big hole with a wonky lamp and you want us to be lookin' for whatever trinket it was you came down for? Don't you think we'd be better off digging our way out the way we came in before we run out of air?"

"We'd be wasting our time, Duggan," answered Stan calmly. "Our air, too." He was amazed at how clearly he was seeing things. As though he was still in that slow motion fall down the shaft. "The way out'll be that way," he nodded towards the far-off gloom. "And our treasure'll be there, too, I'm sure."

"Right," exclaimed Fred again, unable to find anything else to say, but bursting with admiration for his friend's confidence.

Duggan hesitated, weighing up the options. What if Johnson really was right? The way back did seem impossibly steep and he had no idea how far down they had slid to get there. And even if they could somehow scramble up towards the surface, they still had to get through the fall of sandstone with their bare hands. But then, what if Johnson was wrong and there was no other exit? They might never be found alive. He drew in his breath and exhaled slowly. What other choice did they have?

"Oright, Johnson. Your way it is, God help us."

He moved next to Stan and handed him the lamp. They gazed through its petering light to see a dip in the ceiling a few yards out, tightening the cave to a tunnel of about six feet high and four feet wide, funnelling off into blackness. Duggan shivered. Fred glanced behind him and saw their own grotesque shadows looming huge and menacing against the cave wall. He let out an involuntary yelp and grabbed Stan's arm.

"'S'oright, Fred," reassured his pal. "We'll be out in no time, you'll see. And we might even be rich an' all!"

17

ENTOMBED

They stood together, staring into obscurity, the dust settling around them. Stan brandished the gig lamp at arm's length and gazed beyond the visible, his mind clear. Eventually, he led them off, Fred scurrying behind, Duggan bringing up the rear, three hearts pumping as the light bounced weirdly off the walls ahead. They advanced at a walk: the ground beneath their feet compacted. Nobody spoke.

The dimensions of the tunnel remained constant, but after four or five minutes of level progress they encountered a rise in the ground. Momentarily, Stan slowed, passing the lamp from right to left hand before pushing on up the slope, shortening his stride as the gradient increased. After fifty yards the sharp incline became a crude staircase, carved into the sandstone, which Stan attacked with élan. Behind him, Fred's breathing shortened to a staccato wheeze, but he ploughed on up the irregular steps, buoyed by the belief that travel in an upwards direction had to be good. Duggan was of the same mind.

"Johnson," he panted. "You were right. We're on our way out."

Stan did not reply. Ahead of the others and already on a broad landing at the top the stairs, he stood rooted, stock-still, in front of a huge and forbidding gash across their path: a crevasse, perhaps twelve feet wide and the Lord only knew how deep.

"S-s-s-stop," he stammered, just in time. "Stop where you are!"

Duggan piled into the back of Fred who stumbled to his knees.

"Bloodyell, Bill!"

"What's up?"

"Hole," replied Stan in a whisper. "'Normous hole. Right in front of us."

The lamp flickered like a magic lantern show. Duggan eased past Fred on the steps and came to a halt beside Stan to peer over the edge into the void. Fred arrived a few seconds later.

"Now, why would you go to all the trouble of chipping out a load of steps upwards," he chattered, nervously, "only to find there's a blinking big 'ole goin' straight down again?" He leaned over for a better look, dislodging a flurry of small stones with his boot and scattering them noiselessly into the abyss.

"Holy shit," pronounced Duggan. "You can't even 'ear 'em land. Must be a mile deep."

"Depth don't worry me so much as the width," observed Fred, swallowing hard. "I mean, how we gonna get across?"

Stan stood petrified, six inches from the edge, held by the downward lure of his vertigo. At length, knees shaking, he forced himself to shuffle one pace backwards and heaved a sigh.

"You alright, Stan?"

"Not really."

"Height thing, is it?"

"Could say that."

"Me Aunty Ivy gets that. Can't hardly even sit on an 'igh stool no more without 'aving a turn. Gets worse the older you get, an' all."

"Thanks."

"You might want to see a quack about that when we get out of 'ere"

"Have you finished?" interrupted Duggan "We do 'ave more important things to worry about than your Aunty Ivy's dizzy spells."

"Like how we get across?" volunteered Stan in dread.

"Exactly. So what's the dynamic duo's next move, then?"

"*Three-o*, Bill," reflected Fred after a contemplative pause. "We're in this together, right? There's three of us now."

"What?"

"You wanted in, so now we're the dynamic *three-o*, right?"

"Trio," corrected Stan.

"Come again?"

"Trio. It's how you say three-of-something."

"Oh."

"Like a trio of musicians."

"If you say so."

"From *tri*. It's Latin." Stan seized at the educational angle in order to divert his mind from the vertical drop straight down. "You know, like at the beginning of triangle or tricycle. Get it? Trio, triangle, tripod… They've all got three things to 'em."

"Yes, well. Like I said, Stan: if you say so. But can we…"

"Trifle," proclaimed Duggan abruptly, rising to the challenge.

"What?"

"Trifle. 'Aven't you never heard of trifle, you morons? Thing you eat on birthdays?"

"Yes, of course, but I'm not quite…."

"Got three things in a trifle."

"Really?" Fred was intrigued. "Which three?"

"You don't know?" Duggan was flabbergasted.

"Er…"

"'S'obvious. Cake, that's one. Custard, two." He paused in anticipation of triumph. "And prunes: three!"

The others were speechless: Duggan was pleased with himself. "Ask me another," he insisted.

"Can we concentrate on getting across?"

"Well you started it, Johnson."

"Yes, well maybe, but we can't waste our time talking prunes, can we? Need to get across."

A long silence ensued.

"That ladder might have been useful," suggested Fred, "'cept it's on the wrong side." He was looking at a triangular shadow on the wall on the other side of the gulf, to the left of where they stood.

The lamp spluttered again, its oil almost spent. Duggan's eyes widened. "Well! Who'd 'ave thought?"

"That's good," commented Stan to the surprise of the others. "That's very good - that it's over there, I mean."

"Not following you I'm afraid, Johnson. What's good about the ladder bein' on the wrong side?"

"Because it means that someone probably used it to cross over there. See?"

"No."

"No?"

"No."

"If they got over," continued Stan patiently, "then they didn't come back this way, otherwise the ladder would be over here. Get it? Which means," he pursued, "that there must be a way out over there."

Duggan was not convinced. "What if they didn't come back because they just died? You know, without never finding the way out." Stan looked blank. Duggan pressed home his point. "There's nothing good about us being here and the ladder being over there, is there? Nothing at all. We're as good as bollocksed, if you ask me."

A contemplative silence ensued, before Fred calmly proposed a solution. "You could jump it, Bill, then set the ladder as a bridge for us to cross." He turned to face him.

Duggan blanched in the yellow light. "Are you mad, Parker? Jump it? You've got a screw loose."

"Weren't you the one who jumped the canal?"

"Lock, moron. I jumped the lock, not the bloody canal. Christ, Parker, 'ave you seen 'ow wide the canal is, by any chance?"

"Lock, then. But you jumped it, didn't you? And I bet it weren't far off being as wide as this 'ole."

"Not even 'alf as wide, and that's a fact. Jesus, Parker! Are you trying to get me killed?"

"I reckon," ventured Stan after a period of tense silence, "that it's definitely wider than the lock."

"Told you."

"But jumpable."

"Really? Well not by me, Johnson. Jump it yourself. I'm goin' back the way we came."

"Then you're gonna be down here for a long time, aren't you?"

"What d'you reckon, Stan?" enquired Fred, peering towards the other side. "Ten feet? Eleven, maybe?"

"'Bout that."

"Then, blimey Bill! You *must* be able to jump that! What about last Bournville sports day? You won every blinkin' medal going and the long jump's got to 'ave bin one of 'em."

"It was and I didn't," responded Duggan coldly. "Hendry won it. Lanky streak of piss. Did seventeen foot nine to my seventeen."

"Seventeen foot? Well there you are, Bill. What did I tell you? You could stroll over it and not break sweat. Come on now. What d'you say?"

"Still no." He studied the leap nonetheless. "I'd have no run-up, see? You'd need a run-up. Nobody jumps seventeen feet from a standing start."

"We're not asking you to jump seventeen feet, Duggan," reassured Stan. "Just ten, or so. And we could give you a pull to get you started.

You know, like a slingshot, one on each arm."

Duggan looked at the space behind him. Barely six feet to work in before the staircase fell away into blackness. It would give him three paces: if he was lucky. Three short strides, then push off from the very edge. Right foot take-off, left foot landing. It might just…

"Up yours, Parker!"

"Bill?"

"God help us." He drew a breath through clenched teeth. "Let's get on with it."

"That's a boy!"

"I'm not doin' it for you, Parker, you twat. Understand? It's just we don't appear to have no other choice." He paused to draw another calming breath. "Promise you'll tell Kate I love her if it all goes tits up?"

"Er, of course, Bill. But it's going to work out, you'll see. It'll be a cinch."

"Thanks, Duggan," said Stan, placing a hand on his tent commander's drooped shoulder. "It *will* be alright, you know? Fred and me'll give you such a tweak you'll be landed over there before you know you've even taken off."

His forced grin did little to conceal the doubt in his voice. Duggan shuffled to the crevasse and pawed his boot at the edge like a tired bull. He sighed once more, took two full strides backwards towards the stairs and looked over his shoulder to check his position.

"This'll 'ave to do," he said, with passable assurance. "Get your-selves set to give me a yank and then grab hold of me 'ands. We'll go on three."

And on three he went, propelled into space by two muscular strides and a lopsided yank that sent him off well to the left of his intended target to land, in a heap of expletives and a scream of pain, five yards from the ladder. The dust hung thick around his fall.

"Blimey, Stan! He's over!"

"Duggan? Hey, Duggan? You alright?"

"Me wrist. Arghhh."

"What about it?"

"I think I've broke me wrist."

"You sure?"

"No I am *not* sure, Johnson, but as I'm in fuckin' agony and I can't move the thing I would say that there's more than a sportin' chance that it's broke. Oright?"

"Gosh! Sorry, Duggan."

"Can you still pass us the bloomin' ladder, though?"

"Up yours!"

Duggan righted himself in agony and approached the ladder, his left arm dangling by his side, then pivoted it around on itself and lowered it, one-handed, over the gulf between them. The ladder settled into a makeshift bridge, with barely six inches of its length touching the ground at either end.

"D'you reckon it'll hold?" he enquired, adjusting his kneeling position with a wince. "Looks a bit short to me. You sure you wouldn't rather jump?"

"What? And end up crocked like you?" chirped Fred. "Not bloomin' likely. Ladder's safe as houses: trust me. You goin' first, Stan?"

"Nope."

"As you like." Fred hitched up his shorts and spat into his hands. "Hold your end steady, Bill. I mean, as steady as a bloke with one arm can 'old anything."

He grinned at Duggan over the gap and took up a start position on all fours, clasping the ladder stiles in his pudgy hands which he proceeded to slide carefully out across the emptiness. Inch by inch he slid them out along the ladder until the rest of his body was obliged to follow: right leg slanted inwards, knee cap overhanging the stile. He paused for balance, edged forward and pulled his left leg onto the opposite stile. The ladder trembled beneath his weight. He lifted his head to look at Duggan, clamped at his post, and exhaled loudly. No turning back. Stan tightened his grip.

Slowly, minutely, Fred advanced; foot by stressful foot. The ladder sagged beneath his weight, dragging the stile ends closer to the edge. His arms shook. He bowed his head and blew hard. A bead of perspiration dripped from his nose into the abyss. He glanced once more at Duggan, clinging for all his might and pain to the creeping ladder, and he knew. He knew, in that split second, that he was not going to make it.

"Get back, Fred," yelled Stan. "It's gonna slip......"

Stan's cry died as the ladder sank one final, critical inch and slipped from its anchorages, flexing to horizontal and flipping Fred over like a pancake - to fall, with the ladder, into the breach.

"Noooo! Fred!"

"Araaarrrgghhhhhhh!"

Above the screams, a dull thud. Then silence. Then a wail.

"Argghh. Me arse! Jesus! My aching arse."

"Fred?"

"Arggghhhh!"

"Fred? Are you... are you alive?"

"Ooohhhhhh, God Almighty! Broke me bloody arse, Stan. Again!"

"Parker, you twat!" shouted Duggan in relief. "How come you're not dead?"

"Me bloomin' arse is dead, I'm telling you." He spluttered and coughed for several seconds.

Stan grabbed the lamp and approached the edge. From the opposite side, Duggan scrabbled to lay flat on the ground and peer into the crevasse. Fred was lying on his back in a cloud of sandy dust, barely ten feet beneath them. He had landed in deep powder and was clutching his rear end in face-contorted agony. The ladder lay at his feet.

"Can you get up, Fred?"

"No."

"Try, at least, eh?"

"Stan, I could be parrylised."

"How come?"

"You know, broken me back or somethin'."

"Parker, get your arse up out of there before I come down and kick it out with you on the end of it."

"Steady, Bill. Bit of sympathy might be nice."

"Like what you gave me, you mean? Move it, Parker, and let's get out of this shit-hole."

"Prop the ladder up here, Fred," suggested Stan gently. "And I'll come down. We'll switch it over and climb out together on the other side."

Fred laboured to his feet and set the ladder for Stan's descent. The traverse proved to be a simple "down-and-up job," as Stan described it, as soon as they were all standing together on the other side.

"Yeah, well: there might 'ave been an easier way of finding the answer without me 'aving to fall in first." Fred rubbed his backside ruefully; Duggan held his left wrist close to his chest.

"Here, Duggan. Let's have a look at your arm." Stan inspected the injured appendage, prodding lightly at an area of swelling below the thumb.

"Oi, Johnson. Knock it off, will you. Bloody hurts, that."

"I don't think it's a sprain, Duggan. More like a break, I'm afraid. We should splint it."

"Oh yeah? Like with what?"

"What you got in your pockets, Fred? Anything straight? Like a ruler or something?"

Deep rummaging ensued, punctuated by snorts of pain, before Fred eventually produced a steel comb.

"A comb? I've never seen you use a comb".

"That's because I never have. I just keep it for flicking ink balls."

"Ah, right. Yes, well give it here then. And see us your hanky an' all."

Stan tore the handkerchief in two, held the comb against Duggan's straightened wrist and bound the two tightly together, finishing with a neat knot.

"Lovely job, Florence," grimaced Duggan. "Where'd you learn to do stuff like that?"

"Boys Brigade," answered Stan. "At church."

"Yeah, well thanks. Never knew the church was good for healing, but you learn something new every day, eh? What's next?" The lamplight fizzled to series of blinks before flaring brightly once more.

"We've got to get out of here quick or we'll end up with no light at all. Follow me."

Stan picked up the lamp and headed off along the tunnel, the others hard behind. They walked without speaking for two or three minutes before the tunnel veered sharply to the right. Stan adjusted his grip on the spluttering lamp and rounded the bend, keeping it close to the wall to better follow his course. No sooner had the tunnel straightened again than it suddenly ended, dead: blocked by a barred door. They halted, incredulous.

"It can't be." Stan took a few faltering steps. Surely, it couldn't be? Fred and Duggan held back.

"Is it locked?"

"Locked tight," whispered Stan after inspection. "Barred an' all."

It was another huge blow to their morale. Duggan attempted a half hearted shoulder charge at the obstacle, leading with his good arm, but bounced off with a grunt. Fred sat down cross-legged in front of the door and shivered. He looked as miserable as he felt. What now? Stan held the lamp close and studied the iron hinges, bars and girdles that bound the ancient oak. There were five horizontal bars, fixed in place at regular intervals by iron nails. The middle bar sported at its centre a round iron box, roughly six inches in diameter, topped by an ornate shield. Recessed hinges held the door plush to the wall and in such a perfect fit that not even a blade might be inserted. It gave Stan a thought.

"Fred," he whispered. "See us your knife, would you?'

Fred plunged into his pockets and pulled out a penknife.

"Got sumthin', Johnson?"

"Not yet."

Stan scratched and poked away at the central box for a full minute to no avail. Taking a half a pace back from the door, he forced the blade between shield and backplate of the central box in an attempt to lever the two apart. The knife snapped in his hand.

"Crikey. Sorry, Fred," he apologised. "Hope it wasn't valuable."

"Woolworth's finest, mate," grinned Fred. "Worth just north of bugger all. Don't worry about it."

They smiled briefly, but the door loomed massively over the boys' positive intent. Stan's spirits sagged. "Can't budge it," he declared after further trials. "Can't see a lock nor an 'andle." He sat down on the ground next to Fred and exhaled noisily.

"It can't just end in a door, Stan. A brick wall, maybe, or a rock, but not a door. A door means there's somethin' on the other side. We've got to go on. I mean, we must go on. Mustn't we?"

"Of course we've got to go on, Parker, you numbskull. But we're not gonna be able to unless we can open the bloody thing. Right?"

Duggan took a stride towards the door. He had been puzzling over the rod-like bar that ran from top to bottom, perpendicular to the others, passing through the central shield. What was it for? It clearly was not to strengthen or to reinforce. He ran his index finger along its length, upwards from the shield, until it disappeared into a snug hole in the stone above. "A bolt," he breathed to himself. "Double bolt; top and bottom."

His eyes returned to the shield device at the centre of the door where Fred's knife blade was planted in the crack that ran around the circumference. If Johnson couldn't lever it open, he reasoned, then maybe the thing would slide, or swing open, like the keyhole flap on the back door at home. He took careful hold of the shield in both hands and attempted to slide it to the left, without success. Then he tried to the right. This time it yielded easily, ejecting the knife and swinging upwards around a fixed point to reveal a bronze plate beneath, in the centre of which was an oblong indentation. The weak light made it difficult to discern its purpose, but its interior was intricately ridged and cold to the touch.

"Hold the lamp up 'ere will you, Johnson. I've found somethin' a bit peculiar."

As they peered at the horizontal notch, the hair on the back of Stan's neck stood up. He knew straight away what it must be: had to be. His right hand slid to his pocket, fingers closing around the metal object therein. He hardly dared bring it out. What were the chances?

"Fred? You know that cube thing?"

"Yeah."

"I think we've just found out what it's for."

Fred scrummaged in behind to take a look as Stan presented the face of the flattened cube to the slot, instantly feeling it tug at his fingers. It locked into place with a clack.

"Bloody 'ell," murmured Duggan. "A lodestone key!"

"Yeah. Blimey! What's a lodestone?"

"Magnet, Fred," elucidated Stan. "The one attracted the other. Can't just be made of brass, though. Pulled it right in, plush."

"Magnetite," intoned the awestruck Duggan. "Naturally magnetic metal. Read about it, but never seen anything like it before."

"Yeah," pronounced Fred once more. "Blimey. Now what?"

"Now we're gunna try and open the door, aren't we Johnson?"

Duggan nudged Stan, still staring incredulously at the brass plate. The key had fitted so perfectly into its hole that no trace remained. The metal was as smooth as silk. He ran his fingers over the surface, then swung the cast iron cover back into place and gripped the assemblage in two hands. He turned it a quarter to the left. With the softest of clicks, the bolts slipped their anchorages and the door swung into the darkness beyond.

They hesitated a long moment before entering, until Stan had summoned his courage anew and stepped through to the other side, the lamp at arm's length. The others followed close behind.

The impoverished light revealed a room of stone walls and flagstones beneath a vaulted ceiling. At the far end, perhaps thirty feet away, another door, apparently of identical construction to that through which they had just passed. In the far left corner, a narrow staircase spiralled up through the ceiling and to the right, against the wall, they could just make out a crude table, or altar, fashioned from a flagstone set upon two blocks of masonry. The light flickered dimly in the open space. It was hard to differentiate between form and shadow, but it seemed pretty obvious to all of them that something was lying on the altar: a length of material, perhaps, or could it be an ancient shroud? Stan gulped back his mounting fear and headed towards it, squinting for focus, but it was Duggan who saw first what it was.

"Jesus," he proclaimed. "Jesus H. Christ."

Laid out upon the stone like a desiccated fish skin was a wedding dress, complete with skeletal fingers at each sleeve and slippered bones for feet. The fabric was as dry as the human remains it contained, crumbling to the dust of the walls. Eerie shadows, translucent in the expiring lamplight, flitted across the empty satin form, stroking its sunken bodice, playing upon the fractured shoulders, revealing in absent contrast the bride's most gruesome truth: she had no head.

They stood petrified before the altar, staring and uncomprehending.

"What's it m-m-mean?" stammered Fred. "I mean, why's it here?"

"Why are *we* here?" asked Duggan in disbelief. "What kind of deep shit have you two got yourselves into?"

"Was never meant to be this, Bill," implored Fred, his voice cracking. "We thought we was on a treasure hunt. Honest."

Stan's emotions were in turmoil. He at once wanted to run away screaming, yet he felt compelled to take a closer look at the bridal remains. His knees knocked together like music hall spoons. Surely this couldn't be the end? Could it? Maybe it had nothing to do with their quest at all. Just a morbid coincidence. But then, wasn't a headless, withered bride in a wedding dress something you might find in hell? Or Hades? The clue did seem to foretell this and they had unravelled every clue until now. God, this was all so awful. There surely had to be a reason, otherwise the whole thing made no sense…. He took a deep breath.

"Can anyone see…?" He faltered. "Can you see something that might be another clue?"

The lamplight died, plunging them into blackness. The shiver of fear between them became a wave of outright panic. Fred clung tight to Stan's arm, except that it was Duggan's arm. Duggan clung back. They all clung to each other, hearts pounding; disoriented; in shock.

"Anyone gotta match?" asked Stan at length.

"Me," croaked Duggan, fidgeting within the huddle. "Hold tight. I'm not even sure I can find me pocket."

He winced as his bandaged wrist came into contact with someone's elbow. They shuffled around in a slow waltz, desperate to avoid touching the dress and whatever it clothed, eager to free up Duggan's access to his pocket. Finally, a box of *England's Glory* was retrieved and, after much fumbling and swearing, the bright yellow halo of an ignited match swelled around them. In that very second, Fred spotted the skull, impaled upon the blade of a broadsword to the left of the altar. His scream of terror caused the others to scream too, though neither knew why. They clung fast to each other again. The match expired.

"Bloody hell, Parker. What happened?"

"An 'ead. I saw an 'ead," he stammered. "A bonehead, you know? No skin nor face." They could both feel him trembling. "'Orrible, it was. 'Orrible."

"Where, Fred? Where did you see it?"

Fred's voice had gone; stolen by terror. He whimpered softly and began to cry.

"'S'oright, Parker. Take your time. Get yourself back together. There, now. Deep breaths: take a few deep breaths. That's it. When you're ready, tell us what it was."

Fred sniffed back his sobs. "Over there," he whispered at length, pointing into the dark. "Against the wall. L-l-left of the thing in the dress."

"Well done, Parker. Good." Duggan was fumbling for another match.

"It's alright, Fred," soothed Stan nervously. "We'll be alright." He felt like crying, too.

A flame flared. Duggan held the match above their heads. Fred closed his eyes. The broadsword stood on its handle, the blade leaning against the wall with the skull balanced lopsided at its tip, like a tired drunk, shining white in the yellow light. The eye sockets stared straight back, the jaw lolled, unhinged. Stan averted his gaze and almost vomited, catching sight as he did so of something sparkling on the floor near the handle. Duggan yelped and the match went out. They huddled together in the pitch black once more, trying to take in what they had just seen. Trying to rationalise the unthinkable. This was so far removed from a treasure hunt. This was… well… this was somebody's murder!

"We've got to get the police," said Duggan with forced composure. "We've got to find a way out and tell 'em."

Stan's nausea abated and a degree of clear thinking returned, though he shook like a leaf. If only he could retrieve the object he had seen on the ground beneath the skull. It had to be the reason for it all. An explanation. A clue, at least. There simply must be something more.

"How many matches d'you reckon you've got left, Duggan?"

"Four or five maybe. Then that's it."

"Light one of them for me and I'll see if I can get whatever's on the floor. Then we're out of here. Right?" Fred sniffed back another tear. "It'll be alright," Stan assured him. "She's hardly likely to jump up and attack us, is she?" He smiled weakly into the dark.

The match flared phosphorus bright and Stan darted from the scrum to fall to his knees at the base of the sword's cross shadow. An envelope came within his compass and he grabbed it, raising it to his spectacles for inspection. The thick paper was sealed with wax, the copperplate hand bold. The match burned out. "Damn."

Alone and on all fours, Stan could hear Fred's sniffing as Duggan struggled with the matchbox. One more would do it. God help us, one more would have to do it. They still had to get out of there. Brightness flared anew: his last chance. And there it was: a sparkling band around the base of the handle, twinkling yellow in the match's glow. He touched it lightly. Then, with both hands, he yanked the weighty sword handle six inches to the right to free the band. The skull toppled to ground with a *plock* and rolled onto Stan's fingers, just as the match died.

"Arrghhh!" He gasped for breath and steadied himself, planting his hands further away from his body, feeling the ring of jewels within the palm of his closed hand.

"Johnson?"

"Stan? You oright, Mate?" quavered Fred's voice. "Got anything? Eh?"

"Got something," he panted, the blood thudding in his ears. "Let's get out of here."

"Only two left, Johnson. Broke one. Which way's out?"

"Up. We've got to get to the staircase behind us and go up. The other door's useless without a key."

"Behind us? You sure?"

"Yes. Perhaps. Let's stick together, aim for the corner and be ready to move as soon as the match is struck. I mean, straight away. Right? And try not to break it."

At the glow of light they scurried across the flagstones, Duggan cupping the flame in his good hand as they made their way to the foot of the twisting staircase before another plaintive yelp heralded darkness. One left.

"Right," panted Duggan. "I'll go up first, but stay tight. We'll save the match. Hold on to me belt whoever's following me up."

"Can't we use the match now?" pleaded Fred.

"No way. We're hardly goin' to get lost on a spiral staircase, are we?"

"He's right, Fred." Stan's voice sounded calmer. "We'll probably have more need of light at the other end. You go on ahead of me."

They climbed the stairs in line, in darkness, wheeling slowly around. The soles of their boots scuffing abrasively on the sandstone steps; swooshing, swooshing round. Then a thud.

"Bollocks."

"Bill?"

"It's blocked. A roof or summat. Hit me bloody 'ead on it."

"Can you go on?"

"I've just told you, Johnson; it's blocked."

"Is it stone or wood? Feel it with your hand."

"Iron."

"Iron?"

"Yes. And bloody 'ard iron, an' all."

Stan was flummoxed. Dante's line about abandoning all hope rushed to mind. He swallowed hard. "Feel it again. Is it a door?"

"It's above me, Johnson, and it feels pretty bloody solid all over." They heard him grunt. "Can't budge it, neither."

Stan's mind was racing through their options. There appeared to be only one. "Use your match, Duggan, and take a look. It simply can't be blocked."

"I'm telling you, Johnson. It's as blocked as buggery up 'ere."

"Just do it, Duggan, for God's sake. It's our only chance."

The tension was wire tight. Fred actually came close to wetting himself. Stan's heart pounded like a steam hammer. Duggan fumbled the matchbox and fired the last lucifer, blinding in the confines of the stairwell and prodigious in its outpouring of sulphurous smoke. He scrutinised the cast iron plate with watering eyes and saw what Stan had hoped for: a simple bolt opposite an ancient pair of hinges. Tugging firmly at the bolt, he freed the fastening just as the match spluttered to black. Fred tightened his grip on the belt. Duggan steadied himself with a long exhale and pushed up with both hands against the door, levering it open. Light flooded in: relief welled up.

They scrambled upwards and out through a fireplace to find themselves in a brightly lit chamber with a black and white marble floor upon which they collapsed together in a clump of dusty adolescence: shaking, breathing hard and trying to determine exactly where they might be. It did not take long. As Stan readjusted his spectacles, a prostrate knight in bronze armour swam into focus. Fred, raising his nose to sniff back tears of relief, saw the familiar effigy at the same time. They looked at each other in disbelieving silence. How on earth…?

Stan glanced at the envelope in his left hand and raised the metal band up to the light, staring dumbly at the reflections that shimmered around its diamonds. He gazed at the object, awestruck, scarcely comprehending, not daring to imagine the fortune that it might represent. Silently, he extended his arm towards the others, inviting their wide eyes to make better sense of the extraordinary find. Almost immediately, the ringing clatter of hobnail boots snapped them out of incredulity and they swung round to face the staircase, by which access two uniformed police constables burst into the chapel, truncheons drawn.

"You lot from the Cadbury Camp School, then?" enquired the burliest of them.

"Er, yes. Yes, we are."

"Right. Yes. Well, we've been expecting you. At least, there's a bloke upstairs who said you'd be coming." The constable's bemused gaze bounced from the boys to the chimney to the jewelled tiara and back again. "God only knows how he knew," he continued. "But no doubt you'll be able to explain it all when we get you down the station."

He glanced at his fellow officer for support and scratched his bewildered head. The boys struggled to their feet, lining up like grubby accessories to Beauchamp's shining armour and awaited further instruction.

"This way," commanded the second constable. "Follow me."

They filed from the chapel between the policemen, stumbling weak-legged up the steps that Stan and Fred had descended so excitedly barely twenty-four hours earlier, to emerge into the sun-streaked nave. Here sat Young Doran, in the front row of chairs, unblinking eyes fixed on the ragged procession that advanced towards him. As Stan drew alongside, the barge boy dipped his head and tipped the peak of his cap. Stan slowed momentarily and strained a brief smile in reply, relief welling up. It suddenly, amazingly, felt very good indeed to see Young Doran again.

18

TYING THREADS

The boys watched the second hand tick and flop around the clock for the hundredth time: tick-flop, tick-flop, tick-flop. The air inside the room was stuffy, the barred window shut tight. Unwilling to rest his aching backside on the chair, Fred stood against the painted wall, his famished insides rumbling counterpoint to the flop-ticking clock. Behind the brown door, the hum of conversation droned on as it seemed to have done for hours. Why was it taking so long? Fred shuffled to the window to peer between the bars at the black bricks opposite, then returned to lean against the wall. Stan cracked his knuckles. The clock crowded in. Fred set off for the window once more.

Eventually, the door yelped open and Mister Ferguson emerged, dapper in Harris tweed and brown brogues, followed by the limping figure of Mister Barker clutching a sheath of green-inked pages. Stan stood up. Behind the teachers, Inspector Latchford was talking.

"...as I said, an international manhunt will begin immediately and I am confident that this new evidence will ensure that our man is brought swiftly to the gallows. The whole Savage family will be eternally grateful to you… and to your boys, of course. Ah, indeed, and here they are!"

The inspector turned a patronising smile on Stan and Fred and addressed them as five year olds. "Very well done, boys! I shall be sure to ask Mister Cadbury to give you extra rations of chocolate for your efforts!"

He chortled to himself as if he had just cracked the funniest joke in Warwickshire. Stan nodded politely back: Fred glared. Prick.

"I have no doubt, Inspector," responded Mister Ferguson calmly, "that the whole firm will reflect upon the recent discoveries with due pride, once the facts become more widely known. But first, I shall take it upon myself to brief Mister George Cadbury on all that I have learned here this afternoon."

He turned to his young teacher. "There are elements to this story, Mister Barker, that continue to elude my comprehension and others about which I desire to learn nothing at all: the late night absences from camp, for example?"

"Of course, Mister Ferguson." The teacher inclined his head.

"As for you two," the Principal honed in on Stan and Fred. "It is just as well that your total disregard for the rules and regulations of Camp School has resulted in such valuable assistance to His Majesty's police force." He ignored the enthusiastic nodding of the inspector behind him to pursue his admonishment. "Any other outcome may well have landed you in distinctly hot water."

"Yes, Sir," they mumbled.

He studied each of them for a moment, before his grave countenance melted to a smile. "You have done very well, boys. Very well indeed."

"Thank you, Sir."

"Now, I must away and give a helping hand to Mister Pickup at the castle. The poor chap has been holding the fort since dinner and I imagine will be pulling his hair out. I shall leave it to Mister Barker to fill in whatever gaps remain in your understanding of events before we meet again at supper."

He turned to Inspector Latchford, whose hand he shook in farewell, retrieved his hat from the stand in the corner and departed into the afternoon bustle, whereupon the inspector, pronouncing his own goodbyes, retreated to his office and closed the door.

"Well, well," exclaimed Mister Barker. "Who would have thought it? Goodness me. Goodness me."

"Sir?" ventured Stan apprehensively. "Do you think that we might...that is, would you mind explaining what the, er..."

"Of course, Johnson. Of course. But first, shall we repair to a more suitable venue? I couldn't stand one more minute in this dreadful place."

"Me neither," agreed Fred.

The three of them made their relieved exit into the street and sunlight. It was a moment before they spotted Duggan, his arm pinned up in a linen sling, and Young Doran, standing beside him on the opposite pavement.

"Surprised they let you out, Parker," called Duggan across the street. "Lost your records, 'ave they?"

"Yeah? Well I'm surprised they didn't keep you in the 'ospital, an all," responded Fred with a grin. "Haven't they got a looney wing then?"

Within a few minutes they were seated together around the window table in Market Tearooms where Mister Barker ordered cakes and a huge pot of tea. For the first time in hours the boys began to relax and feel more cheerful about life. Fred launched himself upon a slice of chocolate sponge. Mister Barker drew three sheets of inky foolscap from his folder and laid them on the table.

"Well! Who would have thought it?" he exclaimed once more. "What an extraordinary day!" He looked from Stan to Fred and back again. "You did very well this afternoon, boys: very well indeed. I cannot say that the Inspector made life easy for you with his inane questioning, but I am proud of the way you responded and I know that Mister Ferguson is, too."

Stan shuffled on his chair and averted his eyes. Fred grinned sheepishly, his cheeks bulging with cake.

"The four of you have contributed greatly towards the solving of a murder that has remained a mystery to the police for almost ten years. Not only have you discovered the remains of the victim, but you have also been able to provide irrefutable evidence of the perpetrator's identity and motive through the contents of the envelope that you retrieved. Inspector Latchford's subsequent exposé of background facts has enabled me to pull together the loose ends of this extraordinary tale."

They hung upon his words in rapt attention, even when more cakes arrived.

"The remains that you discovered beneath the Beauchamp Chapel," Mister Barker pronounced once the tea had been poured, "were those of Lady Dorothy Ethel Savage, direct descendent of the Beauchamp family of Warwickshire and last seen alive in her home at Wootton Hall on June 30th, 1912. It is believed that she was killed the following day. The letter that you discovered at her resting place proved to be the last piece in the puzzle upon which we have been engaged for three days. It was written and signed by the same hand that we saw on the note from Gaveston's Cross."

He paused to smooth out a sheet of foolscap on the table and to fit a monocle to his good eye.

"Inspector Latchford has obviously retained the letter, but I was able to make a copy of the salient aspects for our benefit. It leaves the identity of the perpetrator in no doubt, for it is no less than a signed confession by the murderer himself."

Fred allowed a morsel of sponge cake to fall from his mouth onto the table.

"And the murderer," continued Mister Barker in conspiratorial tones, "is none other than Lady Savage's husband, one Jeremiah Cornwall; the JC of the note that we examined at Middleton's cottage."

A plume of blue smoke curled up from Young Doran's briar. Stan leaned in on his elbows.

"It appears from his last letter that Mister Cornwall committed his heinous act because, and I quote, he could 'no longer bear her hypocritical lust for control at any price'. Whatever he meant by this, he obviously felt justified in doing away with her in the most barbaric manner imaginable, for he shows no remorse. Indeed, he ended the letter with these words: 'Do not look sadly upon her passing. In life, she killed hope and love: in death, I recover peace'."

Mister Barker laid down his notes. There was a long pause as everyone reflected upon this first glimpse of the killer and his motive. Duggan was the first to speak.

"By barbaric, Sir," he enquired of Mister Barker, "d'you mean cutting 'er 'ead off?"

"Indeed, that would certainly have been a barbaric means of execution, wouldn't it? But it seems likely that Cornwall killed his wife at their home before transporting her body to the secret passageways that you discovered this morning. It was only as he was concealing the body in the underground chamber that he cut off her head with a blow from a broad sword. He must then have impaled the head upon the tip of the sword and decorated it with a dress tiara from his wife's collection."

Fred gulped down a swig of tea.

"Sir?" Stan ventured as the teacher paused. "That's the way old Gaveston was killed, isn't it? I mean, beheaded?"

"Almost, Johnson. The execution was actually carried out by the poor chap being run through with a sword. As with the unfortunate Lady Savage, it was only after death that his head was severed. It is this base decapitation that is depicted in the silver box that you found. It features alongside the Beauchamp family crest in The Rous Roll, too. Do you recall the old book that we looked at together by my tent? The Beauchamp crest has turned up pretty well everywhere we have been since then: in the chapel, for instance."

"And on the bell," contributed Fred. "And on the door in the tunnel, an' all."

"But this time," pondered Stan, "the murder was done *to* a Beauchamp and not *by* one."

"Right, Johnson. And what is more, we know that the victim of the original crime, Sir Piers Gaveston, bore the title Duke of Cornwall."

"So does that mean that Jeremiah Cornwall is a duke an' all?" ventured Fred.

"No, Parker. Jeremiah Cornwall is definitely no duke, nor is he remotely of the same family, but the coincidence of his name clearly provided the inspiration for both the murder and the theme for the clues laid thereafter. It was as though he were acting out a vengeance on behalf of a family that was not his own."

"But why exactly did he bother to set clues?" asked Stan. "What was the point of setting up a treasure hunt when there was no treasure to find? I mean, apart from the tiara?"

"I imagine, Johnson, that he was enjoying a little mischievous sport at the expense of the police force. Or, to be more precise, at the expense of one Inspector Joseph Bray of the Warwickshire Constabulary to whom the first clue was addressed and for whom all subsequent clues were intended. He even went as far as placing a clue upon the grave of a man bearing the same name as the inspector, as you will recall from your visit to Saint Michael's. It would seem that mischief at the expense of the constabulary was his prime motive."

"'Cept that Bray never found the blinkin' clue, did 'e?"

"No he did not, Parker. The police lost the scent early on, failing to decipher the third of Cornwall's clues and spending months in futile pursuit of the man himself, though we now know that he had fled this island within days of the murder."

"And Bray?" enquired Duggan

"Died during the war, I understand."

"Do you know what the clue was, Sir? The one that he didn't get?"

"I do, Johnson, although I can not say exactly where it fitted within the chain of clues that Cornwall laid. Inspector Latchford shared it with us during our interview. It was again written in Esperanto and seemed to set a mathematical problem involving a pair of fractions or, to quote from the clue itself, a problem *rising by stone fractions.*"

"Like ¾ and 1½, for example?"

"Why! Bless me. But how on earth could you know that, Johnson?"

"Because those were the fractions on the stone, Sir: on the milestone where we found the box. I remember us looking at them because we were lost, but we couldn't make nothing of them."

"And the milestone was close to Arising Lane," confirmed Fred. "Kate said. No more 'an a couple of 'undred yards away."

"Rising Lane, Fred. Not Arising Lane."

"Same difference. We got there, right? And we found the clue that the coppers couldn't."

"In fairness, Fred, we didn't really plan to find the clue, did we? More like, we tripped over it accidentally?"

"Hang on a minute, Stan. It wasn't my fault, oright? I've told you: the bloomin' thing was loose."

"Er hem." Mister Barker interrupted gently to pursue his exposé. "Inspector Latchford was able to provide a good deal of background information on the killer which all seems to fit in very well with what we had already deduced." He took a sip of tea and turned over the sheet of paper upon which he had scrawled a few biographical highlights.

"Jeremiah Cornwall," he proceeded, "was a young officer in the second battalion of the Royal Warwickshire Regiment when he met Lady Savage, in 1899, at the regimental ball. He was 21, she was 39 and, despite the age gap, they obviously found meaningful romance together, for they were married in November of that same year. But there was no time for a honeymoon as Cornwall's battalion was straight away sent to South Africa and the harsh realities of the Boer War."

He paused to verify that his audience was still with him. "This, by the way, ties in perfectly with the dating of the rifle cartridge that we examined yesterday evening." Stan nodded silently. Goodness. Was that only yesterday?

As Mister Barker ran through his biographical notes on Jeremiah Cornwall, so Young Doran was searching through his worn notebook for an entry amongst its crammed pages. Presently, he made his first utterance of the afternoon.

"Six hundred."

"Frankie?"

"To the day, Master Barker."

"How so, Frankie?"

"July 1st, 1312," he recited and laid down his notebook. It was open at the page upon which Stan had copied the words from the plaque at Gaveston Cross. "Six hundred years to the day."

"Well I'll be blessed," purred Mister Barker. "So it is."

"Crikey!"

"He must 'ave planned it for ages," observed Duggan. "Nothing spur-of-the-moment about hitting your missus's murder date square on like that after six hundred years."

"Quite."

"Extraordinary."

"'Cept..." Young Doran cut through their reflection. "It's the wrong date."

"Come again, Frankie."

"Gaveston never died July 1st. Greatheed got it wrong."

"Ah! Might you recall when Sir Piers was actually killed?"

"June 19th."

"Are you sure?"

"Died, June 19th: Piers Gaveston, 1312. Duke of Anjou, 1584. Alessandro Marcello, 1747. General N. Greene, 1786. Louis-Jean-François…."

"Quite, Frankie. Yes. Very good. Thank you," soothed Mister Barker.

The incantation ended. Young Doran repositioned his pipe. Duggan rubbed his eyes in disbelief.

"He's a bit useful with numbers and dates, Bill," confided Fred.

Duggan swallowed hard. Mister Barker took another draft of tea, then smiled at Young Doran whose face remained impassive.

"One may well ask," proceeded Mister Barker on a new tac, "why Jeremiah Cornwall was not apprehended and charged on the day of the murder?" He lifted his eyes for a moment to see Fred nodding vigorously. "Well, according to the police, he was in Stockholm at the time and had already been there for several days. He had travelled there as an official member of the British fencing delegation to the Olympic Games, one of whose members was later to provide a strong alibi to corroborate his presence there. Chief Inspector Ellerby, who was leading the investigation into the disappearance of Lady Savage, appears to have accepted his alibi at face value and concentrated instead on pursuing a missing person's enquiry. His naive quackery gave Cornwall the time to make good his escape."

"But had he actually been in Sweden at all?" asked Duggan. "Or was that made up, an' all?"

"Oh, he had most definitely been in attendance at the games, for the police have a photograph of the British team and officials at the opening ceremony whereupon Mister Cornwall is clearly visible. Besides, he was seen by hundreds of athletes and officials throughout his days in Stockholm. But if his arrival in the country had been widely documented, so his departure must have been one of utmost secrecy and perfectly timed. And as we have seen, it was also reliant upon the provision of a false alibi by an accomplice."

"But what about all of the stuff…" began Stan. "All of the objects and clues and trickery that he used? The lodestone key, for example? Or the hidden compartment in the chapel?"

"Or the rifle cartridge?" added Fred.

"I mean, how did he find the time to invent all of that? And to link them altogether?"

"And what about the tiara?" asked Duggan. "Surely it really *was* a treasure hunt if he left a load of jewels to be found with the body."

"Actually, the tiara is not quite as it appears. Do you remember the line engraved in Esperanto upon the rifle cartridge?"

"No, Sir," answered Duggan truthfully.

"He wasn't there, Sir," pointed out Fred. "But I was. It said *all that glitters isn't gold*. Right?"

"Right, Parker. It would appear from Inspector Latchford's files that the great wealth of the Savage family is no more. Was no more, in fact, even before Cornwall arrived upon the scene. The death duties associated with the old Lord's demise had all but wiped out the family fortune, although Cornwall may not have known this at the time. The charade of non-existent old money could be the reason Cornwall engraved the idiom upon his Africa campaign cartridge, although I suppose he could have done so at any time during his marriage."

"And the tiara, Sir…?"

"Another case of glittering rather than golden, I fancy, for it turns out that the tiara is nothing more than plated base metal set with stones of paste. Rather symbolic, don't you think, that he should have placed it on the lady's severed head? A metaphor for the falseness of their lives, perhaps? Or am I reading too much into it?"

"So it's not a treasure then, Sir?" asked Fred, ignoring the rhetoric.

"I am afraid not, Parker."

"Not even a little bit?"

"No."

"Blimey."

There was a period of silence during which Mister Barker poured more tea.

"No treasure at all then?"

"No, Parker."

"Mmm."

"As for the other items," continued the teacher, "I imagine that many of them came from the Beauchamp family collection. The beautiful silver box, for example, must be at least two hundred years old, and the bell the same. And everything about the Beauchamp Chapel, the underground chamber and the tunnels leading to it probably date back five hundred years or more."

"And the lodestone key?" asked Stan.

"That, too, would have belonged to the family. It is extraordinary to think that such a network of tunnels and chambers could have existed beneath the town of Warwick for so long without anyone being the wiser."

"Except the Beechums."

"Except, of course, the Beauchamps."

"Helluva family," declared Duggan.

"Indeed, Duggan. Quite a family."

Conversation continued over a further pot of tea and there was much debate about the remarkable discoveries of the past three days. Such an adventure had been simply unimaginable to Stan and Fred on Saturday lunchtime, yet here they were on Monday afternoon discussing intrigue and murder on equal terms with their teacher in the front window of a tea shop. The others would never believe them!

Two hours later, squashed between their excitable fellow campers on a low bench, Stan, Fred and the injured Bill Duggan were the centre of attention. Where had they been? How did he do his arm in? Was it really true that they had been in jail? Was Ferguson going to send them home from camp? As agreed with Mister Barker, the protagonists resisted all invitations to divulge details of their escapade until the Head had spoken - and the time for such an intervention was nigh. But it was Mister Pickup who took to his feet first.

"Ahem. Thank you, boys. Settle down. Come on now: settle down a bit will you? Husssshhhhh." He pressed an index finger to his lips and held sway. "Thank you. Well, as you will already know, events have recently occurred involving a number of our number about which we know very little. In fact, not withstanding my position as teacher, I myself know nothing at all."

A low hum of agreement murmured through the night air which Mister Pickup took to be a show of support. The fire crackled. He looked around at the eager faces and smiled.

"Fortunately, there is someone amongst us tonight who is imminently better placed to fill in the I's and cross the T's." He paused theatrically. "Mister Ferguson!"

The Head stood and made his way to the centre of the semi-circle of benches. Everybody leaned in to listen.

"As Mister Pickup may have just indicated," he began, before clearing his throat, "I should like to speak to you about an important discovery made this morning by members of Camp School. I intend to reveal the facts of the matter as I learned them from the Station Inspector at Warwick Police Station this afternoon and I should be grateful if you would refrain from embellishing or exaggerating these details when asked to recount them upon our return to the works, next week." He looked around the assembly for a sign of collective understanding.

"Having followed a trail of clues for two days, during which time they displayed many of the qualities taught at Day Continuation School, William Duggan, Fredrick Parker and Stanley Johnson this morning discovered the remains of a murdered person, close to the Collegiate Church of Saint Mary in Warwick."

There was shock on the forms: a brief silence followed by the din of incredulous voices all talking at the same time. Mister Pickup jumped to his feet, shushing for all he was worth, but Mister Ferguson gently took his arm and indicated that he should regain his place and let the ruckus die down of its own accord. He gave them forty-five seconds, then raised his arms above his head.

"Enough, boys. Enough." Order was restored: Mister Ferguson pursued his summary.

"The discovery of the victim was not accidental. These boys, aided and abetted by Mister Barker and Young Doran, had systematically unearthed and deciphered a series of dastardly clues, rather in the manner of Sherlock Holmes."

Stan's ears glowed with embarrassment. He glanced to his right to see Hendry staring at him in stupefied admiration.

"At times, the detective work took them beyond the confines and rules of our Camp School." Mister Ferguson paused pointedly. "You should know that I am the last person to condone the wanton flaunting of Camp School regulations, and you would all do well to heed this fact in the future. However, in this particular instance,

I think it fair to say that the bending of rules was justified." He smiled at the assembly through the dimness of the camp firelight.

"Nine years ago, the family of the victim, the late Lady Savage of Wootton Hall, put forward a reward for information leading to the discovery of her whereabouts. A most generous reward, in fact, for the sum in question was no less than one hundred guineas."

Gasps were heard from the dark benches, the loudest from Mister Pickup. The Head Teacher waited for them to peter out before continuing.

"This evening, Inspector Latchford of the Warwickshire Constabulary has informed me by telephone that the family intends to honour its promise in this regard and to donate the full amount to the upkeep and improvement of the Bournville Day Continuation Schools."

The muted reception from the galleries contrasted markedly with Mister Ferguson's jubilant announcement. He frowned theatrically.

"Hmmm. Oh yes. One other thing." He surveyed the expectant benches. "An hour ago, we received from Wootton Hall a magnificent hamper of chocolates, lemonades and all manner of confections which you are generously invited to share and enjoy during the remainder of our week together!"

As raucous cheering and whistling erupted on the forms and a dozen congratulatory fists pummelled the backs of the adventurers, Fred leaned over to bawl into Stan's ear:

"Now, that's what I call treasure, Stanley! What a bloomin' time we're 'avin, eh? And we haven't even got to Stratford yet!"

THE END

ACKNOWLEDGEMENTS

I began researching and writing this story six years ago, with no idea just how absorbing, difficult, frustrating and challenging it might be. But it was all of those things and more. I am grateful to many people for their support, corrections, criticism, laughter and guidance, amongst them Alan and Alistair Brewin, who dared to publish my story and who contributed much to the way it appears in print. Thanks are also due to Zora Payne, for her fine cover illustration, and to Rebecca at Brewin Books who gallantly corrected a multitude of grammatical errors in my manuscript.

At the very beginning was Nat Waugh, erstwhile English grocer in France, who had the courage to wade through the first draft without recourse to valium and who set me on my way with warm encouragement and subtle changes to almost everything. Then came Norma Boultwood, who hates adjectival strings and who pointed out the same to me with effortless grace and charm. Stanley Johnson's daughter Sheila, my mother, gave helpful nudges in the right direction, as did her husband, George Ellis, who quietly asked all of the right questions. Above all, and well beyond the call, came my dear friend of fifty years, Ian Hayes, who helped shape my story and who lived some of it with me, too.